GUARDIAN ANGEL

GUILD OF SEVENS, BOOK 2

J. PHILIP HORNE

**For news of upcoming works,
please join Mr. Horne's email list at www.jphiliphorne.com
or visit him on facebook.com/jphiliphorne**

ALSO BY J. PHILIP HORNE

The Lodestone (2011)

Guild of Sevens
Joss the Seven (2016)
Guardian Angel (2017)

Cover illustration by Justin Stewart
www.justifii.com

Copyright © 2017 J. Philip Horne
All rights reserved

ISBN: 1544246129
ISBN-13: 978-1544246123

For my mother and father
who deserve every honor

TABLE OF CONTENTS

THE WORLD OF THE GUILD OF SEVENS

Guild of Sevens. The Guild is an ancient organization comprised of leaders from the major families that give birth to Sevens. Each actual Seven is marked by a family birthmark.

The Talents
1. Phasing (pass through solids). Slang: ghost, ghosting
2. Hardening (make body rock-like). Slang: bruiser, bruising
3. Regeneration (heal). Slang: reggie, reggied
4. Telekinesis (move objects with the mind). Slang: telly, tellied
5. Invisibility (become impossible to see). Slang: blender, blending
6. Enhanced Speed (move very fast). Slang: kinney, kinneying
7. Shape shifting (take the shape of an animal). Slang: shifter, shift

Joss Morgan. Joss Morgan is not only a Seven, he's the Seventy-Seven, a once-in-a-generation Seven with all of the talents. Most Sevens have two or three of the talents. Joss's birthmark is a small mark on his shoulder that resembles a butterfly.

The Mockers. The Mockers are a recent crime syndicate with a distributed, networked structure that uses Sevens to commit very profitable crimes.

CHAPTER 1

EAGLE POWERS

I LOOKED DOWN at the green lawn far below, summoned my eagle powers, and leapt. The peak of Thomas's house was at least twenty-five feet high. We'd run the numbers on a website. I had about one and a quarter seconds before I'd hit the ground. Plus, I wasn't dropping straight down. I'd leapt up and out, which had to buy another half second or so. Plenty of time to change into an eagle. A massive bald eagle.

I'd shift into an eagle, because I was a shifter. I was a Seven. I could do it. The fact that I'd failed over and over didn't matter. This time would be different. I'd been failing because nothing had been on the line. That had to be the problem.

I leapt and willed the transformation. Everything that was me stuffed into a mental image of a giant bald eagle. I held that image as I leapt away from the roof, peaked, and fell toward the ground. An eagle, white head and tail feathers, massive wingspan, scaly claws. I could feel it. I was going to shift. My eyes popped open as I thrust my wings down in a powerful stroke.

There were no wings. No feathers. No telescopic eagle vision. My own arms flapped weakly as the ground rushed to meet me.

I expressed myself by saying, "Aaaaahhhhhhhhhhhhhh!" and bruised with everything I had just before I smacked the ground. Bruising I could do. I turned hard as steel and hit the ground with a thud. Grass and dirt rammed past my hardened lips and teeth into my open mouth.

1

~~I lay there, stunned. When I tried to get up, it felt like I~~ was glued to the ground. I couldn't seem to get my arms or legs moving. After a few seconds of struggle, I felt hands tugging on my shoulders, and I popped loose. Standing, I released the bruising and got busy spitting dirt out of my mouth.

"Impressive," Thomas said from just behind me. "Sort of has an abstract art vibe to it."

I blinked away the dirt and grime and looked. A roughly Joss-shaped, three-inch indent in the yard stretched forward from my feet. I grinned, then coughed and spit out some more dirt.

"That's gonna be fun to explain to your mom," I said.

Thomas stepped up beside me and shrugged. "She hardly ever comes out here. Maybe grabs a cup of coffee on the patio in the early morning, but that's about it." He looked at me. "Told you the stress wouldn't do it."

I grimaced. "So what's going on? I'm a Seven. The Seventy-Seven. You saw me shift to an eagle two weeks ago. Why can't I do it now?"

Thomas frowned. "Maybe it's, like, a miracle you did it then. Maybe that's the weird thing, and not being able to do it now, that's normal." Thomas shrugged again. "It's not like we really know how all this works. You can still do the other stuff, right?"

I nodded. "I'm still terrible at tellying, kinneying totally exhausts me, but I can do them. It's like I have a block with shifting."

"Probably." Thomas walked toward the back door, and I followed him into his house. "I mean, given what was going on when you did it, is that surprising?"

I washed my face in the kitchen sink, images flashing behind my closed eyelids. Soaring higher and higher as an eagle. Turning back into me. Dropping like a comet. Busting through the roof of a building and fighting for my life. It had almost been the end of me. I swiped the water off my face and pulled my mind back to the present.

"So we're heading to the mall?" I said.

2

"Don't like to think about it, do you?" Thomas asked.

"Nope." I waved him toward the front door. "Let's head out. Bet the other guys are already there."

"I'll lock behind you," Thomas said. "Meet you around front."

I headed out the front door and grabbed my bike from where it leaned against the hedges. Thomas came through the side gate with his bike. He'd finally retired that ridiculous, tiny bike he'd been riding for three years and had a new mountain bike that was the right size.

"Have you asked Mara about it?" Thomas asked, riding beside me.

"We've texted some." I swerved around a dead squirrel in the road while trying to avoid looking at it. "She's mainly just letting me know where they're at. I mostly text with Isabella." Thomas grinned, but I ignored him and continued. "She thought the whole stress thing should work. Not so much though."

"They still haven't gone back to Mexico?"

"No, her little 'spend a couple days being tourists before going home' is going on two weeks."

Thomas nodded. "They deserve it. Where are they?"

"Not far," I said. "I think somewhere in Oklahoma or Arkansas now."

"Here's a thought," Thomas said. "Is it really stressful jumping off the roof if you know you can just, you know." He wiggled his fingers in the air mysteriously.

"I'm pretty sure I was terrified when I jumped," I said, "but who knows?"

We rode for a few minutes in silence. The mall was a couple neighborhoods over from Thomas's house, next to a highway. We crossed two major streets, but stayed to the neighborhood roads. As we neared the mall, Thomas drifted closer and whispered something.

"What?" I said.

Thomas steered even closer until our handlebars almost bumped. "I said, don't look now, but I'm pretty sure there's a car following us." His voice was barely above a whisper.

I started to turn, but stopped when I caught Thomas glaring at me. "Where?"

"Stopped at that last turn, but they've got a line of sight to us. Black car."

My heart hammered in my chest, and I itched to look back over my shoulder. Who could it be? The Mockers? The Guild? Maybe Thomas was imagining things.

"You sure?" I asked.

"Yeah, pretty sure."

"Okay, I'll check on it."

"What does that mean?" Thomas asked.

I nodded ahead. "We take that right up ahead toward the mall. Soon as we're around the corner, I kinney and blend. Run back, see who it is. You grab my bike and keep riding once I'm gone so it doesn't look like we stopped, okay?"

"I thought you were still terrible at the whole kinney thing," Thomas said.

"I am," I said, "but I've practiced enough to know my limits. I think I can go flat out for at least twenty seconds while blending. Hardest part is the physics."

Thomas frowned at me. "Physics?"

"Actually speeding up is hard. Takes a lot of concentration. But once you're going fast, it's insane. You know how when you ride your bike really fast, you have to lean way over to turn? And you still can't make a really sharp turn? And if you don't lean into the turn, you wipe out? Well, it's like that. Running flat out while kinneying is totally out of control. You have to lean way over, but then your shoes just slip out from under you, and it's practically impossible to turn."

"Oh." Thomas raised an eyebrow at me. "I hadn't thought of that."

"Neither had I when I started out, and it's a good thing I can heal myself or I wouldn't have any skin left. Seriously. Okay, let's take the turn, then grab my bike and keep riding while I check it out."

Thomas nodded, and we rounded the corner onto a

short road that joined the neighborhood streets with a larger road. The houses on both sides had tall privacy fences facing us. We were alone. I slammed on my brakes and hopped off the bike. Thomas caught the handlebars and gave me a quick grin.

"Good luck!"

I nodded. After a deep breath, I blended and kinneyed. Time slowed to a crawl. Twenty seconds. Plenty of time, given I was moving close to twenty times faster than normal. And invisible.

First things first. I knelt and retied my shoes super tight. I wasn't going to run right out of them again. I'd learned that one the hard way. Standing, I glanced at Thomas. He'd pushed off and gotten both feet on the pedals, but that was about it. It was like he was moving in slow motion, but I knew I was the one moving super-fast. I leaned into it and ran.

Each step shot me forward, like I was leaping along instead of running. And each step felt like it might be my last. My arms flailed around and I twisted this way and that to try to keep moving in the right direction. I rocketed back around the corner, barely staying upright by pushing off the curb on the far side of the street.

I'd seen this nature video once of a baby gazelle trying to run right after it'd been born. Its mom was sort of loping along, and the baby gazelle was trying to keep up. It was super awkward, its legs flailing, stumbling around, in a constant state of almost falling. Born to run, but not quite there yet. That was me. I was the baby gazelle. A superhero baby gazelle.

I pushed off the curb and got moving down the street we'd just been on. Ahead of me a black car crawled up the street toward me. Given how fast I was kinneying, the car had to be moving pretty quickly. Thomas had been right. It sure looked like they were trying to get us back in sight.

I ran toward the car, then flailed around as I tried to slow down. I came to a stop just as the car drifted past me. I got a good look through the front windshield, and my mouth popped open. The car glided past me, the two passengers unaware that I stood a foot away. They had to be following us, but why? Were they following Thomas, or me? Or both of us? No time to think. I needed to get back to Thomas.

Turning, I launched myself back the way I'd come and got back around the corner before the car had gone another ten feet. Thomas had pedaled forward a short distance from where I'd left him. I stopped a few feet in front of him and dropped the kinneying and blending.

"Hold up," I said, arms outstretched to catch my bike as Thomas slammed on his brakes. I hopped on my bike and started pedaling. "Come on! Let's get to the mall."

Thomas chased after me and caught up as we rounded the corner. We turned onto the sidewalk along the main street between the neighborhood and the mall. I glanced back down the road we'd left just as it dropped out of sight. The black car was stopped at the previous turn, pulled forward enough to give them a clear view of us.

"Who was it?" Thomas said.

We pulled in at the crosswalk to the mall on the other side of the street, and I punched the button. I was pretty sure the button didn't do anything. I'd never been able to tell for sure that the light behaved any differently whether or not you pushed it, but it made a nice little buzzing sound, so I pushed it three times just in case.

"Joss, who?"

"Remember those two detectives that interviewed us?" I said. "After it all went down with Jordan? Wasn't one of them named Young?"

"I remember," Thomas said. "Yeah, Detectives Young and Malick."

"That's right. It was them. Back there in the car. We're being followed by cops."

"You think they know?"

The light changed, and we headed across the street and into the mall parking lot.

"Doubt it," I said. "How could they?"

"Then why were they following us?" Thomas sounded

worried. "You think they're, like, bad guys? Hunting us down or something?"

I shrugged. "No idea, but I don't like it."

"Yeah, me neither. You sure it was them? Did you get a good look?"

"Yeah. It was them."

We didn't see the car again as we crossed the parking lot and chained our bikes to the steel bike racks. The mall greeted us with a blast of cold air that washed off the summer heat.

"I thought we'd left all that behind," Thomas said, walking beside me toward the escalators.

"Me too," I said, "but I don't think we mention it to anyone."

Thomas nodded. "My lips are sealed. Count on it."

We headed up the escalators and toward the food court. It was going to be great to see the guys again. Sure, my sister had been kidnapped, and the whole thing had been a giant set up to get me to work for the Mockers, but we'd still had a great time together. And we'd learned to fight, which was pretty cool heading into high school. We hadn't hung out for a couple weeks since all our parents had gotten super paranoid. I was pretty sure we'd have a thing now, like we'd bonded or something.

The food court was in sight when Janey stepped out of a store in front of us and waved. I stopped dead in my tracks. What was she doing here?

"Hey, Thomas," Janey said with a big smile.

Thomas hadn't stopped with me, but walked up to her and gave her a high five. "Hey Janey. Whatcha doing here?"

I scowled and walked over to them.

"Mom wanted to do some shopping, so I came with her. You guys going to lunch?"

I stopped beside Thomas, still scowling. "So Mom's checking on us, isn't she?"

"Probably, but she's shopping for real." Janey mimed swiping a credit card. "I need some new outfits for junior high, right?"

"That's right," Thomas said. "You're at the Beedle in a couple weeks."

"I like that." Janey made a point of ignoring me and kept speaking directly to Thomas. "Beedle Junior High. The Beedle."

"So," I said, and waited until Janey looked my way. "You need to get back to Mom, right? Buy your outfits and all?"

"Or she could join us for lunch," said Thomas. "What do you think, Janey?"

"Thanks, Thomas." She was ignoring me again. "That's what I was hoping to do. See all you guys again."

My shoulders sagged. I liked Janey and all, and I still felt bad that everything had gotten so messy, what with her being kidnapped by a psychopath and all, but that didn't mean I wanted her crashing lunch with my buds. Thomas still didn't get it. He just wished he had a brother or sister, and wasn't willing to really think through how bad it could be.

The three of us headed to the food court. Arjeet, Deion, and Frankie were sitting at a table waiting for us. We waved, and they hopped up to meet us. We all gave each other bro hugs before sitting back down at the table. I noticed Frankie had ended up next to Janey.

"Man," Arjeet said. "All together for the first time since..." His eyes drifted over to Janey and he trailed off.

Since my sister had been kidnapped by a psycho and I'd dropped from the sky to rescue her. Not that Arjeet, Deion, or Frankie knew any of the stuff I'd done. The three of them knew Janey had been snatched, but thought she'd been released near our home.

"It's all good," I said.

I looked at Frankie's face. There were hints of bruising around his eyes, but he looked pretty good, given he'd been punched in the face by a beast of a man. I leaned forward and held out my fist. Frankie hesitated, then nodded and bumped it.

"Heard you were the man," I said to him. "Thanks. Sorry

I haven't told you before this."

Janey kept her mouth shut, thankfully. I really didn't want her jumping in on our man-talk.

He shrugged and glanced at Janey. "She's one of us, right? Had to try something, so letting him punch me in the face repeatedly seemed like the best option. Not sure it helped."

Janey beamed, and Deion leaned in. "One of us. I like that. We're like a, a gang or something. I mean, when we go to high school in a week, who's gonna mess with us?"

Arjeet let out a low whistle. "He's right. I know it sucked at the end, but we still learned all that stuff. I mean, I feel like I could..."

"Could what?" I said.

Arjeet wasn't looking at me. His eyes were looking past me, and rising higher and higher.

A heavy hand fell on my shoulder. "It's Joss, right?"

CHAPTER 2

THE APOLOGY

I RECOGNIZED THE voice. Bobby Ferris. Now that was interesting.

He'd humiliated me when I was a seventh grader, and the first thing I'd done as a Seven was seek revenge. Then I'd discovered the horrible truth of Bobby's home life, and ended up trying to help him. Secretly. By pretending to be an invisible guardian angel.

I glanced at Thomas, and he mouthed something about a boat. No, not a boat. The note! I'd totally forgotten about Bobby's note! After helping Bobby, I'd told him if he ever needed me to hide a note in the hole in that big tree in Beckler park. Right after everything had gone down a couple weeks ago, Thomas had found a note from him in the tree. Bobby had asked the angel—me—to do something, but I couldn't remember what it had been.

But Bobby didn't know I was the fake angel, so why was he trying to talk to me? The hand dropped off my shoulder and I stood. Several chairs scraped back as everyone else stood up at the same time. I turned and faced him. He was still big, which wasn't surprising, given most high school boys did the opposite of shrink.

Bobby wasn't alone. Three of his friends were with him. I'd heard Bobby was playing football on the varsity team. These guys had to be his teammates, and they were pressed in around me. Three months earlier, and I'd have probably wet my pants. Not now. I'd been trained. I was the Seventy-Seven. And Bobby had a completely messed up situation at home, which made him seem less scary for some reason.

I glanced around. Deion, Arjeet, and Frankie had all struck that loose, balanced stance that I'd seen so many times at Battlehoop, our fake dojo where we'd learned to fight. Thomas, too, although I was pretty sure he felt the same way I did about Bobby. I smiled. They thought Bobby was here to mess with me, and they were ready to go. Janey had stood up with the rest of them, but was glancing from person to person, her eyebrows pulled together. She didn't have our background from junior high with Bobby.

"Hey," Bobby said in a low voice. "Can I talk to you for a sec?"

He nodded off to the side and stepped that way. Had he somehow figured out my secret? Did he want to ask me about the note? Would he be mad when he found out I'd totally forgotten about it? Or did he have no idea that was me, and just wanted to isolate me so he could pants me again?

I glanced around. The food court was gradually filling as lunch approached, and I drew in a sharp breath when I saw Shelly and a couple of her friends sitting a few tables over. The very girls who'd witnessed Bobby pants me in seventh grade. A pantsing that had gone horribly wrong. He'd gotten the underwear.

"What's up, Joss?" Arjeet asked.

I glanced around again. Everyone seemed tense. I needed to bring it down.

"All good." I stepped around Bobby's friends. "Just need to chat with Bobby."

I walked over to him, ready to kinney, trying to stay relaxed. I figured if I was moving fast enough, there wasn't much he could do to me, but it would attract less attention than, say, turning invisible. When I stopped next to him, Bobby's eyes seemed to look everywhere but at me.

"What's up?" I asked.

His eyes flicked to mine, then away. "I remembered you the other day. Been thinking about stuff, so when I saw you here…"

He trailed off, his eyes still roaming around the food

court. I had a pretty good idea of when he'd remembered me. It'd probably been when I'd yelled at him in my screechy angel-voice, standing in his room, totally invisible, about how he'd mistreated this kid named Joss.

"Okay," I said, and waited.

Bobby's eyes finally settled on mine. "Well, I'm sorry. Didn't mean to get your underwear." He jammed his hands in his pockets, but maintained eye contact. "Probably went a little too far."

I nodded slowly. This was not what I'd expected, but it was probably a good thing. I figured I'd see where it went. "By 'too far' I'm thinking you mean when you stepped on my shorts and underwear so I couldn't pull them back up?"

"Yeah."

"While, uh, those girls"—I nodded toward the table with Shelly and her friends—"watched?"

"Yeah. That part." He finally looked away. "Anyway. I'm sorry. That's all."

"Okay." I looked back toward our two groups of friends. "We're good, and not that it matters to you, but I respect that."

"You respect what? A good pantsing?"

"Uh, no," I said. "Owning what you did."

We stood there for a moment longer, and Bobby stuck his hand out toward me. I might have been a bit jittery, because I immediately kinneyed. A split second later I realized he was offering to shake my hand. I released the kinney and tried to give him a manly shake. That done, Bobby walked off without another word, his friends following along.

I headed back over to the table and plopped down in my chair. Everyone stared at me for a moment, then grabbed a seat.

"And?" Deion said.

"You didn't want us to fight, right?" Arjeet chopped his hands in mock combat. "'Cause I was totally ready to go."

"Who was that, Joss?" Janey said.

"That," Frankie said, "was Bobby Ferris. Biggest kid in

eighth grade back when we hit junior high."

eighth grade back when we hit junior high."

"The one who pantsed Joss," Arjeet said. He was grinning, like it was a funny memory.

Janey's eyes got big, and she cracked a big smile. "Joss, I don't remember you mentioning this."

I glared at Arjeet, and turned to Janey. "It was no big deal. He pantsed me. That's all."

Frankie leaned toward Janey and whispered something. Her eyes got bigger and she mouthed a silent "Oooooo."

"Okay," I said. "So it was a big deal. Anyway, he apologized."

"He what?"

I couldn't tell who had said it. Probably everybody at once.

"He apologized," I said. "Okay? We're good. You saw us shake."

"I figured," Arjeet said, "that you were agreeing to pay protection money to him when we get to high school. And I was feeling disrespected. We don't need protection. Not if we stick together."

Deion leaned over and fist-bumped Arjeet. I sat back and took it all in. The summer had been more or less insane. I'd discovered I had superpowers, and been tricked into committing all sorts of crimes by a Mocker. Then I'd robbed a bank and rescued my sister when she was kidnapped. It was good to be finally hanging out with friends and just being normal.

We spent the next couple hours talking. I didn't forget about the cops following us, but I gradually came down from the intensity I'd felt when we'd gotten to the mall. It was a great time. It felt like the first real day of summer, even though we only had a week left before the start of high school.

Thomas nudged me in the ribs, and I followed his eyes. My mom was hovering outside a nearby shop, acting cool, but glancing our way.

"Janey." I pointed a thumb toward Mom. "I think that's your ride. Tell her Thomas and I are heading back now."

She nodded and stood up. "Gotta go. I'm just gonna say, though, it's pretty unfair all of you are leaving junior high right when I'm showing up."

"Yeah," Frankie said, "but we'll still be in high school when you get there."

Janey smiled at him. A big, warm smile. Frankie smiled back. I really respected Frankie for what he'd done to try to protect Janey, but I was definitely going to have to keep an eye on him.

"So your parents have you on a short leash, too?" Deion said.

"Oh, yeah," I said. "I was surprised they finally let me meet up with all of you."

"No doubt," Frankie said. "Parents can be way overprotective."

"You ride your bike?" Thomas asked.

"Nope," he answered. "Wasn't an option. Mom's lurking in a nearby store. She'll take me home."

"Me, too," Arjeet said. "We're dropping off Deion on the way home."

I smiled. "Moms are in full effect today. All right, Thomas and I have to pedal home, so we're out."

I waved to my Mom as Thomas and I headed toward the down escalator. She and Janey headed out the opposite way.

"That was cool," Thomas said as we rode down the escalator. "Good to hang out without, you know, wondering if we were going to die."

I nodded. My mind had already returned to the cops. Why had they been following us? We hit the bottom of the escalator and headed for the exit.

"And really cool that Bobby apologized," Thomas said. "What did you say to him when you were being the angel?"

I shrugged. "Not much, really. I mean, maybe enough so he'd remember who I was and what he'd done, but that was it."

"I'm betting Bobby's a good guy, you know? Just dealing with tough stuff."

"I hope," I said, "'cause I need to help him. That note,

right? Do you remember what it said?"

"I'll show you," Thomas said.

We headed out the doors into the summer heat, and Thomas fished his phone out of his pocket while we walked over to our bikes. He flipped around for a moment on the screen, and handed it to me while he worked on getting our bikes unlocked. He still used that same insanely long bike lock.

His phone displayed a picture of a wrinkled piece of paper with a handwritten note. Bobby's note. I zoomed in and read.

Bobby here. You told me to write if I needed help, so I'm writing.

My dad's done good the past few days, but it's been hard. He's going to see it through. That's what he said. He's going to do the right thing.

But he's in big trouble. I always wondered where his money came from. He didn't have much, but he never worked. Now I know. He was doing stuff for some sort of criminal organization. Dad needs to get away from them. Get a clean start. You can help with that, right?

"Oh, crud." I handed the phone back to Thomas. "I can just forget about all this, right? I mean, he wrote that to an angel, not me."

Thomas cocked an eyebrow at me, but didn't say anything. We got on our bikes and headed across the parking lot.

"There's only a week of vacation left." I punched the crosswalk button. "Not really enough time to do anything."

We crossed the street and headed back toward the entrance to the neighborhood. Thomas kept his mouth shut, but he didn't need to say anything. My mind was going at a hundred miles an hour. How could I ignore Bobby's note? I'd made a commitment, and that was before Bobby had apologized to me. I was a total jerk if I didn't try to follow through.

We turned into the neighborhood and rode slowly back

to Thomas's house. There was no sign of the black car. By the time we got there, I'd made up my mind.

"Alright, you talked me into it," I said. "Can you invite me over for a sleepover tonight?"

Thomas smiled. "Yeah, I can arrange that."

"Good. I'm gonna pay Bobby a visit tonight and get things moving. See if there's something I can do to help his dad."

"Sounds like a plan," Thomas said. "Come by around dinner unless I text you."

Thomas walked his bike toward the back of his house and I headed home. I had no clue what I'd be able to do for Mr. Ferris, but it felt right to at least try. What I really needed to do was learn to shift. I couldn't get around town on my own. Even Sevens weren't allowed to drive at fourteen. If I could shift into an eagle, it'd be huge. I'd be able to fly around and get places fast. But I couldn't shift, and I didn't know why.

I turned onto Chickadee Place and hit the brakes. There, at the end of the cul-de-sac in front of my house, sat a fancy black car. Not the black car I'd seen this morning with the cops. This one looked expensive, and I recognized it from about two-and-a-half weeks ago. It was driven by Blondie— that was my nickname for him since I didn't know his real name—and Luc, a Seven. I knew Luc was a ghost, but didn't know if he had any other talents.

When I'd first met them, I'd gotten everything twisted around and thought Blondie was a Mocker trying to force me into a life of crime. Now I knew they were with the Guild of Sevens, an ancient organization supposedly dedicated to training and using Sevens for good in the world. Guild or not, I didn't really trust them, and I doubted they trusted me after what went down when they'd tried to confront Janey and me.

They were back at my house. Could this day get any weirder? Cops following me. Bobby talking to me. And now the Guild at my house. Maybe some flying monkeys could put on a show for us this evening.

I was not going to simply walk in with Blondie and Luc at the house. I turned my bike around and cut back to the alley that ran behind our house. We had a big fence around our backyard with a rolling gate across the driveway to the alley, so I dumped my bike in the alley and blended. Once invisible, I ghosted through the fence and headed into the garage. Mom's minivan was in its spot, so she and Janey were already home from the mall.

I held my blend and ghosted into the laundry room through the backdoor. I heard muffled voices coming through the door to the kitchen, but couldn't make out what was being said. After a deep, calming breath, I ghosted through the door and stepped into the family room.

Mom and Dad had their backs to me, standing side by side behind Dad's recliner, facing the couch, where Blondie and Luc sat facing them. Blondie was talking, perched on the front of the couch and looking intense.

"I recognize you value your privacy, but we have to take action. We cannot have an unregistered Seven robbing banks and—"

"That's bunk," Dad said, cutting off Blondie. "You absolutely don't have to do anything. You want this. You want the excuse. You want to use our family's near-tragedy to get what you want."

Blondie sat back, his mouth pulled in a tight line. Luc didn't look too happy, either. I stepped around to the side so I could see my Dad's face and leaned against the wall as I watched. Another man stepped through the wall next to me. He smiled at me and put his finger to his lips.

I decided not to scream, but it was close. After a quick breath to restart my brain, I recognized him. Short dark hair, short beard sprinkled with white hairs on the chin. Snug t-shirt and jeans. It was the Seven that had confronted me on one of my missions, back when I thought I was the one working for the Guild.

He nodded when I swallowed my scream and pointed toward the wall he'd just walked through. I tilted my head in question, and he gestured toward the wall again and stepped through it.

This guy had confronted me when I'd been stealing a hard drive from a laptop in a very secure office. We'd actually fought, and I'd caught him off guard with a couple of my talents and knocked him out. But there'd been a moment when he'd ghosted through me and I'd gained a strong sense of who he was. The main thing I'd sensed was honesty.

My parents were talking to the other two again, but the words were a buzzing sound in the back of my head. I had a chance to possibly meet another Seven. A Thief with the ability to ghost and blend. I had to give it a shot. I followed him through the wall.

CHAPTER 3

STANTON, NICK STANTON

PASSING THROUGH WALLS was harder than doors. Maybe it was because of all the different materials, but I'd always had to work harder to ghost through them. The Seven had looked like he'd just stepped through it. For me, it was more like being up to my chest in water and pushing against the current.

I pushed through and popped out the other side. The Seven was across the entryway by the front door. He waved me to follow before ghosting through the door. I followed him through and blinked in the bright sunlight on the front walkway. Ghosting had the weird effect of neutralizing hot and cold, so the blazing summer heat felt the same as inside, just a cool nothingness.

"Thanks for following," he said.

The Seven was a couple steps down the walk, looking at me. He had to be blending, or he wouldn't have been able to see me. Anyone driving by wouldn't have seen a thing, but no one drives by in a cul-de-sac anyway.

"Name's Stanton," he said, and stuck a hand out to shake. "Nick Stanton."

I was still ghosting, but I took his hand in mine and shook it. The rules around the Seven talents were mostly a mystery to me, but I did know that if two people were ghosting, they sort of cancelled each other out, just like two Sevens blending could see each other. His hand felt totally normal me.

"Should I call you Mr. Stanton?" I asked.

"No, let's just go with Stanton."

21

"You could tell I was still ghosting?"

"Piece of cake," he said. "You just have to learn how to spot it, and it's a little more subtle since we're both blending. But take a look."

Stanton changed. He looked the exact same, yet somehow more solid. He held his arms out. "That's me, blending, not ghosting." He changed again. "Blending and ghosting."

It was subtle, but I could see it, and now that I was thinking about it, I'd noticed when he was ghosting the first time we'd met, at least when I hadn't been ghosting myself. I nodded to him.

"So, Joss, let's chat for a moment, while Brian and Luc talk to your parents."

"Blondie's name is Brian?" I frowned. "Seriously?"

Stanton gave a crooked smile. "Yep, Brian. Look, I'm guessing this summer has been pretty crazy for you. We've pieced together a lot of it."

"What do you mean?" I tried to relax my face and not react to the icy feeling that had just clenched up my stomach.

"Guessing you came into your powers this summer," he said, "and based on the timing, I'm thinking that Mocker helped push you along pretty hard. Hold on"—he held up his hands, like he was trying to calm me down—"I get it. You don't know if you can trust us, and Brian and Luc didn't exactly make things better. But hear me out, okay?"

He was right. I didn't trust the Guild, and I'd been getting ready to bolt, but I felt something for Stanton that I hadn't felt very often this summer. I trusted him. Or I wanted to.

"Keep going," I said.

"Thanks." He nodded and smiled. "We've seen the bank robbery film, and that warehouse that looked like it had played host to a war, and the mini-apartment where Jordan's men were holed up. And none of it makes any sense. He robbed a bank with you, but tossed all the money in an alley? And what made that impact crater in the warehouse? And who was being held at their hideout? It was pretty obvious two women lived there, and they'd bolted. Left everything behind."

He stopped talking and looked at me, waiting. I wasn't ready to give him anything, so I waited, too. It got a little awkward, but he finally started talking again.

"You're not going to join the Guild, are you?"

I shrugged. "I'm thinking not today."

"Okay." Stanton looked me straight in the eyes. "That's probably for the best. Here's what you're going to get from me, Joss. The honest truth. I may not tell you everything, but I want you to have someone you can trust. And the Guild is, it's, ah, this ancient thing that I sometimes feel exists for its own sake. It does a lot of good, but I don't think it's the worst thing if there are some unaffiliated Sevens keeping it honest." He cracked a big smile. "Of course, I'll deny all of this if you talk to Brian."

"But what's the point of it?" I asked.

"The Guild?"

I nodded.

"Well," Stanton said. "At its noble core, to make the world a better place. To aim the efforts of extraordinary people toward where they are needed most. But any organization tends to start to exist for its own sake given enough time, and the Guild has had plenty of time."

"So what stuff outside of its 'noble core' does the Guild do?"

Stanton looked away and didn't speak for a moment. His voice was quieter when he did.

"It makes a tremendous amount of money for the powerful families."

"Oh," I said. My stomach seemed to relax for the first time since we'd started talking. "That's pretty normal, right?"

Stanton looked back at me. His eyes seemed sad, but he nodded. "Yeah, that's normal."

"So what sorts of things do Sevens do to make all that money? Can you give me an example?"

Stanton shrugged. "Sure. One of the most mundane is

hiring out Warriors as ultra-high class bodyguards."

"Warriors?"

"Yeah. Like, we're Thieves, right? Blending and ghosting together make the Thief. So Warriors are a mix of bruising and kinneying or sometimes bruising and reggying. In fact"—Stanton's hand drifted up as he spoke and rubbed his jaw—"based on what happened when we met, I wonder if you don't have some Warrior in you."

I felt real trust for Stanton, but I wasn't ready to go there. I wasn't going to acknowledge that I was the Seventy-Seven to anyone with the Guild. But I loved the idea of the Warrior. It totally made sense. To move fast, hit hard, heal easily. That was me, if I could ever get really good at kinneying and reggying.

Suddenly, a thought popped into my head. The ice surged back into my gut.

"Stanton," I said, "why were you in my house to begin with? You were blending and ghosting, weren't you? So my parents don't even know you're here."

"True," Stanton said. "I was supposed to keep an eye out for you. Let the guys know if you were lurking around, blending. Blenders can see blenders, right?"

If they'd needed Stanton, that meant Luc couldn't blend. Good to know.

"So you weren't supposed to pull me outside and talk to me?"

"Nope. And as far as I'm concerned, I never saw you, okay? I want you to have your space, to figure things out."

He put a hand on my shoulder and I flinched. I still wasn't used to having someone touch me while I was ghosting.

"I'm serious. Take your time. But please, please don't get into another mess with a Mocker. Keep your nose clean, okay? The Guild's really uptight about Sevens operating outside their control, so try to keep a low profile."

I nodded. "Sure. Low profile. That's me."

His eyebrows lifted, and his grip on my shoulder tightened slightly.

"From now on, that is," I said. "Totally under the radar."

Stanton dropped his hand. "Good enough. Listen, I hid a business card inside your pillowcase. It's got a mobile number on it. You can reach me on it if you need to, but don't use it unless it's important. And leave a message. I can't take a call most of the time."

I was opening my mouth to answer when the front door swung open behind me. I stepped out of the way just as Brian and Luc swept past me and headed down the walk to their car. My parents followed them out the door and stood a couple feet from me, watching them go.

Stanton nodded to me and turned to follow the other two. While they got in the front seats, he ghosted through the rear door and disappeared behind the tinted glass. At least, he disappeared to me. My parents had never seen him.

I stepped through the wall back into the house, cut to the family room, and dropped my ghosting and blending. I heard the front door shut and my parents walked into the room.

"Joss!" my dad said. "Have you been here, uh, hiding?"

Dad had stopped near the door to the entryway, but Mom walked over and gave me a quick hug. I didn't want to tell them about Stanton—not yet, at least—but I didn't want to lie either.

"I was only in here for a moment and didn't really hear anything. It was the two guys from the Guild, right?"

"Yes," Mom said. "They're... perceptive."

"They'd pieced together some of what happened," Dad said, "and are pretty much assuming that you were the mystery person who popped into view during the bank robbery."

I nodded. "I mean, we were trying to get the Guild involved, so I guess it makes sense."

Mom sat down in her recliner. "Have a seat, Joss."

Crud. Dad made his way to his recliner while I plopped down on the couch. Things were just getting back to normal. I'd finally been able to hang out with my friends today, and now the Guild had to come along and get my parents all worried again.

"The Guild wants oversight," Mom said.

"Of what?" I asked.

"Everything, I'd guess," Mom said. "But mostly you."

Dad held up a hand to stop me from speaking. "We told them no."

Right on cue, Janey stepped into the room. "That's right. They can keep their paws to themselves. How'd his nose look?"

In the past couple weeks, my parents had squeezed a lot of details out of Janey and me, including the whole encounter with Blondie and Luc where Janey had kicked Blondie in the face. I knew his name was Brian, but I'd gotten used to calling him Blondie and decided to stick with it.

Dad's mouth quirked up in one corner at Janey's question. "It, ah, appeared to be healing well, if perhaps a bit crooked."

"And you can believe," Mom said, "that was a topic of conversation. The gall of those men trying to confront you by the side of the road. Served him right."

Janey flopped onto the couch beside me, smiling.

"But Joss," Dad said, "we're not really sure what's best for you. The past two weeks we've been processing what all took place, and coming to terms with you being a Seven—"

"The Seventy-Seven," Janey said.

Dad nodded. "True enough. So we've talked a lot about the past with you, what all happened this summer, and the present, trying to understand your powers. But what about the future? What's best for you going forward? Do you just go to high school and pretend to be—well, 'normal' isn't the right word, but you know what I mean."

"Joss," Mom said with a glance at Dad, "we don't want to alienate the one group of people on the planet that might be able to help you learn to be who you were meant to be."

"I can get by. I don't need them."

That's what I said, but was it true? I didn't like Blondie and Luc, but they weren't the Guild. They were just one small part of it. The Guild might be able to help me truly learn to use my talents. To overcome my block and shift again. To learn to kinney for hours instead of seconds. To telly with real strength. Even the talents I'd thought I was really good at needed work. Stanton had ghosted so effortlessly. Could he teach me if I joined the Guild?

My mind snapped back to the room. Janey had just said something about kicking Blondie in the face again.

"No," Dad said, the corner of his mouth twitching up, "you're not kicking anyone in the face. Well, you absolutely have my permission to kick anyone in the face who tries to accost you on the road. But you won't have to. They've agreed to come through us from now on, okay?"

"Did you have to agree to something, too?" I said.

Mom and Dad shared another glance.

"Yes," Dad said. "We agreed to consider their request, and to meet with them once a week to check in on things while we consider it."

"We wanted to close the door for now," Mom said, "but not lock it forever. Does that make sense to you?"

"Yeah, I get it," I said.

"I don't," Janey said. "I'd have told them to stuff it."

"Janey," Mom said, "I understand why you feel that way. But this isn't just about you."

Janey put on her frowny face, but kept her mouth shut. Right at that moment, I remembered my plans for this evening.

"Hey, since we've gotten things kinda back to normal," I said, "and I've only got another week until high school, I was hoping to go have one last sleepover at Thomas's tonight. Can I go?"

Mom opened her mouth to speak, but then closed it. Dad's mouth had pulled into a tight line.

"We have some concerns," Dad said, "based on what went on this summer."

"But Dad," I said, "sleeping over at Thomas's didn't really have anything to do with it."

"Maybe," he said.

"I can live with it." Mom was speaking to Dad, not me.

Dad gave her a long look, and nodded. "Okay, you can go. But remember your promise. No new Seven adventures without talking to us first."

"I know," I said. "Haven't I asked before doing anything new to practice my talents?"

"You have," he said. "Just keep it up."

"Yes, sir," I said. "I'm going to go get my stuff ready to go."

I stood and noticed Janey was staring at me, her eyes narrowed. That couldn't be good. I gave Mom and Dad a quick smile and headed for the stairs. Upstairs, I shut my bedroom door, but didn't lock it to avoid suspicion. After stripping down to my underwear, I blended and ghosted. An arm's-length from the door, I pushed my way into my bedroom wall and ghosted up it. Once inside something solid, ghosting came down to mental effort. I could glide up the wall by thinking about it as long as enough of me was in the wall itself. I'd blended so nobody would see part of me sticking out the other side of the wall.

I ghosted up into the attic and released the blending. I was standing on a large piece of plywood behind the AC unit. It was dark, but I knew right where to find what I needed. After all the craziness had gone down a couple weeks ago, nobody seemed to remember or care about my 'work' clothes that I'd been given for going on missions. I had a matching black shirt and pants made from a stretchy material. The shirt had a tight pocket on the chest for holding loot against my body, and a small hole right below it. I'd earned that hole by taking a bullet. The pants had cool pockets on the thighs with a knife on one side and mulitool on the other. Then there was the pair of boots that zipped up the front and had a split between the big toe and other toes. Like a ninja. Last was a ski mask-looking thing made from the same black material as the other clothes, but with a lighter weave.

I took a deep breath and released my ghosting. The attic heat hit me like a hammer. I bent down and reached under some insulation to retrieve a large, sealed plastic bag. Working slowly in the dark, I untied the bag and put on the work clothes. I wished there were a better way to do this, but if I had ghosted back down out of the attic holding the clothes still in the bag, I would have come out below with a handful of torn material. Ghosting and the other talents only worked on whatever was right next to my skin, and that could have weird effects if you tried to carry something larger while ghosting or blending.

Dressed, I ghosted and felt immediate relief from the pressing heat. I blended and dropped back down through the attic floor and down the wall. I stepped out into my room and released the blending and ghosting.

I don't know how I'd missed her. I must have been looking down at the floor as I ghosted down the wall. Whatever the case, I jerked my head up when I saw motion across the room. Janey stood up from where she'd been sitting on my bed, her arms crossed, a big smile plastered on her face.

"So, Joss, here's where you tell me what you're up to, or I go straight to Mom and Dad."

CHAPTER 4

A PRIOR COMMITMENT

"WHAT ARE YOU talking about?" I pulled the mask off, dropped it on the floor, and tried to act natural. "I'm just going over to Thomas's."

Janey stepped up to me and jabbed a finger into my chest. It couldn't have been on purpose, but she poked me right in the shirt's bullet hole.

"Start talking, or you can explain this"—she gestured toward my outfit—"to Mom and Dad."

"Okay!" I said. "But back off!"

Janey went back to my bed and sat down. I took a seat on my desk chair.

"You know that guy at the mall today?" I said.

"Bobby?" she said. "The one who pantsed you in seventh grade?"

"Yeah. Bobby Ferris. When I first learned my Seven stuff, I had this idea to get even with him, okay? I went to his house, blending and all. I was gonna haunt him or something. Like, make him pee himself."

Janey's eyes went wide. "That's horrible! You get these powers and that's what you want to do with them?"

"Pretty much. Not too proud of it, either. Anyway, I went to his house and, well, it was bad. Drunk dad trying to punch him bad, so I left him alone. But it got me thinking that maybe it'd be good for him, and good for me, if I could figure out how to help him. So I did."

"Wait, what about his mom? Where was she?"

I shrugged. "I don't think she's on the scene. Don't really know anything about her."

"Okay." Janey shook her head. "So what'd you do?"

"I went back and pretended to be his guardian angel. Dumped all his dad's liquor and told him he had to treat Bobby better. The weird thing was, his dad acted like he agreed. Like, it was a good thing this invisible angel was telling him to fix stuff."

I swung around and rummaged through my desk drawer while I kept talking. "I told Bobby to contact me if he needed more help.

I found the note, still in the plastic bag, and took it to Janey. She was staring at me like I was nuts. I ignored it.

"I told Bobby, you know, as a fake angel," I said, "that he should contact me by leaving a note in that big tree at Beckler Park. Well, after everything went down, we found that."

I handed her the bag, and Janey slowly pulled the note out. Her eyes flicked back and forth across the page as she read it. When she finished, she put it back in the bag and handed it to me.

"What're you going to do?" she said.

"I'm going to help," I said, "or try to. I'd totally forgotten about the whole thing until I saw Bobby in the mall today."

"But you can't." Janey got to her feet. "You promised Mom and Dad. No new Seven stuff."

"This isn't new," I said. "You see the note. It's a, uh, prior commitment."

The words popped out of my mouth, and I wasn't sure if they sounded right. I'd been thinking it, but saying it made it sound like I was being dishonest. But I'd made a commitment, and if I told my parents they'd just shut it down.

Janey sat back down on the bed and stared at me for a moment. "That's genius. Evil, but genius. And it's for a good cause, right?"

"Absolutely."

"All right. I'm in. Let's do it."

"Wait," I said. "What're you talking about?"

"You include me," she said, "or I go to Mom and Dad."

"But, uh, but." Words failed me. "You can't help. I've got to do Seven stuff."

"We'll see," Janey said. "For now, you're gonna tell me what's going on. So start with tonight. What's the plan?"

"But, you… what?"

"What's the plan? Tonight. What're you going to do?"

I shook my head. "There's no plan. Not really. I'll go to Thomas's house and head over to Bobby's place from there. He lives pretty close by. Try to figure out what comes next. That's all I know."

Janey hopped up and patted me on the shoulder. "Then that's good enough for me. Just report back tomorrow morning and let me know how it goes."

With that, she swung open the door and walked out. I flipped the door closed and suppressed the urge to scream. I settled for waving my arms above my head in frustration. I had just been blackmailed by my twelve-year-old sister. I wasn't even doing anything bad. Sure, I was cutting it pretty close with my promise to my parents, but it really was a good cause. And she'd get me busted if I didn't keep her in the loop. There was no justice, and nothing to do about it.

I stripped off my work clothes and stuffed them in the bottom of my backpack before packing in the rest of my clothes and bathroom stuff. Once done, I pulled on a snug pair of shorts and lay down on my bed. All my clothing was pretty tight now. Mara had taught me Sevens almost always wore tight clothing to avoid problems when using their talents. The last thing I wanted to do was leave part of my pants behind when ghosting through a wall, so I'd followed her advice.

I'd also discovered, sort of accidentally, a really cool trick with reggying. Right before we'd gone to rescue Janey, when I'd been pretty beat up, Mara had told me to get in bed and reggie with everything I had. I'd done it, and it had put me into a deep sleep for over an hour. When I'd woken up, I'd felt about a hundred times better. A few days later, I tried it again when I wasn't injured, but just wanted some good rest. I'd reggied, slept a bit, and it had felt like I'd slept all night. Since then, I'd been doing it every night. I could grab an hour of sleep a couple times a day and feel great. It was how I'd made time to practice my talents so much the past few days. While the neighbors slept, I'd be outside kinneying and running around like a maniac.

I lay down in my snug shorts, closed my eyes, and practiced the tactical breathing I'd learned at Battlehoop. In a couple minutes, I felt calm and was ready for the next step. I took one last breath, and reggied. A moment's warmth, and I was out.

I woke about forty-five minutes later, refreshed and feeling great. It was still an hour or so until I needed to go to Thomas's, so I practiced flipping through some of my talents. Ghost to bruise. Bruise to kinney. Kinney to blend. Blend to ghost and bruise. On and on. Different combinations, faster and faster. Blending and ghosting were still fast and pretty easy, but bruising was right there with them, and kinneying was radically faster than it'd been a couple weeks ago. I couldn't kinney for long, but I could get going in the blink of an eye now.

After that, I grabbed my backpack and headed downstairs. No one was in the kitchen, so I grabbed a mug of leftover coffee and reheated it in the microwave, making sure it wasn't too hot. I wanted to be able to drink it fast. I added a touch of sugar—maybe three heaping spoonfuls— and a splash of half-n-half, and downed it. Between my reggie sleep and the coffee, I figured I was good to go if I had to stay up all night.

That done, I tracked down my parents and said goodbye to them. As I headed back through the family room to the backdoor off the kitchen, I ran into Janey. As I stepped around her, she took a big sidestep and blocked me.

"What?" I said.

"Just wanted to say goodbye," she said. She leaned in close. "And remind you. Full report tomorrow."

I glared at her. She smiled back. I shook my head and stepped around her. I might have kinneyed just a little bit to make sure she couldn't block me again. Janey was freaky quick, and I knew it bugged her that I could move faster than her when I wanted to. In fact, it was probably good for her. A gentle reminder to help her stay humble.

I biked over to Thomas's house and pulled up by his privacy fence's side gate so I could take my bike around back. It was locked. I knew he used a carabiner instead of a padlock to secure it, so I set my bike down and glanced around. The fence was set back between Thomas's house and their neighbor's, so I was more or less out of sight. With no one around, I ghosted through the fence. Once through, I unlocked the gate, pulled my bike through, and locked the gate back up.

I walked to the back of the house with my bike and almost stumbled in a rut or something. I looked down and saw a hollowed-out indent in the shape of me. Oops. Had it really only been this morning that I'd squashed my face into the dirt? I continued to the back door and leaned my bike against the brick side of the house under the patio roof.

I knocked, and Thomas let me in.

"You're early," he said as we headed to the kitchen. "Mom won't be home until super-late. I guess we can get something to eat."

"You think that's a problem?" I said. "Will she want to see me? I was thinking I'd head over to Bobby's around sunset."

Thomas pulled some hotdogs out of the fridge and stuck them in the microwave on a plate. "Not a problem. I'll cover for you."

Once the hotdogs were ready, we sat down to eat them with some apples and carrots. I hadn't planned to tell him about Stanton, but once we were eating it all came out in a rush. It helped having someone else know what was going on, and Thomas was my best option.

"Pretty crazy day," Thomas said when I finished.

I nodded. "That's what I was thinking."

After cleaning up, I grabbed my backpack and we headed upstairs to play XBOX. It was a nice break, but I kept losing. It wasn't like we played the same game over and over, either. I lost at everything.

"Pretty distracted, huh?" Thomas said after his character kicked mine off the screen.

I nodded and checked my phone. It was about 7:00 PM. "I think I'm going to head over, see what my options are."

"Might as well," Thomas said. "Wake me when you're back if it's late. I'll have a sleeping bag set up for you."

"Will do. Gonna change into my work clothes just in case."

Thomas nodded. I grabbed my backpack and headed into the bathroom. A few minutes later, I was back, dressed in black from head to foot. I had the mask tucked into my chest pocket with my phone. Thomas cracked a grin when I stepped back into the game room.

"That outfit is awesome," he said. "Like you're a scuba ninja."

"Whatever. I'm out. Be back whenever."

I blended and ghosted through the wall. I came out onto a section of first floor roof and released the ghosting. Jogging to the edge, I leapt out over some hedges below and landed on the grass in a shoulder roll. Now that I could heal myself, I was willing to take risks that might have terrified me before. The odd thing was, the bad stuff didn't end up happening. No broken ankles. No concussions. We'd done a ton of training on how to fall properly at Battlehoop, and it had paid off.

I ghosted through the side fence and went out to the street. It was a fifteen-minute walk to Bobby's house, but I figured I could jog there in six minutes. 420 seconds. That meant if I kinneyed full speed and ran, I could probably get there in under twenty seconds. But that would also tire me out, and I didn't know what was coming next. I decided to save my energy and walk, but ghost the whole time to avoid the summer heat.

At Bobby's house, I cut through the front door and headed to the family room, past the living room and dining room on either side of the entryway. Mr. Ferris was coming toward me from the hallway on my left, rubbing his face like he'd been asleep. He was a pretty big guy, though not as big as Bobby. His dark brown hair had looked more like a bird's nest than hair when I'd last seen him. Now it was neatly trimmed and short.

At Battlehoop, we'd learned to fight, but we'd also learned what we called ninja skills. How to walk silently. That sort of thing. I put the training to use and stepped lightly forward out of Mr. Ferris's way. He walked by me to the kitchen, and I headed down the hallway to Bobby's bedroom. The door was closed, so I ghosted through it. On the other side, I stopped in shock. Just froze up and forgot to breathe for a moment.

Bobby lay on his bed messing around on his phone in the middle of a tidy, well-kept room. What had happened? The other two times I'd been here, the place had been trashed to a level that scared even me. I waited a moment to regain my sense of balance with the world before I spoke.

"Bobby," I finally said in my angel-falsetto, "I got your note."

Bobby leapt up at his name, eyes wide and wild. He looked around, and the lines in his brow disappeared as he sank back down to sit on the edge of his bed.

"Hey," he said in a rough voice, "you, uh scared me. I mean, I'm glad you're here. I guess it's hard for you not to surprise me, you know, with you being invisible."

"I understand, Bobby. You're, uh, very brave. Now, about the note. You said your dad needs help. That he's doing well, but in trouble with some criminal, uh, endeavor. That he wants help."

Bobby looked down at his feet, and his face scrunched up like he was in pain. I waited, but he didn't say anything.

"Bobby?"

Bobby mumbled something, but I was still next to the door and too far away to hear.

"Bobby," I said, and my falsetto cracked a bit. "What's going on?"

Bobby squared his shoulders and stood up, looking at a point about two feet to the left of me.

"Well, uh, Dad's sobered up, you know? Or he's trying to. And he's done really well with it. Turns out he'd been working with this, uh, I don't know, organized crime or something. Real low level work. But since he cleaned up, they've given him a promotion or something. And he's decided he likes it. The crime. The money. All of it. He thinks there's a future in it. And he doesn't really want your help anymore."

CHAPTER 5

MR. FERRIS'S NEW JOB

I WAS STANDING, invisible, in Bobby Ferris's room, my junior high arch enemy, pretending to be a guardian angel, and he was telling me that his dad was doing well in organized crime and, thanks for the help, but no thanks.

"He doesn't want my help," I said in my angel voice.

Bobby shook his head. His eyes looked misty, like he was about to cry. I did not want to see him cry.

"I guess that's it, then," I said. "I'll let myself out."

He jumped to his feet. "Wait! You have to help him. Please."

What exactly did Bobby expect? How was I supposed to help a guy, who didn't want help, leave a criminal organization I knew nothing about?

"Bobby," I said, using a very calm, high pitched, squeaky voice. "How am I supposed to help him?"

"You're… you're an angel. Can't you figure something out?"

Except I wasn't an angel, and I was beginning to regret ever pretending to be one.

I sighed. "When's your dad working next?"

Bobby tried to smile but failed, and settled for scrubbing his eyes with the back of a hand. "Tonight. He was grabbing some dinner and heading out. Said it would be a long night. Something big's going down this week."

I worked it over in my mind. I figured I'd give it a shot for one night. Sneak along in the car and see what he was up to. Maybe think of a way to mess things up so badly that Mr. Ferris would have to look for work somewhere else. I imagined different things that might be going on, and what I could do to stop them.

"Are you still here?" Bobby said.

He was sitting down on his bed again, squinting and looking around the room, as if squinting would help him see me when I was blending.

"I'm here, Bobby, but I'm leaving now. I'll go with your dad when he leaves"—I held a hand up to silence Bobby, who looked like he wanted to interrupt, but of course the hand didn't do any good because I was invisible, so I just kept on talking—"and make sure he doesn't know I'm with him! Maybe I'll be able to help."

Bobby smiled and nodded. "Thank you. Thank you so much!"

I didn't see much point in staying any longer, so I backed out and ghosted through the door to the hallway. I could hear Mr. Ferris banging around in the kitchen, so I figured I had a little time. What I needed was a chance to stop blending so I could save my energy. If I went outside I'd sweat like crazy, and the thought of getting sweaty before riding in the car with Mr. Ferris didn't seem smart. He might smell me. It had happened before, and I didn't plan to ever be detected again by someone's nose.

I ninja-stepped to the kitchen. Mr. Ferris was standing at the counter eating what looked like mushy pizza. Reheating pizza in the microwave was the worst. I cut across the kitchen and through a doorway into a short hall. There was a bathroom to my right and a pretty big laundry room to my left that had another door on the opposite wall. That had to be the door to the garage.

I picked the bathroom. The door was wide open and the lights off. I went in and ghosted through the clear glass door to the shower stall. Thankfully, it hadn't been used in ages and was dry. I sat down in the corner, which gave me a clear line of sight of the laundry room and back door, but left me in deep shadows. I released the blend and took a deep, slow breath. I was getting a lot stronger at blending and ghosting, but they still wore me down over time.

The shower tile was cool on my back and legs. My black work clothes blended into the shadows. It was pretty much the perfect spot to hide out and rest. I pulled my mask out of my chest pocket and put it on, just in case.

Mr. Ferris banged around in the kitchen for a few more minutes, before it quieted down. He was probably getting ready to leave. I closed my eyes and rested. I had no idea what I was doing. I had this nagging thought in the back of my mind that this might count as flagrantly disobeying my dad, but I kept telling myself it wasn't something new. It was a prior commitment.

The back door banged shut and my eyes snapped open. Had I dozed? I jumped up, ghosted and blended, and ran for the garage. I popped through the backdoor in time to see Mr. Ferris close the driver door on an old SUV that barely fit in the trashed garage. Stuff was piled everywhere. Scraps of wood. Rusted tools. A bunch of folding lawn chairs that looked like they'd spent a year at the bottom of the ocean. At least five bikes, all with parts missing.

I ran over to the vehicle and ghosted through the back door as the engine started. Thankfully, the inside of the SUV was clear. I ghosted through the back seats into the cargo area and lay down. The vehicle jerked into motion, and Mr. Ferris backed it down the driveway into an alley. I made sure I was out of sight behind the seats and released my blend.

Riding in a car without a seatbelt felt strange. I lay on my back behind the back seats with my legs curled to the side, staring at the car's ceiling, and seeing flickers of motion and light out of my peripheral vision through the surrounding windows. It was full dark now. At some point Mr. Ferris flicked on the radio and, unfortunately, it was a country station. My mind wandered.

Had I been a normal kid just three months ago? Eighth grade conquered and gearing up for high school? Before I learned what my butterfly tattoo really meant. Before the tests, and the talents, and Battlehoop, and Mara, and Jordan. Before cops followed me to the mall, and the Guild forced meetings with my parents.

Would I walk away from all that if it meant I was no longer a Seven? There'd been that moment with Isabella and Gary—who I still thought had the lamest gangster name ever—when I'd have gladly given it all up. But I'd gotten through it, and the bank robbery, and the battle for Janey. I was pretty sure I wasn't the same person anymore, and I didn't think walking away was a real option, even if it was possible, which it wasn't.

The SUV lurched to a halt, and the music died as Mr. Ferris killed the engine. I blended and sat up just in time to see Mr. Ferris swing open his door and hop out. I ghosted through the side of the car and looked around. We were in the parking lot of a worn out apartment complex. It looked like every other street lamp lighting the cars had given up or was doing a poor job of it. Puddles of shadows hid the spaces between the three story apartment buildings.

Mr. Ferris crossed over to a sidewalk and marched toward the nearest building. I hurried after him. He headed up the nearest flight of stairs and knocked on the first door. I caught up and stood off to the side, still blending. Mr. Ferris knocked again, but this time it was a lot closer to banging on the door with a fist.

That's when I noticed his other hand. It was behind his back, up under the ultra-light jacket he was wearing, grasping a gun that was tucked into the back of his waistband. I moved closer and got ready to kinney if things went sideways.

Mr. Ferris kept banging on the door, and right when I was pretty sure he'd established no one was home in the apartment, or any of the other apartments in the area, the door cracked open. A burst of words came through the crack, but I couldn't understand them. Maybe an Asian language, and pretty high pitched, so probably a woman. Mr. Ferris pushed on the door, but it didn't move, like something was holding it open a crack but no more. It was probably one of those door chains.

More words spilled out of the apartment, and Mr. Ferris

shouted something back. In the same language. I was stunned. He'd spoken much slower, but still. Mr. Ferris had spoken Korean, or Vietnamese, or something. I hadn't expected that.

Whatever he'd said worked. The door closed for a second, there was a scraping sound, and it swung all the way open. Mr. Ferris still had his hand on his gun, but when an Asian woman shorter than me stepped out, he tugged the jacket back over the gun and dropped his hand to his side. I took a deep breath and tried to relax. She was wearing long pants and a sort of bathrobe-looking shirt. She didn't look old or young to me, just somewhere in the middle.

The two of them argued in hissed words and large gestures for a few minutes, but she finally pulled the door closed and produced a key from some inner pocket to lock it. I followed them back to the SUV, and ghosted into my spot behind the back seats while they got in the front. As soon as Mr. Ferris started the car and pulled out of the parking lot, I released my blending. All this blending and ghosting was tiring me out. I figured we'd be in the car for a while, so a cat nap wouldn't hurt. I closed my eyes and did my reggie-sleep trick.

My eyes popped open. The near total darkness was broken by a greenish glow coming through the windows on one side of the SUV. There was no motion, no vibration of the engine. We were stopped, but I could hear what sounded like a loud engine idling somewhere outside. How long had I been asleep? I felt great, but hadn't planned to sleep for more than a few minutes. I blended and sat up to look around. It was hard to see, but the SUV was empty. Not good.

I ghosted out of the vehicle into cool, indoor air. The engine sounds were much louder. I stood on a smooth concrete floor in the middle of a massive space. The green glow came from glow sticks scattered on the floor around two eighteen-wheelers. The second one barely showed behind the first from where I stood, and they both had their engines running.

Motion flickered at the edge of my vision. I jerked around and saw two men walking at the very edge of the faint greenish light near a wall of the building. They drifted out of sight into the shadows and I started breathing again. Sure, I was invisible, but my brain still had trouble with the concept, and I did not want to be seen right now.

Taking another look around, I figured out I was in a warehouse. The ceiling was at least twenty feet above, and on the far side of the SUV I could just make out giant storage racks set in rows, retreating into the darkness. The SUV was parked near two other cars, maybe fifty feet from the two eighteen-wheelers.

The two people came back into sight over near the storage racks, walking slowly across the warehouse floor. Was one of them Mr. Ferris? What was going on? And where was I? I decided to answer the last question first.

I ghosted back into the SUV and released my blend. I pulled my phone out and wedged in facing the rear seats, so that the phone was in a little triangle of space between me, the seats, and the floor. I unlocked it and was relieved to see it was only 10:00 PM. I hadn't slept that long. I pulled up the map app, and the little blue dot showed that I was near downtown, but off to the west. I mapped a route home. It was seventeen miles, but there were a couple highways that went most of the way.

That was no good. Even if I ran flat out kinneying, I doubted I could move faster than twenty times my normal speed. Maybe a top speed of three hundred miles an hour. Incredible, but even at that speed it would only be five miles in a minute, and I could only kinney like that for half a minute or less. So running home was out.

I flipped off my phone and stuck it back in my chest pocket. The problem would have to wait. First, I needed to figure out what Mr. Ferris was up to in this warehouse, and who these other people were. And how to shut it all down.

I blended and ghosted back out of the SUV. The two men walking the perimeter were back at the wall near me. I walked lightly toward them at an angle to intercept them. My eyes were seeing some spots from the brightness of my phone, but by the time I was ten feet from them it was obvious neither of them was Mr. Ferris. From their size and shape, they were big men. Really big. And somehow I doubted the shadowy shapes they clutched were water guns. Probably the real thing.

Why, why, why was I doing this again? Did I have some bizarre need to put my life in danger? Or was I just incredibly stupid? Had becoming a Seven done something to my brain? Maybe that was it. Sevens had always existed to make the world a better place or something like that. Maybe Sevens were addled so they'd ignore the risks and be all brave.

While I stood there silently asking myself questions, the two men moved off along the wall into the shadows. I glanced around. Three vehicles parked in a row. Two eighteen-wheelers, engines running, surrounded by glow sticks. Then I noticed something new. A set of steps led up to shadowy doorways at the back of both trucks' trailers. Whatever was going on, it had to be happening inside those trailers.

I walked toward the trucks. I'd find out what they were doing in there, and I'd put a stop to it. Somehow. It would come to me. It had to.

The door at the back of the trailer farther from me burst open, and a man spilled out along with a dim, red light. Between the red light from the trailer and the hazy green light of the glow sticks, we practically had a gangster Christmas thing going on. In the faint light, I could tell he was wearing a suit, and was big, but not much else. He was holding something in his hand. He jerked it to his mouth, and more light fell on it. A walkie talkie.

"Everyone. Get back here. We're compromised. A cellphone's transmitting somewhere in the warehouse."

The walkie talkie squelched to silence. My hand drifted up and felt the flat shape of the phone in my pocket. Oops.

CHAPTER 6

THE WAREHOUSE

MAYBE ONE DAY I'd enjoy feeling scared and confused, but I wasn't there yet. My heart ticked up to a gallop, and my breathing got shallow and fast. What was going on? A second man I didn't recognize came out of the trailer right behind the first guy with the walkie talkie, and the door to the other trailer burst open.

Mr. Ferris stood framed in the doorway by a harsh, white light. I squinted and looked away to keep my night vision, but in that moment I'd seen he was wearing a full set of blue scrubs, like the surgeons on TV. It was a good thing I'd looked away, because I noticed the two men patrolling the perimeter jogging directly toward me. I hustled over to the first trailer, where Mr. Ferris still stood in the doorway, and scooted underneath it. From there, I could see walkie talkie guy and the other guy from that farther trailer as they walked toward the back of the trailer I was under, as well as the two patrol guys inbound.

A crack of yellow-green streetlight opened in the dark wall across from me. It widened into a doorway, and two shapes entered. The door closed, and the shapes disappeared for a moment in shadows, before the men showed up in the wedge of white light shining from the doorway in the trailer above me.

Mr. Ferris came down off the steps and closed the door behind him, cutting off the white light. Soon, all seven men stood in a tight circle, lit only by the glow sticks. Mr. Ferris was definitely in scrubs.

"Okay, here's the drill."

That was walkie talkie guy. It was hard to tell the men apart, but I recognized his voice.

"Let me see your phones," he said. "Unlock 'em. Gonna make sure they're on airplane mode, then we're gonna leave 'em right here to be sure. I'm doing it, too, see?"

"Walt," one of the men said, but walkie talkie guy—Walt—cut him off with a slashing motion.

"I'm doing it, too, see? Now!"

There was some grumbling, but I saw seven little bursts of light as phones were unlocked and inspected. A minute later, all the phones were on the floor in the circle of men.

"Three nights," Walt said. "And no second chances. You hear me? I've been puttin' this together for a long time, and nothin's gonna screw it up. I'm not tellin' Mr. Silver I blew his investment. Art here"—Walt's arm jerked up toward the man next to him—"swears he picked up an active cellphone a moment ago on his scanner, okay? So let's assume someone's here, and let's find 'em, and take care of 'em. Eddie, how they comin'?"

"They're telling me they've got over half of it prepped, so maybe an hour, maybe a little more, and we can roll."

That had definitely been Mr. Ferris's voice. I hadn't thought of him as an Eddie, but I was flexible. Eddie had said "they," so there was more than one person in the trailer above me, not just the woman he'd picked up. What were they prepping, and what was that whole "three nights" comment about?

I ran through the facts. Eddie thought he was part of some big criminal thing. Someone believed it was important enough to have armed goons patrolling the place. They needed another hour tonight and probably another couple nights to finish whatever it was they were doing. I wanted to ghost into the trailer above me and see what was going on. It had to be a lab setup.

"Make it one hour tops." Walt's voice snapped me out of my thoughts. "Here's what we do. You guys stay paired up. Eddie, stay with the scrubs. Art, set us up, then get back into control."

Art reached over to both shadowy pairs of men and handed them something that looked a lot like a walkie talkie.

"Okay, it's like playing the hot and cold game," Art said, holding up another of the devices, and handing it to Walt. "You'll feel it vibrate more when you get closer, and vibrate less when you're farther away. So you've got to triangulate, okay? You all come in from different directions, and figure out where it is in the middle."

Oh, crud. No time to investigate the lab trailer. Things were about to get very hot for me when they turned those scanners on. I needed to get my phone into airplane mode, but if I opened it here, they'd see the light from the screen. I turned, scooted out from underneath the trailer, and headed for the rows of giant shelving at the edge of the light. I was walking softly, and that meant I was walking slowly.

"Hey, mines buzzing," a voice said behind me.

"Mine, too." Another voice.

"Spread out, three different directions," Art said.

"Get back in control," Walt said. "We'll find 'em."

I kept walking, hoping the scanners weren't very sensitive and it'd take a while to figure out who was closer to me.

"Mine's definitely getting weaker." The voice was further away.

I turned around and walked backwards. A pair of men were over near the cars, and a second pair were almost out of sight in the shadows near the wall. I didn't see Walt.

"Yep, definitely weaker." The voice had come from the pair near the wall.

"Let's go." Walt's voice came from somewhere on the far side of the control eighteen-wheeler, barely audible over the sound of the diesel engines. "Toward the shelving!"

Fear tugged at my stomach with a sickening pull. They were on to me. At that moment, I realized I was being dumb. I was sneaking around and trying to walk quietly when there was no way anyone could hear me over the sound of the rumbling engines of those two trucks. I turned and ran.

The shelves loomed ahead in the darkness, and the cogs in my brain made another slow turn. I was running blind. What if I ran into something in the dark and brained myself? But I was a Seven. I ghosted and kept running. It took extra concentration to run while ghosting because my feet kept trying to sink into the floor, but I figured it was worth it.

What was my plan? Was I going to keep running and head right out of the back of the warehouse? What about my promise to Bobby to help his dad? Promise seemed like a strong word. Maybe I'd just said I'd do my best. Having a bunch of armed men zeroing in on me felt like I'd done my best, but was it? I was the Seventy-Seven. I had all seven talents, so why would I bail at the first sign of trouble?

The warehouse shelving reached up on either side at least twenty feet as I ran into one of the huge aisles. Big shelves held bulky shapes clustered together in dark, shadowy masses. I slowed to a stop and looked back. I was a dozen paces into an aisle. I could see one pair of the men coming my way, but they were still a ways off.

I needed to think. If I was going to force Mr. Ferris—Eddie—out of this thing, whatever it was, I needed to disrupt the whole operation. But I couldn't ghost and blend forever, and they were tracking my cellphone. I needed to shake them loose, then do something dramatic. A plan popped into my head. It was simple, but to the point. I took another look into the gloomy darkness of the top shelf above me. It could work. So, no putting my phone into airplane mode. Instead, a distraction.

When I kinneyed and ran, I covered huge amounts of ground with each step. What if I kinneyed and jumped straight up? I looked back toward the trucks, and saw the silhouettes of the men moving down my aisle toward me. I stopped ghosting and kinneyed. Feet planted, I jumped hard, aiming at that top shelf.

It worked. I held the kinney so I'd have time to react as I floated higher and higher. I gradually slowed down, but it looked like I might make it. The top shelf loomed into view, and my heart sank. I was hosed. A huge wooden crate pretty much blocked off the shelf right where I was heading.

I'd aimed myself almost perfectly. At least, it would have been perfect if there hadn't been a giant wooden crate walling off the shelf. I could tell I'd peak right about the moment I smacked into the side of that crate. If I was going to pull off my plan, I needed to leave my phone up there to keep the men busy looking for me. Well, that didn't mean I had to actually land.

I pulled my phone out of the pocket as I leveled out and sailed gently into the crate. At least, it felt gentle to me, since everything was moving so slowly. I reached with one hand to fend off the crate while I set my phone on top of it with the other. Success! Then I started falling.

Somehow, I hadn't really thought through what would happen on the way down. And what I really hadn't planned for was my foot catching the lip of the top shelf. But it did, and I tumbled backwards end over end as I fell. My life was so ridiculous. I did slow motion cartwheels in the air as I fell toward the concrete floor two stories below.

I was twisting as I rotated, and as I swung around I got a good look at the two guys coming down the aisle toward me. They were moving in super-slow motion, but seemed to be lifting their heads up to look at the crate where I'd just put my phone. Oh, crud. My gentle encounter with that crate, when played at normal speed, had probably made a ton of noise.

Maybe that was to my advantage. It had put the focus on that shelf, which was the point of putting my phone up there. So now I just had to survive my landing. Bruising would save me for sure, but it would also make a lot of noise and mess up the whole "find my phone" trick I'd just set up. So bruising was out, but if I didn't do something soon, I was pretty sure I was going to discover what it felt like to break my bones in slow motion.

Speaking of which, why didn't my bones snap when I kinneyed? Moving that fast had to put intense pressure on my body. I'd just proved it by jumping twenty feet straight up. This whole Seven thing was still one giant mystery to me. And the floor was getting closer.

I settled on ghosting and released the kinneying. Time snapped back to normal, and I whipped around and slammed into the floor. I was almost upright when I hit the concrete, but I didn't really hit it since I was ghosting. I came to a stop buried up to my chest. There'd been no pain. No sense of broken bones.

The two bad guys walked toward me and stopped a few feet away, still looking up into the darkness where they'd heard me hit the crate. I ghosted out of the concrete, released the ghosting, and ninja-stepped away from them, back toward the trucks.

"Guys!" one of the men behind me said. "Little help here."

Walt came running into the aisle with the other pair of men just behind him. I stepped to the side and let them past, then ran back toward the trucks, hoping the engine noise was loud enough to cover the noise. I cut across the open area, past the trucks, and pulled up at phones, clustered on the floor. One of the phones was still lit, showing its home screen.

I grabbed it and touched the screen to keep it from locking. My plan was going to work. I took it off airplane mode while I walked over to the wall. A moment later, it was on the network. Time to create some chaos. I dialed 911.

"You've dialed 911. What's your emergency?"

The woman's voice on the phone was friendly, even cheerful. I'd never dialed 911 before, so I hadn't been sure what to expect, but this was not it.

"Yes, ma'am," I said. "I've got an emergency."

"And what is that emergency?"

I frowned. Good question. Maybe I should have hammered out some of these details ahead of time.

"Sir, what is the nature of your emergency?"

"I'm trapped in a warehouse," I said. "Lots of guys with guns. I've seen six or seven of them."

"Is your life in immediate danger?" Her voice had gotten tense.

"I'm hiding right now. I stole one of their phones. Can you trace it? Figure out where I am?"

"We're working on that right now. Can you give me any more information? Are all the men in the warehouse with you?"

"The ones I've seen are," I said. "I think that's all there is."

The door to the control trailer burst open, red light spilling out once more. I immediately mashed the phone up against my chest to make sure it was blending with me. I didn't need Art to see a phone suspended in midair.

"Sir? Sir?" a tiny, distant voice said. "Are you there?"

Art jerked his head this way and that, put his walkie talkie to his mouth, and turned back into the trailer as he started speaking.

"Pretty sure we've got a second cellphone active." His voice came through the open trailer door. "Any luck with that first one? Over."

I set the phone face down on the floor, and turned its volume all the way down.

"Yeah, we've got a problem." Art's voice again. "This second phone's on an active call. Over."

"I'm comin'." That had been Walt's voice on Art's walkie talkie.

I edged toward the trailer. As I got closer, I heard other noises coming from inside the trailer. Not noises. Voices, but warped sounding, like over a cheap radio. I heard Art cuss, then cuss some more.

"Just picked up a response to a 911 call on the police scanner," Art said. "Our address. We've got cops inbound. Over."

Walt came tearing into view from the shelving and ran straight into the red-lit control trailer. I heard him talking to Art, but their voices were low and I couldn't make out the words aside from some more cussing. They were mad. I smiled.

Walt stepped out of the trailer and put his walkie talkie to his mouth. "Eddie. Out here. Now. Everyone else, get over here. Forget that phone."

The door to the other trailer opened and Mr. Ferris stepped out, shutting the door behind him.

"Man, it's dark out here," Mr. Ferris said.

"Shut up," Walt said. "Where we at? If we had to roll right now, how much'd we lose?"

"We can't leave!" Mr. Ferris said. "They're in the middle—"

"How much!" Walt stepped over to Mr. Ferris and grabbed him by the scrubs. "How much would we lose?"

The other four men ran up, saw Walt raging at Mr. Ferris, and decided not to interrupt. They stood in a knot off to the side and waited.

"I'll find out," Mr. Ferris said, "but at least thirty percent. Should we lock it down? Once we do that, we're done. We lose what we lose."

"Keep 'em working," Walt said. "The moment I give the word, get 'em to pack it up."

Mr. Ferris nodded, and Walt pushed him toward the trailer. Mr. Ferris stumbled, caught himself, and ran back into the trailer. I had the good sense to shield my eyes while the door was opened this time.

"Let me spell this out," Walt said, his voice intense. "We lose a third of this batch, and Mr. Silver, he's gonna deep six us. You get me? Dead men walking, that's what we are. So I don't care what it takes. We gotta buy time. I figure we make it out alive if we get to eighty percent or more, so we need thirty minutes."

"What's our protocol?" one of the men asked. He had his gun out and was inspecting it in the weak light from the glow sticks.

"Anything goes," Walt said. "Stretch it out as much as possible, but I'm gonna take dead cops over me being dead, see?"

Dead cops? An icy fist clenched my stomach. What had I done?

CHAPTER 7

SERVE AND PROTECT

"GET THOSE SCANNERS goin'," Walt said. "Find this other phone that's callin' 911."

"Uh, Walt," one of the men said. He was kneeling by their pile of phones on the floor. "There're only six phones here. Shouldn't there be seven?"

Walt cussed a blue streak. "What's goin' on? How's this happening?"

I stepped away from them toward the shelves. What was I going to do? I couldn't let them kill any cops. It would be my fault. I'd called 911 thinking it would solve my problems. Instead, I'd made a big mess of things. And I still didn't know what was going on in the lab trailer where Mr. Ferris was working.

It would have to wait. I needed to get my phone back in case I had to make a run for it. I turned and ran toward the shelves. The men were still talking, but the truck engines quickly drowned out their voices. I headed down the aisle and found my spot. There was no way they could see me wearing black, so I released my blending before kinneying to keep it as simple as possible. My first jump was terrible. Not high enough, and at the peak I was about five feet over from the crate. Jump number two nailed it, and I grabbed my phone off the top of the crate. I tucked it into my chest pocket before ghosting and letting go of the kinney.

I plummeted back down to the concrete floor and sank in a few feet before coming to a stop. That was a seriously cool trick. I ghosted out of the concrete, flipped my phone to airplane mode, and stuck it back in my pocket. Now I just had to figure out how to keep those cops from getting hurt. I blended and ran back toward the trucks.

The men were spread out in pairs again using the scanners. Art was with Walt, and all three pairs were zeroing in on the section of wall where I'd left the phone after calling 911. Walt must have seen it, because he pounced forward and grabbed something off the floor. I edged closer to overhear them.

"It was still on the call with the police," Walt said, looking around at the other men. "Just hung it up. Whose phone is this?"

That led to a bunch of denials and general muttering before one of the men stepped forward to take the phone.

"I didn't do it, Walt," he said, "but that's my phone. Y'all know I was over there"—he hooked a thumb toward the shelves where I'd just been—"with you."

"I know, Frank." Walt's eyes narrowed. "Eddie, then?"

The men turned as a group to look at the trailer Mr. Ferris had entered. And that was when I realized it really hadn't gotten as bad as it could get. No, not only had I put some cops' lives at risk, but I'd managed to frame the very man I was trying to help.

Art stuck a hand out and grabbed Walt's arm. "Don't think it was him, Walt. I was on the radio with him a few times while you guys were looking for the other phone. I could hear the three labbies talking in the background. Didn't understand any of it, but he had to be in that trailer the whole time."

My knees got weak with relief. Back to only one problem to solve. Walt stood there, not speaking, and the other men waited.

"This here is the kind of stuff I've heard about," he said at last, "talkin' to Mr. Silver. We need to get through tonight, then I pull up with 'em tomorrow. Maybe we got an out even if we don't get more of the stuff cooked."

"So what's our play with the cops?" Frank said.

Walt pointed to the control trailer. "Art, get back in there and find that bottle of vodka we stashed. Now." He turned to Frank as Art ran for the trailer. "Get sloppy with the bottle. Make sure they can smell it on your clothes and breath. Then get outside and wait for 'em. When the cops show up, play it off as a prank call. It was your phone. Get yourself arrested for drunk 'n disorderly if you have to. Oh, and gimme your gear."

"Will do, boss," Frank said as he reached inside his light jacket and retrieved a gun to hand to Walt.

Art came back out of the trailer carrying a large, clear bottle, and handed it to Frank, who started dumping it down his front and drinking large gulps of it.

"Don't get too much down the throat," Walt said. "We need you sharp if things get ugly. Okay, let's see. Art, get our back door open and pull your rig into it to block it off. Hopefully the cops'll come in straight from the front, but we got to be ready to roll. Rick, stay near yours and be ready. Rest of you, let's go."

Art got in the cab of the control truck, and a moment later the eighteen-wheeler lurched into motion. It pulled forward and drove out of sight down one of the aisles between the huge shelving. Their "back door" had to be some kind of cargo entrance on the far side of the warehouse. One of the other big guys went over and got in the cab of the lab truck. He stuck his hand out the window and gave a thumbs up.

Walt nodded to him, and waved the other men after him. "Okay, let's set up. Frank, you're out in the open. Nothing dramatic until I give the word."

Walt, Frank, and the two other men headed out the door I'd seen them use earlier. That left me alone with three cars, some glow sticks, and an eighteen-wheeler. Time to find out what was going on in that lab trailer. I ran over to it, leapt up the steps, and ghosted through the door.

The light was blinding. I held the ghosting along with my blending while I let my eyes adjust. Once I could see, I dropped the ghosting. It was cold like the frozen section at the grocery store. The trailer looked like a chemistry lab from a science fiction movie. Mr. Ferris sat on a stool in the corner off to my right in a clear space. An aisle stretched from me to the far end of the trailer. All sorts of equipment and gadgets, large and small, lined both sides. Tubes, beakers, scales, vats, giant cylinders, and other stuff crowded together, with bits of noise and steam coming from some of the devices.

The woman Mr. Ferris had picked up at the apartment was wearing a white lab coat, oversized glasses, and a surgical mask. At least, I assumed it was her. I couldn't really see enough to know for sure, but the other two working with her were pretty obviously men, even though they were dressed the exact same. They exchanged a quiet stream of words in that language I'd heard her use with Mr. Ferris. I couldn't understand what they were saying, but I could tell they were mad. Just then Mr. Ferris yelled something, cutting over their conversation, and all three turned to him for a moment before returning to work with a lot less talking.

What were they making that was so involved? Then again, did it matter? It had to be something bad, whether drugs or bombs or whatever.

The walkie talkie in Mr. Ferris's lap crackled to life.

"Two patrol cars inbound. Maintain radio silence until I give the word. Eddie, keep 'em working. Over."

Mr. Ferris picked up the walkie talkie and brought it to his mouth. His eyebrows pulled together like he was thinking hard, and he slowly lowered the device back to his lap. I smiled. He'd almost answered a direct order to shut up. I looked around the trailer one last time. I wasn't hit by a burst of insight. It still made no sense. I shook my head and ghosted through the door behind me.

The warehouse was nearly pitch black to my eyes after the searing bright light inside the trailer. The faint green glow was barely visible as I tried to blink away the spots of color dancing in my vision. It had to be brighter outside. I kept ghosting in case I hit anything and ran for the warehouse wall. It made me realize that ghosting would be a great way to avoid stubbing a toe when going to the bathroom at night, though I wasn't sure what would happen if I ghosted while actually taking a leak. I'd definitely have to do an experiment to find out.

I hit the wall and pushed through. It was slow going. I was wearing myself out with all the blending, ghosting, and bursts of kinneying. Outside, the moon shone brightly, revealing a narrow strip of grass separating the warehouse from a large parking lot. Headlights swept past me. Two cop cars turned into the far side of the lot and were rolling this way. There were no sirens, and no flashing lights. Several cars were parked in nearby spaces, and Frank was making a scene of stumbling around between them. I saw Walt crouching behind an SUV off to my left with one of his men. The other guy hid behind a car off to my right. None of them would be visible to the cops.

Holding my blend, I walked toward Frank. The cop cars came in fast, and they parked at angles so that the two cars made a V, the wide end open toward Frank. Two cops got out of each car, their hands on their gun belts.

"Sir," one of the cops said calmly but forcefully, "put the bottle down and get your hands in the air."

Frank stumbled, looked around, and made a big show of seeing the cops for the first time. He set the bottle on the pavement and stood back up slowly, raising his hands.

"Whazzup?" Frank said, his words barely understandable.

I stopped about ten feet away from Frank and waited, ready to move. Two of the cops glanced at each other before approaching him together. My eyes were finally adjusting to the night, and I saw that one cop held his taser and the other his gun. The remaining two cops spread out on either side and walked forward with them.

"We had a call to 911. You know anything about that?" taser cop asked.

"Oh, ya. I preshed those buttons." Frank, it turned out, was great at slurring his speech. I'd never been around drunk people, but from what I'd seen in movies, he was doing a pretty good job of faking it.

"You? You called 911?" Taser cop was really close to Frank now, and his partner had let go of his gun to reach for something at the back of his belt.

"Yesh. I. Did." Frank gave each word serious emphasis.

Taser cop shook his head, and his partner whipped a pair of handcuffs out. The other two cops stayed to the sides, scanning the warehouse. I was so conflicted. I'd hoped to get the cops here to bust up the whole operation, but was now hoping they'd just drive away. But if they did, it left me with the problem of disrupting the big chemistry experiment going on in Mr. Ferris's trailer.

"Hands behind your back, sir," taser cop said, and he and his partner stepped forward and each took an arm to help Frank obey in a hurry.

A moment later, Frank was cuffed and the men were searching him. Taser cop came up with Frank's cellphone a moment later. He held it in front of Frank's face.

"This yours?"

"Shink so," Frank said, and let his head roll down onto his chest.

"I need you to unlock it, okay?" taser cop said. "I'm going to ask you to use a finger to unlock it when I hold it behind your back. Do you understand?"

Frank lifted his head for a moment and eyed the cop. "Yesh."

They got the phone unlocked, and taser cop flipped through the screens. "Last call was to 911. It's the right number. This is our phone."

"Doesn't make sense," said his partner. "Dispatch said it was a kid."

Frank's head jerked up at that, and I thought he was going to break character. Instead, he spoke in a weird, higher pitched voice. "Oh, helpsh. Helpsh. I'm just a, uh, a kid. I needs helpsh."

Okay, that sounded nothing like me. There was no way that was going to fool anyone.

Taser cop shook his head and grabbed his radio. "Dispatch, this is Adam Twelve. Code Five. We've got a suspect on a prank call. Over."

Ridiculous, but it was probably good news.

There was a pause, and his radio squelched to life. "Continue."

"We have a suspect with the phone that made the 911 call. We'll administer the breathalyzer, and bring him in. Over.

Good call, Mr. Policeman, good call. The cops would take Frank and leave, and sure, I'd be back to square one, but at this point square one looked a lot better than squares two and three.

"Please walk the property," dispatch said. "Check for any open points of entry and anything suspicious. Over."

Taser cop shook his head and looked at his partner, who shrugged. "Let's do the breathalyzer, then secure him in the car." He looked between the other two cops. "Smith. Jeffers. Can you start checking things out?"

"On it," Smith said.

Oh, crud. The two cops, Smith and Jeffers, headed straight for the door that Walt and his crew had just used to exit the building. That meant it was probably still unlocked. And that meant Walt couldn't afford to let them get to it, or they'd see what was going on inside. And the path to the door went right between the two cars where Walt and the two guys were hiding.

What was I supposed to do? I couldn't let these cops get gunned down, but there was no way Walt would let them open that door. I felt stuck, unable to act, because I had no clue what to do. Then everything happened at once.

Walt stepped out from behind the SUV, his gun out.

"Now!" he yelled.

I didn't think. I didn't weigh the odds or count the cost or any of that stuff my parents were always telling me to do. I acted. I was probably ten feet off to the side of the two cops, and maybe twenty-five feet away from Walt. I dropped my blending and screamed.

Magically appearing out of nowhere wearing all black and a full mask while screaming did the trick. Walt jerked the gun toward me and I bruised with everything I had left. The cops both went for their guns, though I was pretty sure they were going to do that anyway with Walt on the scene.

I kinneyed and leapt, aiming for a spot a few feet above Walt, rocketing toward him as I curled up like a cannonball. Hopefully gravity would do the rest. Weakness down in my bones swept through me. All this blending and ghosting and reggying and now bruising was wearing me out. I needed to hold the bruising, but the thought of doing that while kinneying the whole time made my head hurt. I took a last glance around and saw the other guy standing up behind the car across from Walt. I dropped the kinney.

Time snapped back to normal, and I shot over Walt by several feet. He must have ducked really quickly or something, because there was no way my aim was that bad. I arced down and slammed into the grassy strip around the warehouse, digging a shallow trough into the dirt before banging into the wall of the building.

I leapt to my feet, still bruising, just in time to get shot about eight times. I'm pretty sure Walt and the two other guys were doing the shooting, and the good news was I was getting better at bruising. None of the bullets stuck. They bounced off, but knocked me around so that it probably looked like I was doing some crazy dance. I decided to roll with it and flopped to the ground. I thrashed around for a little before laying still, facing out toward the men.

Everyone was in motion. The cops were diving for cover behind their cars. Frank was running for the warehouse door, his hands still cuffed. Walt and the other two guys were heading the same way, crouched over. Based on the angles, I guessed that the SUV sat roughly between the cops and the door, so they were probably getting some protection from it. I made sure no one had a gun pointed at me, dropped the bruising, and blended.

When I stood up, a wave of dizziness washed over me, and I staggered back against the warehouse wall. I was definitely overdoing it. Once it passed, I jogged over to the cops. They were on their radios, basically calling in

Armegeddon and requesting SWAT backup. I figured that gave Walt and his crew a few minutes to get out of there. Hopefully they'd take it and we could put an end to the insanity for at least one night.

I headed back to the warehouse, but when I tried to ghost through the wall, I only managed to walk into it and hurt my nose. I was too worn out to ghost and blend at the same time. I glanced back at the cops. A couple of them were looking toward the warehouse, so I lay down and stretched out against the warehouse wall, dropped the blending, ghosted, and rolled through the wall.

Once inside, I let go of the ghosting but didn't bother blending since I was in deep shadows. Walt's team had been moving fast. The cars were all gone, and the eighteen-wheeler was pulling away from me and heading down the aisle.

I stood up and tried to get my brain moving again. I was miles from home, just about out of energy, and the cops were going to come down on this building like a sledgehammer. I needed to get out of there, to get back to Thomas's house, but my ride home in the back of Mr. Ferris's SUV was already gone. The back of the trailer disappeared into shadow ahead of me, and it felt like hope was driving away with it.

CHAPTER 8

YOUNG & MALICK

"COME ON, JOSS," I said to the empty warehouse. "Get your butt in gear and do something."

Red lights flashed at the far end of the aisle where the eighteen-wheeler had driven. Probably its brake lights. An impulsive thought hit me, and I started running toward the lights. While running I kinneyed as well as I could, which wasn't great. I was going maybe ten times my normal speed. It would be enough.

I zoomed toward the red lights, shelves towering on both sides of me, like I was running down the length of a dark canyon. The truck came into view as I raced closer to it, and I saw a faint halo of night sky around the bulk of the trailer. I'd been right. There was some sort of giant cargo door.

The red lights cut off, and I was plunged into darkness. Then the trailer, creeping along from my kinney point of view, cleared the huge doorway it was driving through and light from a nearby street light flooded in to show me the way.

I sped out of the warehouse, once again doing my best impersonation of a superhero baby gazelle, and leapt. I arced up and forward, onto the truck's trailer. For once, something went right, and I actually landed on top of it. Then something went terribly wrong. I didn't stop, but shot forward, sliding across the top of the trailer at an angle.

I was so stupid. Of course I'd slid. I'd probably been running a hundred miles an hour when I'd leapt. I wasn't going to instantaneously stop when I landed. That was as far as I got thinking through my mistake when I launched off the side of the trailer up near the cab and went tumbling toward the pavement far below.

I had a choice to make, and only a second to work it out before I was flattened by a high-speed impact with concrete. I had to let go of the kinneying to either ghost or bruise. If I ghosted, what if I came to a stop deep underground? I'd never ghosted into the earth, because I was scared I'd lose my way back to the surface. But if I bruised, I might be seen.

It was a pretty easy decision. I wasn't scared of the dark, not much, but the thought of being blind and lost underground was pretty freaky. I curled up in a ball, dropped the kinneying, and bruised.

I hit the ground and bounced, spinning end over end. And then I did a true superhero move, though I'm not sure it counted since it was complete luck. I popped out of my tuck as I flew through the air, crashed to the ground again, and happened to land on my feet. I skidded to a stop about fifty feet later. Like a boss.

While I did all that, the truck had slowed down at the edge of the small parking lot I was now standing in and was turning away from me onto a road. I put my hands on my knees for a moment, took some deep breaths, and kinneyed once again. I ran to the eighteen-wheeler as it inched around the turn and slowed down to match its pace. I was not going to make the same mistake again. I leapt, and this time I landed neatly on top of the trailer.

I dropped the kinney and collapsed onto my back, looking up at the stars as the truck rumbled along. I pulled out my phone and flipped off airplane mode. The little blue dot on the phone's map showed us gradually getting closer to the highway that led back toward my house. I felt one last turn and a steady acceleration as we pulled out onto the highway. Something had actually gone right.

I kept an eye on the map and tried not to fall asleep. It was a warm summer night, but the rush of wind that enveloped me as we got up to highway speeds was almost chilly. Amazingly, the truck exited onto the highway that

J. Philip Horne

went right next to the mall where my day had started. I jumped off as it zoomed past the mall and used my new favorite trick of ghosting to soften the landing. I had almost nothing left, but managed to kinney in short bursts so I could sprint the length of each street as I headed back to Thomas's house. It was still full dark, and I was dressed in black, so I didn't blend. Not that I could have if I'd wanted to. If someone saw me, they were just going to have to deal.

I ghosted through Thomas's front door and crept upstairs. He was in his bed, but he'd laid out an air mattress, sleeping bag, and pillow for me on his bedroom floor. I collapsed on the sleeping bag and tugged my mask off. I was at the end of the line, with no energy left, but I dug deep and reggied.

"Wake up. Joss. You alive?"

It felt like an earthquake or something. What had happened? Were people worried I was dead? I cracked an eye open, and immediately closed it. The light was so bright.

"Joss. Wake up!"

The earthquake continued. I tried again and got both eyes open a crack this time. Thomas was leaning over me, kicking the air mattress. I decided that made more sense than an earthquake. I flopped an arm over and grabbed his shin to stop the kicking.

"What time is it?" I asked, trying to wedge my eyes open further.

"9:30. You never woke me up when you got home. What happened?"

I rubbed my face and sat up. "Can I get some coffee?"

Thomas glared at me.

"I'll give you the scoop, okay?" I said. "But it ain't pretty, and we need to go to my house first. And I need coffee."

Thomas threw his hands in the air. "I'll make some coffee, but why your house?"

"Janey blackmailed me. I need to tell her what happened, too, and I'd prefer to do it once. Mom and Dad are both at work today, so we can talk there."

67

"Why do you do that, Joss?"

"Do what?" I was starting to wake up, but I had no idea what he was talking about.

"Make her blackmail you," Thomas said.

That woke me up. I climbed to my feet. "Make her blackmail me? Like, it's my fault she's gonna rat me out if I don't include her?"

Thomas shook his head and turned to head downstairs. "She wouldn't need to blackmail you if you'd just include her to begin with. I'll get the coffee."

Thomas had the craziest ideas of how having a younger sister worked. I changed, packed up my stuff, and took my backpack downstairs. Thomas was in the kitchen with two cups of coffee. He'd put a lot of milk in them to bring them down to a temperature that we could actually drink, and enough sugar to make it taste good. I still hadn't figured out why adults liked to drink something that tasted terrible and was hot enough to leave scars in the mouth.

"So?" he said. "Did you do it?"

I held a hand up to stop him while taking a big swig of coffee. "When we get to my house. And I've been thinking about it. We need to go see Bobby Ferris."

"What?" Thomas's arm was frozen, the coffee mug halfway to his mouth.

"You'll hear about it soon enough, but last night was bad, and I don't like the idea of playing him along with the angel stuff. People could have died last night, Thomas. I just feel like I"—I shook my head, looking for the words—"like I need to come clean with him."

"You think that's a good idea?" Thomas asked. "Another person knowing about you?"

I shook my head again. "It's a terrible idea, but I'm not up to any more lies, okay?"

Thomas nodded. "I get it. So we go there, then your house?"

"That's the plan."

Fifteen minutes later, we pulled up in front of Bobby's

house on our bikes. I dumped my backpack by our bikes in the front lawn, and we walked up to the front door.

"You sure, Joss?" Thomas asked.

"I think so," I said. "Let's just get it over with."

"Okay." Thomas reached out and knocked on the door.

We stepped back and waited. I was sort of hoping no one would answer, but the door opened a few seconds later. Bobby stood there staring at us.

"Hey, Bobby," I said.

"Hey, man," Thomas said.

Bobby nodded his head in greeting. "Uh, what do you guys want?"

"We need to talk," I said. "About your guardian angel."

That did the trick. Bobby's eyes bugged out, and he made some choking sounds. I leaned in and tried to figure out what he was saying. I was pretty sure it was something like, "How boo you snow."

"How do we know?" Thomas asked.

Oh, that made a ton more sense. I'd thought Bobby was losing it. Bobby nodded, still moving his mouth with no sounds coming out.

"Can we come inside?" I asked. "I need to show you something, but I'd prefer it not be out here."

Bobby looked at me for a moment, his eyes still wide, his mouth calming down, and stepped to the side, opening the door wider. Thomas went in first. I followed and closed the door behind us. We looked around, but Mr. Ferris wasn't in sight. We were in the entryway between a small living room and dining room. I figured this spot would work as well as any.

"Your dad home?" Thomas asked.

Bobby nodded and pointed toward the bedrooms. "Asleep."

"Okay, Bobby, there's no easy way to do this," I said, "so get ready to be shocked. I'm, uh, your guardian angel."

Bobby stared at me with that same mixture of shock and confusion. I realized I may have said that wrong.

"I'm not really a guardian angel," I said. "I was

pretending to be one. I, well, I was trying to help you."

"I'll vouch for him," Thomas said.

Bobby's eyes narrowed. His face looked a lot meaner when he was squinting. "What kind of joke is this?"

"No joke," I said. "Here, watch this."

I blended. Bobby screamed, lurched backwards, bounced off the wall, and caught his balance just before he ran into me. I released the blend which, of course, meant I popped back into view. Bobby screamed again, and this time he actually lost his balance when he hit the wall. Thomas stepped forward and grabbed his arm to keep him from falling over.

"So, that's me," I said. I went to my angel-falsetto. "Once invisible, I talked like this." I blended again, and kept the falsetto. "See? Like this. Your fake guardian angel."

I dropped the blend and the falsetto. Bobby's face was turning a shade of purple. It looked like he'd stopped breathing. Thomas was still holding his arm and gave him a hard shake. Bobby's eyes finally pulled away from mine and found Thomas, and he gasped for air.

"That's it," Thomas said. "You gotta breathe."

Bobby honestly looked like it'd been too much. I felt sorry for him.

"Look," I said, "I'm sorry. I wanted to help you, but I didn't know how to do it. So I went in as an angel. I didn't want to trick you or anything. I really did want to help."

Bobby's eyes were round, and he reached out toward me. I stood still and let him paw me, like I was some piece of furniture he wanted to navigate around in the dark.

"How?" Bobby gasped.

I shrugged. "I found out I could do this stuff at the beginning of the summer. And, just to be clear, you have to keep it a secret, okay?" I gave him a hard look. "I'm serious. I won't put up with anyone talking about this stuff."

Bobby nodded vigorously. "But, how do you do it?"

I shrugged again. "Don't really know, but I can."

"Wait," Bobby said. "Why'd you decide to try to help me? This was before we talked at the mall."

"Right," I said, and looked away. "Well, I sort of came by your house to get even for the whole pants thing, but then I saw your dad, uh, you know, he wasn't doing well. And I felt bad about the whole thing and decided to try to make it right."

"So, that's a lot," Bobby said.

"Yeah, and here's the deal. I'm telling you because I tried to sort things out with your dad last night, and it was insane. As in, the people with your dad tried to kill some cops."

"What?" Bobby and Thomas asked together.

I held a hand out toward Thomas. "I'll fill you in, okay? But hold on." I turned to Bobby. "Listen, I know this is shocking and everything, but I need your help on something."

I couldn't tell if Bobby had heard me. He had this weird, dreamy expression, his mouth hanging open.

"Bobby?" I said.

"So," Bobby said, "you're like a real superhero. For real."

I glanced at Thomas. He was smirking. I gave him a hard look.

"Pretty much," I said, turning back to Bobby.

"More of a mediocre hero," Thomas said. "He's still sorting things out."

"What the heck?" I said.

Thomas smiled at me and shrugged.

"What else can you do?" Bobby asked. His color looked a little more normal.

"I'm not really going to go into it," I said. "Well, I'll show you one more thing."

I ghosted down into the floor up to my neck. Bobby's eyes rolled up into his head, and Thomas had to grab him in a hug to keep him from falling. By the time I'd ghosted back up, Bobby seemed to have recovered.

"I'm not showing you this stuff to show off, okay?" I said. "I'm trying to help your dad, and I need your help. Can you do that? Can you help me?"

Bobby still looked a little wobbly, but he nodded.

"Good. I'm going to give you my phone number, and I

need you to text me when you know what your dad's plans are for this evening, okay? I'm guessing he's gonna head back out tonight, and I need to know when. Can you do that?"

"It's a lot to take in," Bobby said.

"But can you help?"

"For my dad?" Bobby nodded. "Yeah, I can help."

"Let me ask you something," I said. "Did you know your dad could speak some language? Maybe an Asian one?"

"Maybe," Bobby said. "Probably. When he was young, he was in the military and stationed somewhere in Asia. He, uh, well, it's weird. I think he learns languages really easily. He's picked up Spanish the past few years, even though he was, uh"—Bobby mimed taking a sip from a bottle—"all the time."

"Okay," I said, "that makes sense. That'd explain why he was suddenly important to his, ah, employer, if he knew the right language. So you're gonna help me, right? Let me know when he's heading out?"

Bobby nodded. "What's your number?"

I gave him my cellphone number, and Bobby entered it in his phone.

"So what are you gonna do?" Thomas asked him.

"Text Joss as soon as dad's up and I can figure what's his next move."

I nodded. "And do you tell him about me? Do you ever tell anyone about me?"

Bobby shook his head. I shook my head, too.

Thomas looked from me to Bobby. "We good?"

Bobby glanced at Thomas, and looked back to me. "I still don't get it. I never thought that, you know, there were actual superheroes."

"I'm not a superhero, Bobby"—I ignored Thomas when he said "That's the truth" under his breath—"I just happen to have some really, um, unusual talents. Gotta do the best I can with them. So text me today, okay? It's really important."

Bobby nodded, but his eyebrows had pulled together.

"So what happened last night?"

"Not now. We need to go, okay? Just text me."

Thomas and I got out of the house, though Bobby stared at me the whole time as we got on our bikes and rode down the street. I figured Thomas was going to pepper me with questions about what the heck I'd been thinking to tell Bobby. The truth was, I wasn't sure why I'd done it. Just felt right. But Thomas kept quiet until we made it around the first corner and rode out of sight of Bobby's house.

"Those cops are watching us again."

That wasn't what I'd been expecting. "You're kidding, right?"

Thomas shook his head. "They were at the other end of the street. Saw the nose of the car."

Could nothing let up? This was getting ridiculous.

"Okay, that does it," I said. "I'm gonna talk to them."

"Wait. What?"

"I'm gonna talk to them. Wait here."

I hit my brakes and dumped my bike on the sidewalk. I'd just about had it with people making my life a confusing mess. I was trying to help a kid in a bad spot, and everything had to be so totally out of control. I was sick of it. I cut across the street so I could head back to the corner we'd just come around without being seen. I might have kinneyed just a little bit so I could get behind a tree in the corner lot before they showed up.

Sure enough, right on cue, the black car pulled up nice and slow to the corner. I stepped out from behind the tree and walked over to the car and knocked on the tinted driver's window. There was a pause, and it rolled down halfway. Detective Young gave me a hard look, and Detective Malick didn't look any happier in the passenger seat.

"Hi, officers," I said. "Remember me? You came by my house a couple weeks ago to ask us questions about that guy who kidnapped my sister. Any particular reason you're following us?"

Young looked at Malick for a long moment. She gave a

quick nod, and Young dropped the car into park. I stepped back as they both swung their doors open and got out.

"Call your friend over," Malick said as she came around the front of the car to stand by Young.

I looked back and saw Thomas standing where I'd left him. I decided to play along and waved him over. I could tell he was looking at me like I was nuts, but he set his bike down by mine and walked over to us.

"Officer Young," Thomas said. "Officer Malick."

"Thomas," Malick said. "Okay, let's get down to brass tacks."

Adults used the weirdest phrases. I was pretty sure I knew what a brass tack was, but that expression made no sense.

"The, ah, events of a couple weeks ago," Young said, "don't add up. Not even close."

"Not that we expected them to," Malick said, "given Jordan Johnson was involved. He's why we got involved in the first place, but we'd have been pulled in eventually given the facts of the case."

What did that mean? I knew the "facts of the case" were bizarre. They'd probably seen bank security cam footage that showed me appearing out of nowhere when I was hit by the taser, dressed in all black and wearing a mask. And the actual building where we'd rescued Janey wouldn't have made any sense. Silver mesh covering the floors and the walls, a massive hole in the roof and an impact crater below it. But why would that sort of weirdness mean they would have been put on the case? And it sure sounded like they'd already known who Jordan was.

The two cops stood staring at us, like we were supposed to start talking or something, but Thomas and I kept our mouths shut. They glanced at each other.

"So we've got a bank robbery, a kidnapping, and several dead bodies," Young said, "but no explanations. Oh, we have some suspicions as to who offed Jordan and his guys. But the rest is just a mess."

"Not that we're surprised by any of this." Malick said.

"Comes with the territory, right? I'm sure you understand."

I was starting to feel very uncomfortable. They were dropping hints, like they knew something, and they were acting like we knew it, too.

"Are we being interrogated for an ongoing investigation?" Thomas asked. "My mom, who happens to be a very well connected, successful lawyer, told me not to talk to any police without her present. As my lawyer. To ensure my rights were protected. Also, I can promise you she'll be interested to learn you are following us."

I think my eyes might have bugged out a little while he spoke. Thomas was full of surprises. The two cops hadn't reacted at all, though, and that worried me.

"Thomas," Young said. "Have we asked you any questions? I rather doubt anyone can claim we're interrogating you if we don't ask any questions. I think you've misunderstood our intent. We're not here to put pressure on you. We're here to help."

"See, we're pretty sure," Malick said, "that one of you has some abilities that might fall outside of what is considered normal, and that those abilities attracted Jordan's attention in the first place."

My jaw dropped open.

CHAPTER 9

DIRTY DOZEN

I STARED AT Malick. Was she implying she knew about the Sevens?

"What do you mean?" said Thomas.

"She means," Young said, "that we work cases that have an element of the extraordinary. We aren't part of the local police force, though we often work closely with them."

"So you're, like, the FBI?" I asked.

"We're agents at the Fed level," he said, "but not that org. No, we work with the DOSN."

He'd pronounced it as a word, like doe-sin. Alarms went off in my head. I'd heard that phrase before. I reached for it, and found the memory. The day I'd gone on my first mission for Jordan. Mara had said something about the Dirty Dozen. The DOSN. Or she'd mentioned them. She hadn't actually given me any real information.

My eyes narrowed. The Department of Seven something or other. I must have mouthed the words by accident, because Malick cracked a grin and nodded.

"That's right, Joss. Department of Seven Normalization. We don't really go for all the nicknames you might have heard, so we'll stick with DOSN."

"Wait a second," Thomas said. "You're not cops? How'd you get inserted in the investigation and interview us?"

Young shrugged. "We do it when needed. Our department carries a bit of influence."

I took a step back. I was starting to breathe too fast. What did they want with me? Were they going to take me away to some hidden government lab and experiment on me?

Sure, Mara had mentioned them, but we'd never circled back to talk about them and I had nothing to go on.

"Joss, calm down." Malick held her hands out, empty. I guess that was supposed to put me at ease. "We're not going to do anything. I understand our department doesn't have the best reputation with Sevens, but that's not why we're here."

"We're agents in a task force that operates somewhat independently," Young said. "If you can help us do our job, we can wipe any reference to you"—he looked straight at me when he said this—"because it is you, right? We can make sure there's no record of you that might end up with the main department. But we need your help."

"Wait," Thomas said, looking from me to Young. "Was that a threat? That he has to help you or else? And what are you talking about? Seven of what?"

Young shook his head. "No more pretending that you two don't know what I'm talking about. And it was just an offer to help him in exchange for his help. Take it however you want. Joss, can you help?"

Thomas stepped over to me and hissed in my ear, "Don't talk to them. Let's get out of here."

I wasn't so sure. I was getting past the initial rush of panic, and was curious. If they didn't hunt down Sevens, what did their task force do? Why had they been investigating Jordan? I needed to know more. I put a hand on Thomas's shoulder and nudged him back.

"I'm not saying I have any idea what you're talking about," I said, "but this whole DOSN task force thing. What exactly is it?"

"We were created about five years ago," Malick said, "to deal with a new threat, the Mockers. Made sense to put it under the DOSN, but we have a more specific mission."

"So you don't, like, hunt down people that are, what did you call them? Sixes?"

Young and Malick shared a look, and both of them smiled when they looked back at me. I felt like they were looking at me like I was a little kid that had to be treated nicely. I didn't like it.

"That's cute, Joss," Malick said. "Sixes. It even works with DOSN. Props on playing dumb, and please, keep doing it if it makes you feel better. But no, we are not specifically tasked with finding Sevens, though when you find Mockers, you find Sevens. These Mockers tend to be very bad, and very dangerous. Like Jordan."

"But Jordan's dead, right?" Thomas said. "We saw it on the news, like, two weeks ago."

"And who killed him?" Young asked. "Have you thought about that? How did they move that fast when Jordan cracked? We think there's another Mocker here in town. And what about Jordan's Sevens? Are they free agents now? Lots of questions, boys, and we're not going anywhere until we have answers."

"Shouldn't you be talking to our parents about this, not us?" I said, but I regretted it immediately. I didn't want them talking to my parents. It would just create problems for me.

"Sure," Young said. "But we don't really think they're the ones who actually know what all went down. Can you two help us? I really think it's for your own good. There's a Mocker out there who was willing to put a bullet in Jordan's skull, and he's going to figure out you're involved soon enough."

Jordan. The gift that just kept giving. I grabbed Thomas's arm and pulled him back a couple steps.

"Give us a sec, okay?" I said to them.

Malick nodded. "Please. Take your time."

I turned to Thomas. "What are you thinking? 'Cause I'm thinking that they're making sense. There's another Mocker out there who's gonna come for me. I heard something last night about a crime boss who had people working for him who had unusual talents, and when I heard it, I thought, Sevens."

Thomas glared at me. "What the heck, Joss? Why didn't you tell me?"

I glared back. "I'm gonna tell you. And Janey, right?

That's why we were headed to my house."

Thomas gave me a hard look, and shook his head.

"Sometimes," he said, "it's a real pain being your friend."

"Hey boys," Young said, cutting through our discussion. "I thought you might be interested in one scenario we pieced together around Jordan's death."

That got our attention. Thomas and I turned back to the agents.

"See, Jordan had two gunshot injuries that, as far as the M.E. could tell, he received several hours before the kill shot," Young said. "Ballistics matched the injuries to a gun found at the site that'd been wiped. No prints."

Thomas tightened up as Young spoke. I needed to distract him. Get him to relax.

"So no prints mean nothing to investigate, right?" I said. "What's the point?"

"Well, it's interesting, isn't it?" Malick said. "You have someone shooting Jordan in a very non-lethal way, and working pretty hard at it given all the slugs we pulled out of the wall that must have missed him, a few hours before a very lethal shot was taken. Implies there were two separate incidents, right? One that resulted in Jordan being incapacitated. The second, well, having a more permanent outcome."

"So we dug through the background for everyone associated with Jordan," Young said. "Wouldn't you know it, Thomas, we discovered you're quite the marksman. We've spoken to the owner of that shooting range you go to with your dad. He says you're the most natural born shooter he's ever seen. High praise, really."

The conversation felt like a noose tightening around my neck. I glanced at Thomas. He looked stiff, a blank expression etched on his face.

"Good to know," I said, "and thanks for all the info, but we need to get to my house before someone starts worrying about us." I grabbed Thomas's arm. "Let's go."

"One sec," Young said.

He stepped forward and pulled a small, white card out of a shirt pocket. He held it out to me.

"Contact info," Young said. "We're going to get to the bottom of this, and when you figure out that it's in your best interest, give us a call."

I hesitated, stared at the business card for a second, and grabbed it.

"Thanks," I said as Thomas and I turned away and headed to our bikes.

I stuffed the card into a pocket of my backpack, and we headed out. I glanced back as we pedaled toward my house. Neither agent had moved. They stood there watching us as we rode down the street and turned a corner.

"Didn't like that one bit," Thomas said. "But I guess we knew something was up since they've been following us."

"Yeah," I said. "I wish Mara had told me more about the Dirty Dozen. I'm feeling exposed."

"Is that what Sevens call the DOSN?" Thomas asked.

I shrugged. "That's what Mara told me."

We rode the rest of the way in silence. My mind felt like it was overheating as I worked over what Young and Malick had said, and what had happened the night before. It was like I was pedaling as fast as possible, but there was no chain connecting the gears and the bike wouldn't move. I couldn't seem to wrap my head around everything that was happening.

Thankfully, my actual bike did have a chain, so pedaling worked pretty well and we got to my house in a few minutes. We cut through the side gate, left our bikes in the garage, and headed inside. I went straight to the family room and dumped my backpack on the floor.

"Janey!" I yelled as I flopped onto the couch.

I heard the thump-thump-thump of her coming down the stairs, and she rounded the corner into the room.

"Hey Janey," Thomas said. "Joss says you blackmailed him. Good work."

Janey's face split in a big grin and she sat down in Mom's recliner. "I do what I can. So what happened last night?"

I was about to speak, but Thomas held up a hand to stop me.

"Maybe we should see if we can get Mara on the phone," he said. "Given how you said it got pretty crazy. Might help to loop her in."

I nodded. "Good call."

Thomas stared at me and shook his head. "Just terrible."

I played back what I'd said. Oh. I hadn't meant to drop a pun into the conversation. My talents for humor apparently didn't take actual thought.

I fished my phone out of my pocket and dialed Mara. I flipped on the speaker phone and set it on the coffee table. Janey and Thomas crowded in on the other side, sitting on the floor. It rang once, twice, and she picked up.

"Joss? What's up?"

"Hey Mara. Got you on speaker phone with Thomas and Janey. You got a sec?"

"Yeah, I do," Mara said. "But if you're doing the speaker phone thing, I am, too. Hold up."

There were a couple clicks and a thump, and Mara's voice came back on, sounding thinner and more distant.

"You guys still there?" she said.

"Hi, Mara!" Janey said. "We're here."

"Hola, Janey!" a new voice said.

"Isabella!" Janey yelled. "Hey!"

I totally lost control of the conversation for a minute as everyone checked on how everyone else was doing. I was surprised how great it felt to hear Isabella's voice. Sort of comforting, but also exciting. I held a hand up to try to quiet Janey down. She'd launched into a ridiculously detailed description of each day since we'd last seen Mara and Isabella. She ignored me. I finally spoke over her.

"Hey! I need to fill you guys in on the situation."

Janey cut off when I spoke, but stuck her tongue out at me. The other end of the call went silent for a moment.

"The situation?" Mara asked. "Joss, it's been two weeks. How can there already be a situation, let alone the situation?"

In the background, I heard Isabella say something in Spanish, and Mara laughed. I ignored them both.

"Here's the deal," I said. "You remember the note I got from that kid, Bobby? About helping him if he needed it?"

"Yeah," Mara said. "You showed it to me the day we left."

"Okay, well, after that, I totally forgot about it until yesterday morning. We ran into Bobby at the mall, and I remembered it, so last night I slept over at Thomas's and tried to help out."

"Are you saying," Mara said, "that your parents were okay with that?"

"Not exactly," I said. "But they weren't against it either."

"Sure," Mara said, "because they didn't know about it, right?"

"It doesn't really matter." I glared at the phone, but I don't think Mara picked up on it. "Listen, when I got to Bobby's, his dad didn't want help anymore, but Bobby still wanted me to help."

"Joss," Isabella said, "were you the pretend angel? The ángel guardián, how do you say, guardian angel?"

"Yeah, that's me," I said. "The guardian angel."

"Okay," Mara said, "back to the story. How did this become a situation?"

I told them everything as best I could remember it. What I'd done. What they'd said. What had been in the trailer. How I'd been shot, but managed to keep everyone from killing each other. How I'd escaped and gotten home. I finished and waited for a response.

Thomas shook his head. "What. The. Heck."

"Joss, bringer of chaos, destroyer of normal." Janey was smiling. She actually looked happy about the whole thing.

"Joss," Mara said, "that's insane. So…"

The phone got quiet for minute, then Mara came back on.

"Maybe a weaponized biohazard of some kind. But some sort of exotic, designer drug is most likely."

"Does it matter?" I asked. "As long as I shut it down,

we're good, right?"

"Maybe," Mara said. "And Mr. Ferris, he's acting as the handler since he knows the language, so I'm betting the chemists or whatever they are have been kept isolated. Language barrier, foreign culture, easier to control. Okay, anything else?"

"We've had those two cops following us," Thomas said. "The ones who came to the Morgans' house a couple weeks ago. Except they're not cops. They're with the DOSN."

Mara said something in Spanish that must have been pretty extreme, because I heard Isabella gasp in the background. There was a long pause.

"Anything else you need to tell me?" Mara said.

"Well," I said, "they aren't really with the Dirty Dozen. Something about a crime task force focused on taking down Mockers. Oh!" I suddenly remembered something Walt had said. "Walt kept talking about Mr. Silver, how he'd heard about really strange stuff with him. And that if they didn't get this batch done, Mr. Silver would finish them."

There was another long pause.

"You think that's important?" I asked.

"We're on the way to town," Mara said. Her voice was pitched slightly higher, like she was really tense. "Listen, Joss, I'm sending you a link to an app and some info to sign in. It'll let me track you with your phone. Get an accurate location for you, just in case. But you need to stay put, okay?"

"Why? What's going on?"

"Silver's a Mocker, Joss," she said. "I'd put money on it that's who finished off Jordan. I used to hear Jordan talk about him. He's bad news. Don't go near him, you hear me?"

"Sure, Mara," I said. "I'm not reckless or anything."

Both Mara and Isabella snorted. I looked to Thomas for support, but he just shrugged. What the heck? I wanted help, but I hadn't expected everyone to act like I was helpless and out of control.

"I've dealt with a Mocker before," I said, frowning at the

phone.

"That's not quite how I remember it," Janey said.

I turned my frown on her, but she just shrugged.

"Joss, you must listen to Mara," Isabella said. "She cares for you. She is very upset about this man, this Silver."

"He's got Sevens," Mara said. "Dangerous ones, okay? Maybe a Warrior. Look, just sit tight. We'll get there tonight."

"Okay," I said. "Uh, goodbye."

"*Adios*," Isabella said and the call went dead.

"So," I said.

"Yep," Thomas said.

My phone buzzed. It was a message from Mara with instructions for the location app. I installed it and got logged in with the info she'd given me.

"You're not really gonna quit, are you?" Janey said.

Thomas and I looked at her.

"Say what?" Thomas said.

"I said, you're not quitting, are you?"

Thomas and I looked at each other. He shrugged, and I turned to Janey.

"We just heard Mara pretty much panic and head for town," I said. "'Cause this Silver guy's that scary."

"And you're scarier," she said. "Plus, he's just a name. He's not gonna be there."

"Huh," I said. I wasn't used to Janey pushing me, but she had a point.

"Janey," Thomas said, "don't you think it would be a better idea to pull back and loop in your folks? Or at least wait for Mara?"

"I think Joss is what he is," Janey said. "If he's not using his powers for good, if he's just sitting around, isn't that a waste? Why'd he get the powers if he's not doing anything with them? You think Mara would sit around and wait?"

"What about Mom and Dad?" I said.

"Mom and Dad'll come around," Janey said. "They think they're supposed to protect you. I mean, that's normal. But what if being who you're supposed to be means doing stuff that's risky? Like, being a superhero?"

Thomas and I sat there, staring at her. I think my mouth may have been hanging open. She glanced at Thomas and her cheeks got a little red.

"I've been thinking it over." Janey stood up and started pacing. "How can parents be parents, or"—she waved a hand at my phone, still sitting on the coffee table—"Mara be Mara, and you"—she jabbed a finger at me—"still be who you're supposed to be?"

I leaned toward Thomas and spoke quietly. "I think she just lost me."

"You're supposed to be a superhero!" Janey said. "So be one! Mom, Dad, Mara, they're just thinking about you like you're a kid."

"Janey, I think Mara's worried about more than that," Thomas said. "She sounded, I don't know, disturbed by this Silver guy. He's got Sevens. And Joss"—Thomas reached over and grabbed my shoulder—"sure, he's the Seventy-Seven, but he actually is a kid."

Janey's mouth pulled into a line as Thomas dropped his hand. My mind was racing. Janey, in spite of being my little sister, was making sense. When Mara had told me to sit tight, it'd made sense, too, but it had bugged me. I was a once-in-a-lifetime superhero. I could do stuff. Hadn't I been the main reason Jordan had been stopped? Hadn't I been the guy who'd freed Isabella? Hadn't I just managed last night in spite of all the insanity?

I looked up at Janey. She was wearing her determined look, eyebrows pulled together. I made up my mind. I had promised to help Mr. Ferris. I had the power to do it. I just had to get in there and destroy that eighteen-wheeler with the lab. Whatever was going on, Walt had been pretty clear they couldn't afford to lose it. If I busted it up, Mr. Ferris would be out of a job. He'd have to look for something else. Hopefully something legit.

It would be simple. No messing around. No figuring everything out. I'd blend and ghost into the trailer. Then I'd bruise and reggie to tear the place apart. In and out in no time. They wouldn't know what hit them.

I smiled and nodded at Janey. I'd see it through. And I'd soon discover it was the worst decision of my life.

CHAPTER 10

GO BIG

"I'M DOING IT," I said. I gave Janey a quick nod, and she smiled.

"What does that mean?" Thomas looked from me to Janey. "What are you doing? What Mara told you to do? Why's Janey smiling?"

"I'm gonna finish what I started." I gave Thomas my earnest look. It usually helped when I was in trouble with my parents. "Look, Silver's out there, but he's not gonna be there tonight. If I can get in there again with Mr. Ferris, I'll just tear the place down. Destroy the lab. I bet I can do it in under five seconds. Kinney and bruise. Then I'm gone. They won't know what hit them."

Thomas stood up. "That's insane, Joss." He held a hand up to stop me from interrupting. "I know you can do it. That's not the issue. No one's saying you can't do it. They're saying you could get killed or hurt or something. That stuff could go very, very wrong."

"Go big or go home," I said.

"What does that even mean?" Thomas threw his hands in the air. "But sure. Go home. Oh, look." He waved his arms around, pointing out the room. "Hey, look! You're home! Stay home!"

I stood up. I didn't like being yelled at when I was sitting down. And I was feeling angry.

"Chill, Thomas." My neck was heating up. "I'm gonna go big. It's what I do."

"Joss, no," he said. "Mara's on the way. Just wait for her. Heck, she might be here before you even head out."

I nodded. "If she is, cool."

"But otherwise, you're gonna go in."

"Yep."

Thomas shook his head and turned to Janey. "You could have died a couple weeks ago. We all could've." He turned back to me. "I can't do it. I can't just play along. All you have to do is wait. Help's on the way."

I took a deep breath and tried to calm down. Thomas was a good friend. He didn't deserve my anger.

"Waiting could make the whole thing worse, Thomas," I said. "It'll just give them more time to respond. What if Mara gets here, and we go in together, but now we've got Mr. Silver involved? I need to hit them now. Tonight."

"I don't like it," Thomas said.

"You don't have to," I said. "Look, you don't have to do anything. I'm not asking you to go with me."

Thomas's mouth pulled into a line. He looked angry. "Yeah. I guess I'm not really even a sidekick am I?"

"That's not fair," Janey said. "Without you, I don't think Joss and I would be alive."

Thomas looked from her to me, his eyes narrowed. His shoulders slumped and the anger seemed to drain out of him.

"I don't like it," he said.

"Fair enough," I said. "You can tell me 'I told you so' if everything goes wrong, okay?"

"That's not what I want. Look, I can't do anything else here. I don't like it, but it's not my call. I'm heading home, okay? Text me if you hear from Bobby."

"Will do," I said. "Thanks, man."

Thomas looked at me, and I smiled at him. He didn't return it, but he didn't glare at me either. I counted that as a win.

"All right. I'm out." He turned and headed for the garage where he'd left his bike.

Janey and I watched him go.

"I was hoping he'd agree with me," she said, turning to me. "You think we're wrong?"

"No way."

But I wasn't really sure. Thomas had been right there with me from the beginning. The letter with the butterfly seal. Battlehoop. Everything. It didn't feel right to have him walk away thinking I was wrong. I worried that maybe, just maybe, I actually believed he was right, and that I was being stupid. I shook it off.

"We just have to figure out when things are going down tonight," I said, "and how I get out of here without Mom and Dad freaking out."

"Getting out's no problem. They've got that thing to go to with Dad's work tonight. They'll be home for a little, but then they're out super late. I'll figure out how to cover for you when they get home."

I held my fist out to her and she bumped it.

"I guess we just wait around," I said. "Hopefully Bobby'll text me soon."

"Okay, but let's spar while we wait."

For the past couple weeks, Janey and I had spent time each day practicing the forms we'd learned at Battlehoop and sparring with each other. I wasn't sure we were making each other better, but we weren't getting worse.

We geared up with pads and thin gloves. I'd accidentally destroyed a pair of regular boxing gloves when I'd ghosted through a wall wearing them. Only the stuff closest to my skin stayed with me. We headed out to the backyard where we had a loose circle marked off with a long piece of rope. Janey and I started with stretches and moved into our forms. It was sort of like a slow motion pretend fight. Then we sparred.

We fought normally at first, her speed against my size and weight. I was definitely getting the hang of using my size to outmatch her, in spite of her quickness. After that, I practiced using my talents defensively. I'd ghost and let her hand pass through me on a strike, or bruise to take a blow. We'd done it enough that I was no longer shocked by the jolt of insight every time we overlapped when I was ghosting. Lastly, I kinneyed the tiniest bit to get faster than her, and let her practice fighting someone who was bigger, heavier, and faster. I figured if we kept it up, by the time she got to high school she'd practically be a superhero, too.

My phone chimed, and I ripped my gloves off so I could fish it out of my pocket. It was a text from Bobby. Janey stepped over to me so she could see my screen.

dad leaves tonight at sunset

There was a pause, and then another chime.

still weirded out

Another pause, another chime.

You being a pretend guardian angel

I think I knew what he was saying. Guardian angels weren't exactly an everyday sort of thing, but seeing me disappear and sink into the floor had to have been even weirder. I texted him back.

I'll be there. You get used to it. Just keep it secret.

I waited for a minute, but didn't get any more texts from him. I shot Thomas a text to update him.

goes down tonight at sunset

His answer wasn't exactly wordy.

Okay

I looked up at Janey and shrugged.

"You got this," she said. "Get in there, tear it up, get out."

I nodded. The sun was like a fiery blanket, and I was pretty much soaked in sweat. I did not need to head into tonight exhausted.

"I'm gonna grab a shower," I said as we headed to the back door, "and grab a little sleep. Can you wake me up before Mom and Dad get home if I'm not up?"

"Yeah, I'll do that," she said.

The shower felt great. After dressing, I lay down in my bed and did my reggie power nap trick, only I didn't quite fall asleep. I floated in a dreamy place, but my mind kept going. It wouldn't stop.

Was I making the right call to go in on my own? Thomas and Mara both thought it was a bad move. Janey was on my side, but she was twelve. Was I really going to take her view over theirs? And what about my parents? I couldn't even talk to them about it. They'd told me I had to talk to them before doing any new "Seven" stuff, but the whole thing with Bobby wasn't new.

I had this bad feeling in my stomach that they wouldn't see it that way. That they'd think I'd lied to them, or at least deceived them. It was like my dad was standing there with me. I could hear him say his whole thing about deception.

"Joss, you don't have to lie to deceive. You just have to lead someone away from the truth."

Had I led my parents away from the truth? Pretty much. Yeah, they were not going to be happy with me. What was I supposed to do? I'd made a commitment to Bobby and I couldn't just dump him, but if I told my parents they'd shut it down for sure. But if I didn't tell my parents, and they got wind of it, then what? All sorts of bad stuff for sure.

I must have finally fallen asleep, because the next thing I knew, Janey was shaking me awake.

"Hey. Mom just pulled into the garage."

I blinked, and swung my legs over to get out of bed. "Thanks."

She didn't move. "So, how are you doing it?"

I looked at her, my head cocked to one side. "Doing what?"

"Keep going. I know you've been up most nights for a couple weeks now."

"You know that?"

"Yeah, I know that," Janey said.

I figured there was no point in not telling her. "I reggie. Like, big time. Right before we busted you out, I was done for. Mara told me to lay down and reggie, and next thing I know Mom's waking me up and I feel great. So I've been doing that every time I go to sleep."

The faint sounds of a door closing drifted into my room.

"Mom," Janey said. "Let's go."

We headed downstairs together. We found Mom standing at the entrance to the family room from the kitchen, her hands on her hips. She saw us and raised her eyebrows. I looked around for the problem. Oh. My pads and gloves stretched in a line on the floor from where she stood across the room to me.

"Right," I said. "Uh, sorry!"

I got busy picking up. As I dumped my stuff in its basket in the laundry room, Mom called from the kitchen.

"Whose day was it to empty the dishwasher?"

My shoulders slumped. "That's me!"

Mom's head popped into view. "Joss, kindly get it together."

"Yes, ma'am." I gave her my winning smile, but she just shook her head.

A week earlier, I'd tried to do my chores in record time by kinneying. There were two problems with the approach. First, it'd still felt like it took forever. When I kinneyed, it felt to me like the world slowed down, not that I was moving super-fast. Second, I'd accidentally ripped a cabinet door off its hinges. Mom and Dad hadn't been pleased. Dad had been busy the past week, so it was still sitting in the corner of the kitchen. I figured that was the silver lining. It was a lot faster putting up the glasses without a cabinet door to open and close.

I emptied the dishwasher. Dad came home with some pizza for Janey and me. We ate while Mom and Dad got ready.

"Be good to each other," Dad said as he and Mom headed for the garage. "We're going to be out late, so get to bed at a reasonable time."

"You bet," I said.

Janey gave them a big thumbs-up and waved to them as they left.

"Piece of cake, just like I said," Janey said.

"You called it."

I pulled my phone out and looked up what time the sun would set. Around 8:15. I figured I should get to Bobby's a solid hour before then just in case, which meant I needed to leave pretty soon.

"Okay," I said to Janey, "here's a question. How do I get there?"

She shrugged. "Ride your bike."

"So where do I leave it?"

"I don't know. Isn't there an elementary school somewhere over there?"

I pulled out my phone again and opened the map. Sure enough, there was an elementary school a street over from Bobby's house. I held my fist out and Janey bumped it.

"Okay, I'm grabbing my stuff and heading out." I stopped. "Wait a sec. If I'm riding my bike, I need to stay in normal clothes, right?"

"Yeah, Joss. The neighbors don't want to see a ninja-guy riding a bike. I'm just guessing and all, but—"

"I get it," I said. "I'm out."

I grabbed a water bottle and some snack bars, and ran upstairs. Once my backpack was loaded with my work clothes and supplies, I headed back downstairs to get my bike. The ride was hot. For about two seconds, I thought about ghosting to get some relief from the heat, but thankfully figured things out before I went through with it. How could I ride a bike I couldn't touch?

I headed past Thomas's house, went on past Bobby's street, and turned left at the next one. The elementary school was a few houses in. I rode around behind the building and found a door. After locking my bike to a ramp handrail that led up to the door, I gave its handle a pull, but it was locked. I dumped my backpack just to the side of it and ghosted through the door. The inside was dark, but it was gloriously cool. The interior of the door had one of those push bars on it, so I gave it a push and the door swung open.

It was pretty much perfect to have an air-conditioned base of operations. I changed into my work clothes, pulled on my mask, and stuffed all the clothes I'd been wearing into the backpack. I loaded up my snacks into various pockets so they were right up against me, but the water bottle was a problem. It was too big. If I ghosted through something with a big ole water bottle bulge, I'd leave some of it behind, and that meant it would tear up my work clothes.

I settled on taking a nice, long drink and stuffing it back in the backpack. I wasn't really sure what to do with the backpack when I was done, but finally stuck my head out of the door and looked around. The back of the school faced a playground and field, with tall wood fences lining an alley on the far side. No one was in sight. I stepped out, kinneyed, and jumped up onto the roof with the backpack. I left it leaned up against some big metal thing, maybe a vent hood, and hopped back down, doing my ghosting trick for a soft landing.

It hit me that if I could ever get strong enough as a Seven to keep going all day with my talents, I really would be a superhero. And I was getting stronger. Maybe not every day, but at least every week felt better than the week before. I ghosted as I thought about it to cut off the oppressive heat, blended to avoid the whole ninja-walking-through-the-neighborhood thing, and headed to Bobby's house.

When I got there, it was a repeat of the previous night with one big exception. Mr. Ferris was in the kitchen eating, but Bobby wasn't in his room. I found him in the front rooms, walking around slowly and whispering my name. I was still blending, but had dropped my ghosting once inside out of the heat, so I reached out and flicked his ear to shut him up.

Bobby jumped and made a squealing sound.

"Bobby!" Mr. Ferris yelled from the kitchen. "What're you up to?"

"Nothing, Dad," Bobby said as he looked around for me.

I shook my head. Leaning in close, I said, "Act normal."

Bobby jumped again, but thankfully he didn't squeal this time. He looked around and gave a big thumbs up toward the front door. He walked to the family room, and I followed him.

"Just heading back to my room," Bobby said to his dad, who was standing at the entrance to the kitchen, a piece of pizza in his hand.

"You going to eat?" Mr. Ferris said.

"Oh yeah," Bobby said. "Be right out."

Mr. Ferris turned and disappeared into the kitchen. I gave Bobby a gentle push and he got moving. We walked back to his bedroom and he closed the door. I glanced around. The door to the bathroom was closed. The curtains were pulled. I dropped my blend.

Bobby jumped for the third time. "Whoa!"

I held a finger up to my mouth, though with my mask on it was more like holding up my finger to the bottom part of my head.

"Whoa," Bobby said quietly. "That's your superhero costume?"

I pulled the mask off. "I don't have a superhero costume. These are my work clothes."

"Right." Bobby nodded. "But shouldn't it have a cape?"

I grimaced. "No. No capes. It's not a superhero costume, okay? Besides, a cape would get destroyed the first time I ghosted through something."

Bobby's eyebrows lifted, and his eyes widened. "Cool. But I still think it should have a little more to it. Maybe a letter on the front, and different colors. What's your superhero name?"

"Bobby, I don't have a superhero name." I stepped in close to him. "I don't have a superhero costume. I'm not running around saving people, okay? These are just my work clothes."

"Sure," Bobby said, "but I'm pretty sure that's what a superhero costume is, isn't it? Work clothes? I just think yours need an upgrade, that's all. I mean, they're kinda boring. And what's that hole in the middle of the chest? It's almost a different color black around it."

"It's where I got shot, Bobby, and the shirt was stained. By my blood. Can we drop it now?"

Bobby's eyes had gotten wide again while I spoke, and he went over and sat down on his bed. "You can survive being shot in the chest? You really are a superhero. I mean, that's awesome. Maybe go with, uh, let's see. How 'bout

Bullet Boy?"

"Bullet Boy?"

"Yeah, for a superhero name. Then you'd need to work a B into the front of your costume, or maybe"—he jumped to his feet and smiled—"a bullet. Like, an icon of a bullet."

"Bullet Boy." I was feeling an odd mix of irritation and maybe a little pride. "I'm not going to call myself Bullet Boy. I don't need a costume. I don't need a name. I'm just going to wait here for your dad to leave, okay? Can you get out there and come get me when he's heading out?"

"Sure thing, BB," Bobby said and headed for the door.

"BB?" I shouldn't have asked.

"BB. Short for Bullet Boy," Bobby said, and he pulled the door shut behind him as he headed out of the room.

I threw my hands in the air in frustration. I wasn't going to be called Bullet Boy or anything else.

Unless Isabella liked it.

Where had that thought come from? What the heck? I shook my head and sat down on the floor to do some stretches. I figured I didn't have long to wait, but I might as well do something with the time. A few minutes later I heard steps thumping toward the room. I blended just in case and sat still.

Bobby burst into the room. "Joss, Dad's in the garage."

He looked around frantically. "Joss? You here?"

I stood up and released my blend. "Here."

Bobby tensed when I appeared, but didn't jump. He was getting better. I pulled my mask on. "Okay, I'm out."

I blended and ran toward the garage. I ghosted through the door just as Mr. Ferris started to back down the driveway. I followed him and ghosted into the back of the SUV when he stopped in the alley to put it into drive. A moment later I was laying in my spot behind the rear seats and released my blending.

From there, things were a repeat of the previous night. I stayed in the SUV when Mr. Ferris went into the apartment to get the woman. I was trying to minimize how much I used my talents so I could keep my strength up. After a couple minutes of waiting, Mr. Ferris came back with her, and we were driving again. I didn't bother trying to pay attention to where we were. It was too hard to keep track of the turns looking up through the windows. I mainly saw street lights flashing by.

Eventually, we pulled into a parking lot, and after a short wait, drove into a building through a large opening. I blended in case we drove by anyone who could see into the SUV. Mr. Ferris pulled to a stop, and I sat up to look around.

We were in another warehouse, with a high ceiling and concrete floor, though it didn't look nearly as big as the one from the previous night. The same two cars were parked nearby, but a third car was with them this time. A short distance away, the two eighteen-wheelers were surrounded by green glow sticks. The space we were in looked empty other than the vehicles. I spotted a couple guys walking the perimeter near some doors on a side wall. The big entrance we'd driven through was already closed up with what looked like a steel rolling door.

I ghosted out of the car. Time to get busy. I was going to tear that eighteen-wheeler lab apart. I'd have plenty of time to figure out where I was and how to get home once I was done. That made me think of my phone, and that made me realize I hadn't flipped it to airplane mode. They were going to spot my phone again.

Still blending, I ducked down on the far side of the SUV where no one was in sight and pulled my phone out. Once it was in airplane mode, I stuck it back into my pocket and stood up. Taking a deep breath, I did a couple deep stretches and got ready to charge the lab.

Something hard slammed into the back of my head down near the base of my neck. The world turned black.

CHAPTER 11

MR. SILVER

I FLOATED IN a gray mist, feeling at peace with pretty much everything. Silent gray mist and cool air. A bright pinpoint of light stabbed into my eyes. I blinked and turned away, but the light followed me, always directly in front, blindingly bright. It stabbed through my closed eyelids and found its way to the base of my skull.

The light took root and grew into a terrible pain. I wanted the cool mist back, but everywhere I looked, the light pierced me. The pain gnawed at me, defying my efforts to get away.

I opened my eyes, and this time it seemed to be real. I wasn't in a gray mist, but the pain was still there, drilling into my skull. I tried to reach up to massage my neck, but my hands were stuck. I blinked, and the room came into view.

The concrete floor looked familiar, but I wasn't in the warehouse. Or, at least, not the main space with the eighteen-wheelers. Maybe this room was on the other side of one of those doors I'd seen. It was large, maybe twenty-five feet square. The wall to my left had a row of windows high up near the lofted ceiling. Two men, really big men in dark suits, stood on either side of a door directly in front of me. I didn't recognize them from the previous night.

The pain in my skull was overwhelming. I reggied, but nothing happened. I tried again, putting every scrap of concentration I could muster into it. Again, nothing. I looked down, and fear clenched my stomach. Heavy silver manacles encircled both my wrists with a silver bar attaching them together, about six inches apart. A heavy, silver chain ran from the bar down to another silver bar that was driven into the concrete floor.

What did this mean? What was happening? The pain in my head kept breaking up my thoughts. I had to get control of myself. I started doing tactical breathing, a slow cadence of breathing in, holding, and breathing out. It took a solid minute, but I gradually mastered the pain and started to process what had happened.

I'd obviously been hit with something in the back of the head and knocked out. And whoever had done it had landed the blow precisely, even though I'd been blending. That meant they'd gotten impossibly lucky, or they'd been blending, too, and could see me. They'd knocked me out, and tied me to the floor with silver, which drained all my powers. Whoever had done it was a Seven or had a Seven with them, and knew to use the silver.

A wave of dizziness and nausea washed over me. I closed my eyes and fought it, trying to maintain my breathing and my thoughts. Big time crime. Sevens. Using silver. It all added up to a Mocker. Which was about as bad as it could get. Fear threatened to overwhelm me again.

Knowing I was out of options and possibly about to die finally calmed me down. The pain even seemed to recede a little. Things couldn't get worse, so I figured I might as well do my best and see what happened.

The nausea passed, and I opened my eyes and looked around. I was still wearing my mask, but I couldn't feel my phone against my chest. Twisting around, I took in the rest of the room. There was nothing to see. Just me, the chair, the silver chains, and the two guards by the door. I leaned over and peered under my chair, and was happy to see my phone sitting on the floor, along with my multitool and knife that had been in my pants' pockets. So that was one bit of good news.

The door opened. A huge man walked in dragging a small metal chair behind him. He was wearing a dark suit and a bright green lucha libre mask. I blinked, trying to clear my vision, because what I was seeing made no sense, but the mask stayed put. One of the guards pushed the door closed while the man walked straight to me, the chair screeching across the concrete. He flipped the chair around to face me and sat down. I struggled to understand, to make sense of the green mask with it's gold trim around the mouth and eye holes, but came up empty.

His dark eyes stared at me for a moment, and it felt like they could see right through me. Then he twisted around to face the door, and I could see his mask was laced up the back with what looked like a gold shoelace.

He barked a single word. "Out!"

The two men by the door both slipped out and pulled the door closed. I was alone with a crazy man, chained to the floor with silver. Completely helpless. If the pain had been any less in my head, I would have been terrified. Sure, I was breathing pretty fast, and I felt like I was going to throw up, but I was pretty sure the nausea was from the injury and not raw fear. I was somewhere past fear.

The lucha libre crazy-man turned back to me and leaned forward with his elbows on his knees, his hands clasped together.

"We're going to take our masks off now," he said. His voice was big and deep. "Well, I'll take yours off for you."

He reached over and plucked my mask off in one motion, dropping it in my lap. He reached behind his head and started untying the laces on his mask.

"You ought to know," he said, "that no one sees my face and lives." His hands were still busy with the laces. "Unless they are in my inner circle. Only five people are in my inner circle right now. My wife. My daughter. My accountant. My Thief. And my Warrior."

In my mind, I was screaming, "Leave it on!" but nothing came out but a quiet hiss, like the air leaking slowly out of a balloon. This man had to be Mr. Silver, and Mr. Silver had to be a Mocker. And he'd just claimed to have not one, but two Sevens working for him. And if I saw his face, I was going to die. And he was going to show me his face and there was nothing I could do about it. His hands stopped fidgeting behind his head, and he grasped both sides of the mask and pulled it up and off.

I wanted to look away, but couldn't. He had a broad face to go with his broad body, clean-shaven and bald. I wasn't sure how old he was, but he wasn't young. Creases pulled at the corners of his dark, sunken eyes.

"You're a bit of a mystery to me," he said. "I've got to think you're that Thief Jordan acquired, but if that's the case, then I also think it's likely you took Jordan down and necessitated my cleaning things up."

I thought I kept my face the same. No movement, no reaction, but Mr. Silver gave a tight smile and sat back.

"Yes," he said, "I see I'm correct. Very impressive. You can't be past your early teens." He leaned forward again, his elbows on his knees. "Make no mistake, though. You got lucky, and it will not happen again. I don't know how you found my"—he paused and pointed a thumb back over his shoulder toward the door—"little operation here, but you're mine now, and I am going to come to believe you are totally loyal to me, tonight, or I'm going to kill you and everyone you love."

He stood up in a surprisingly quick motion given his size and looked down at me. "I'm going to leave you here for a moment to think about it. When I come back, you're going to tell me everything I want to know, or you're going to die. And your parents. And any siblings you have. And anyone else I choose. Do you understand?"

Somewhere in the deep corners of my mind, a spark of defiance caught fire. I had no idea how to get out of this mess, but I was not going to play along like some scared kid. Even though that was exactly what I was. I stared up at him and gave him my best look of defiance.

He smiled, which made my stomach lurch and achieve a new level of fear. So much menace in that smile. He slowly pulled on his bright green lucha libre mask and laced it up in the back.

"I prefer," Mr. Silver said, "to be wearing this when I'm

forced to be violent."

That did not sound good. I tensed, but there was nothing to do and nowhere to go. His hand lashed out with incredible speed and slapped me so hard across the face it knocked me off the chair. My ears rang and the left side of my face was fire. I tried to reach out and catch myself as I fell, but my arms hit the end of the chain and I slammed onto my side on the floor. My head bounced off the concrete, and my vision went black.

"You see, a lot of kids think adults won't lay a hand on them." His voice sounded like it was far away and sort of tubular, like he was talking through the cardboard roll in the middle of paper towels. "I need you to know that I don't feel any such compulsion. That my threats are real."

I felt him grab my arms and yank me back up into the chair. I blinked, and my vision started to clear, though it felt like I was looking through binoculars, all dark around the edges. I could feel myself leaning back the way I'd just fallen, but couldn't seem to figure out exactly which way was up.

"Now, let's try this again." The lucha libre mask filled my vision as he leaned in close. "I'm going to leave you for a little, and when I come back, you're going to tell me everything, or you're going to die. But it won't be quick. I'll give you lots of chances to change your mind. Do you understand?"

I checked, but my spark of defiance had been smothered. My head sagged down so I didn't have to look at his vile face.

"Yes, sir." I said.

"You'll look at me when you speak," he said.

Of course. He was doing something to me, I could tell. Breaking me. I knew it, but I couldn't do anything about it as long as those silver manacles encircled my wrists, and I didn't think they were ever coming off. Not while I was still alive.

I pulled my head up and looked into those dark, evil eyes. "Yes, sir."

He nodded and stood. "I'll give you an hour or so to think about it. I'm in no rush. We have all night."

With that, he turned and strode to the door. He pulled it open and was gone. My two guards stepped back into the room and one of them closed the door. The back of my head still throbbed with pain, but the fiery pain where he'd slapped me was distracting me, along with the stabbing pain on the other side where I'd bounced my head off the concrete.

I needed to think, to come up with a plan, but I couldn't do it. Too much pain and fear. The fear was like a creature coiled up in my guts, gnawing at me. Mr. Silver was going to kill me, and my family, and probably my friends. He'd said he'd do it, and I believed him. He'd squeeze me for the info, and I'd give it to him. Who I was, where I lived, all of it.

Less than two days ago I'd felt like my life was almost back to normal. I'd even hung out with my friends for the first time since everything went down with Jordan. Now I sat chained in a room, under guard, with some psychopath coming to torture me or something, and probably kill me. How had I gotten here? Did I have an eighth talent? A superpowered ability to mess things up royally?

Minutes ticked by, though I wasn't sure exactly how long, since I didn't have my phone to check the time. Then it hit me. My phone was under my chair. My phone, with the app that would tell Mara where I was. It was a long shot, but as long as my phone was on, maybe she'd check on me once she got to town. She might already be in town. I had no idea what time it was, since I didn't know how long I'd been unconscious.

Hope was immediately smothered by despair. I'd put it into airplane mode. I had to get it back on the network. I leaned over and acted like I was trying to reach my head with my chained hands. I actually was, because it felt like my head was cracked open. I groped around on my head, and felt the huge bump on the back of my head and a smaller one on the side. While checking my head, I glanced

J. PHILIP HORNE

under the chair, and my heart sank. Sure, my phone was under the chair, but it was way to the back. There was no way the chain would let me reach it.

I was doomed. Beaten up, and waiting for even worse. I started crying. Not big, blubbery, loud crying, but scared, helpless, quiet tears. It wasn't a proud moment, but the searing pain in my head and fear constricting my chest made it hard to breathe. I couldn't hold it back.

A motion caught my eye, and I blinked away the tears in time to see one of the guards tap the other one and point at me. Then, the unthinkable. They laughed. At me. A kid, chained down, crying.

The spark of rage and defiance was rekindled, and it blossomed into a burning fire. I had no plan, and no hope. The pain still ravaged my head, but the tears dried up and I felt a murderous hatred. Part of me tried to tame it, redirect it. It's not like I thought hate was a good thing, but I was losing control. I'd make them pay. I'd bring them all the hurt and fear I was feeling. But how?

The window high up on the wall off to my left shattered, and a huge ball of dark fur burst into the room. As it arced down toward the nearest guard, it uncurled, and I saw a vision of beauty and hope. A giant gorilla, limbs spread with terrifying reach, fell upon the nearest guard with violent force, taking him to the floor, and slamming into the second guard.

There was a flurry of brutal, furry motion on the floor. Then it was over. With a weird twist, Mara rose from the two motionless guards. I'd seen this look on her face once before, and it was more than a little scary. Like some mythological goddess of war standing on a battlefield. I might have been a little scared of her myself, and she was on my side.

Mara grabbed Mr. Silver's chair and jammed it under the doorknob of the door. She flashed back into her gorilla form and hammered the chair with a giant fist, then flipped back to herself. I was pretty sure no one was coming through that door any time soon.

107

"Joss, you look terrible," Mara said.

She was wearing a green shirt that said THIS SHIRT IS PURPLE. Somehow, seeing one of her ridiculous t-shirts was comforting. She strode to me and took my head in her hands.

"Not doing so well," I said, and held up my shackled hands to show her.

"I know it's bad," she said. "I saw some of it." She nodded toward the broken window and continued. "Been here for a few minutes doing some surveillance. But I think we're good. Give me a sec."

I nodded, and Mara went back to the guards and started rummaging through their jackets and pants. It took her a moment, but she stood back up and held a small keychain for me to see. She crossed over to me, and worked the keys in the manacle keyhole one by one. The third key clicked over when she turned it, and the manacles popped open.

I leapt up, and was hit with a massive wave of vertigo. I stumbled to the side and collapsed to the floor. I didn't bother trying to get up. Instead, I reggied. Healing swept through me, and my eyes uncrossed. The absence of pain was amazing.

I climbed wearily to my feet. I felt great, but I was exhausted. Mara stood facing me, holding out my mask. I took it and pulled it into place. She stuck the stuff from under my chair into the various pockets on my work clothes and patted me on the shoulder.

"We need to get out of here," Mara said. "No chair's going to hold that door if a Warrior decides to come through it. Listen, I'm parked about a mile away. Just head toward the moon, okay? It's pretty low on the horizon. I'll find you."

"Got it," I said.

Mara shifted into a hawk or falcon. I didn't really know how to tell them apart, but she was definitely some sort of large bird. She took off, flying toward the wall opposite to the windows to gain elevation and circling back toward the broken window. I blended, and as I took my first step toward the outside wall, something slammed into the other side of the door with massive force.

I kinneyed and time slowed. The door buckled, and the chair that had been wedged under the handle shot out like a cannon ball. The door itself tore loose from the wall as it folded nearly in half and spun through the room. Mara was above it all, maybe ten feet from the window. Everything was in motion.

I stepped to the side out of the path of the chair and door as they careened toward the far wall. A large man stepped into the room, wearing a fitted hoodie with the hood up, jeans, and boots. He was kinneying. He had to be, because, to my eyes, he was moving normally, though he leaned into his movements like he was in super-low gravity. It was a graceful version of my superhero baby gazelle running.

His eyes locked onto the empty shackles. Mara was now five feet from the window, up near the high ceiling, then four feet, then three. She was going to make it. He glanced around, and jerked his head up. Toward Mara the bird. He crouched and sprang.

The moment he left the ground, I knew. It was a perfect leap. He'd catch her just as she cleared the window. Then she'd probably die. There was no time. My instincts kicked in. I shot a hand out and grabbed the chair as it sailed past me.

Swinging in a broad arc, I whipped around and launched the chair up toward the broken window, redirecting the chair's momentum and adding some of my own. It rocketed toward the man as he stretched out, reaching for Mara. She cleared the window, the top half of the man followed after her, and the chair slammed into his hips.

He had to be bruising, because the chair folded around him as it slammed him into the wall, stopping him cold. He cursed, and I ran.

CHAPTER 12

SILVER BULLET

I GHOSTED THROUGH the wall opposite the windows and stumbled into a room just like the one I'd left, but with no windows. I dropped the kinney, took a moment to catch my breath, and ran across the room. I ghosted through the wall and found myself in yet another room. This one had windows high up on the wall opposite me. It had to be the other side of the building.

After grabbing a few quick gasps of air, I ran to the outside wall and ghosted through it. I came out of the building into a large parking lot with two or three street lights casting pools of dim light. Several shadowy figures were fanning out off to my left. The moon wasn't in sight, but I didn't let that slow me down. I ran straight across the parking lot away from the building, blending and hoping for the best.

The best didn't happen. I tripped over something in the dark and slammed down to the pavement, crying out in pain and surprise. Guns started firing behind me as I stumbled to my feet and got moving again. I reggied, and my bloodied knees started working again. I was running. I was going to make it. I was nearly to the edge of parking lot. Beyond it was a tangle of dark bushes and short trees.

Pain exploded in my left leg just below the knee. It yanked me out of myself, as though I was suddenly watching myself stumble forward, my left leg acting like it had a second knee below the first one. I collapsed to the ground in the deep shadows by the trees and bit my fist to keep from screaming. I couldn't hold my blending. The pain was too much. Men were running toward me across the parking lot. Above me, a bird let out a loud cry. I reggied and my vision went black.

I didn't really pass out. I figured I was awake because I'm pretty sure I wouldn't have dreamed about my body thrashing around as it failed to knit back together. I lay on the ground and shook, waiting for the men to overtake me. Suddenly, giant talons encircled my hips and chest. Mara the giant eagle swooped back into the air with me dangling below her. My bad leg bounced off a tree limb as she cut just above the trees and angled away from the pursuing men. I screamed because it seemed like the right thing to do. Gunfire erupted behind us, but she was moving fast and the shots tapered off.

After that, it was smooth sailing, except for the part where I was being yanked around and shaken with every beat of her wings. I tried screaming some more, but it didn't really help, so I settled for moaning. My leg was on fire, and the fire consumed me. I lost track of where we were, though I was pretty sure she'd gained a lot of altitude.

A few minutes later, Mara dove toward the ground, flared her wings out at the last second, and dumped me in a patch of grass next to a fast food restaurant. I lay on the ground and tried to keep my sanity. I was crying and gasping and writhing. The leg hurt.

I let my head tilt over toward the restaurant and saw Mara walking toward me, a black bag dangling from one hand, her little silver car parked back behind her under a solitary street light. Isabella burst out of the passenger door and ran past Mara to me.

"Joss!" Isabella knelt down beside me in the grass and took my hand. "You are okay?"

"No, he's not," Mara said. She dropped into a squat beside me and rummaged through the bag. "Joss, you reggied already, right?"

I yanked my head up and down and moaned again in response. Isabella's hand tightened on mine, and I gripped it like my life depended on it. Mara pulled something out of the bag and started tugging at my leg.

"Hold him down, Isabella," Mara said. "Joss, they were firing silver. I've got to pull it out so you can reggie."

Isabella said something sharp in Spanish, and Mara responded harshly.

"*Lo siento*," Isabella said, and leaned across me with all her weight, holding down my arms.

Weight pressed down across my legs, and I spent the next minute exploring new levels of pain as Mara dug into my leg with forceps. I tried not to cry. I tried not to scream. I tried not to thrash. But I failed on all counts.

Then it was over, the weight released me, and I reggied. Sweet relief flooded through me as the wound knit back together. The pain was replaced in a moment with a profound weariness. It was a good trade, but I was pretty sure I had nothing left to use my talents. I tried to ghost and proved myself right.

"That was cutting it close," Mara said from off to my side. "I wish you'd waited for me."

It felt like I'd been kicked in the stomach. In everything that had happened, I'd forgotten that I'd gone against Mara's advice. Thomas had been right. My tears, just vanquished, started back up, so I closed my eyes tight and tried to breathe evenly.

"Oh, Joss," Isabella said, so quietly I almost hadn't heard. Her hand came to rest on my shoulder.

"We're still too close," Mara said. "I need to get you home. Can you get to my car, or do you need me to carry you?"

"I'll do it," I said, but I wasn't sure.

I struggled to a sitting position and pushed myself slowly up.

"We need to hurry," Mara said. "Let's go."

She headed for the car and I followed with Isabella falling into step with me. We got to the car and Mara opened the rear door for me. I got in and flopped across the back seat. Mara closed the door behind me and she and Isabella got in the front seats.

"What happened?" Isabella said the moment their doors were closed.

I didn't have the will to talk about it yet, and Mara stayed silent while she started the car and got it moving.

"Joss? You okay?" Mara asked me once she was on the road.

"No," I said. "I mean, sure, I'm not about to die, and my leg's healed, but I don't feel okay."

I saw the silhouette of Mara's head nod. "Makes sense. You need some rest, and then maybe reggie again. We'll get you home."

"But what happened?" Isabella asked.

I gave her a thirty second version of my evening. I didn't really do justice to Mr. Silver, but I tried. Mara filled in some details for the parts after she arrived. I got a couple quick glances from Mara as she drove when I mentioned redirecting the chair to hit the Warrior. When finished, Isabella turned toward me. Her face was in shadow, but a splash of light flashed across her face and I saw tears sliding down her cheeks.

"All good now," I said, and forced myself to smile.

In the next flash of light across her face I saw a smile. It was beautiful. It made me believe that I could overcome ten Mr. Silvers. Or at least two of him. But not tonight. I was so tired. So fragile. I needed real sleep. I pulled out my phone and checked the time. Just after midnight. If I slept a couple hours, woke up and reggied, and slept some more, I'd be fine by morning.

"Joss," Mara said, "have you thought about what comes next?"

"Nope," I said. "Zero thought. Why?"

"Because"—she said the word slowly, like she was talking to someone who wasn't very smart—"you've got a couple problems. First off, Silver's seen you face. He'll figure out who you are. He'll finish what he started."

At her words, I wanted to panic. To fear what came next. I really did, but I just didn't have the energy. First sleep, then panic.

"He's got a Thief and a Warrior," Mara said. "You ran, and that was the smart play, but you can't go toe to toe with him."

"I stopped him from getting you, didn't I?"

"Sure," Mara said. "So you think you can take him? Joss, Warriors usually don't use their talents and leave it at that. They bulk up. They train. No offense, but you're still a kid."

"I'll bruise," I said. "So he'll knock me around. I can blend and run."

"One," Mara said, "he won't just knock you around. Joss, what happens when you're ghosting and you touch another Seven ghosting?"

"It's like we're not ghosting."

"Right. And if you're blending, and you see another Seven blending?"

"Yeah," I said. "I can see them."

"And when you're bruising," she said, "and another Seven who's bruising hits you, what do you think's going to happen?"

I had a sudden insight, and it felt like my stomach was full of ice. "It'll be like we're not bruising."

"Right," Mara said. "Those three talents all work the same. You're not invisible when you blend. It's more like you're a little out of phase with reality. But someone else blending is out of phase in the exact same way, so you end up in the same place and can see each other. Make sense?"

"Yeah, I get it."

"It's the exact same thing with ghosting and bruising. If you fight a Warrior, your bruising will cancel each other out. It's going to be like fighting a well-trained grown man. Like fighting Jordan, but without any talents. What do you think would've happened if you'd fought Jordan one-on-one without any talents?

I reminded myself that I didn't have enough energy to panic. Isabella must have noticed I was breathing pretty fast because I saw her reach a hand out and put it on Mara's arm. Mara had been about to speak, but stopped. There was no point, though. My dad always said that hiding from reality didn't change it.

"Okay," I said, "so that's point one. What's point two?"

Mara glanced at Isabella, who shrugged and let her hand drop.

"Point two," Mara said, "is that even if you run, even if you get away, Silver's going to go after your family. It's what Jordan did to me. It's what he did to you. It's what Mockers do. So running's not going to cut it."

It was all so unfair. I was trying to help out a kid who was in trouble, and everything was falling apart. Was this going to be my life now that I was a Seven? Stumbling from one disaster to another? My parents didn't even know what I'd been up to, and I'd planned to keep it that way, but if Silver came after them they'd find out. Everyone would be in danger, and they'd know it was my fault.

I didn't say anything. What else was there to say? I slumped back into my seat and closed my eyes. I'd thought I would have it all sorted out by the time Mara got to town. I'd thought I'd wake up tomorrow and be done with it. That high school would be the worst thing in my future, not a homicidal crazy guy who wore a bright green mask hunting down my family. It was the stuff of nightmares.

Thankfully, Mara and Isabella left me alone for the rest of the drive, though Isabella glanced back at me about every thirty seconds. Once we got to my neighborhood, I gave Mara instructions to get to the elementary school so I could pick up my stuff. When we got there, she pulled into the school parking lot and parked the car. They both got out of the car and followed me around back.

"Oh, crud," I said, looking up at the roof above the door.

"What's up?" Mara asked.

I pointed at the roof. "Backpack's up there, but I've got nothing. Can't get it."

Mara gave my arm a brief squeeze and flashed into an owl. She flew up out of sight, and a moment later a chimpanzee jumped off the roof and landed at my feet holding the backpack. As I reached for it, the chimpanzee morphed into Mara.

"Thanks," I said.

"You bet," Mara said. "Come on. I've got some rope in the back with our luggage. I can tie your bike to the roof. I'll get you home."

"That'd be great," I said as I unlocked my bike from the railing.

A few minutes later we pulled to a stop in front of my house. After helping me get the bike down, Mara gave me a quick hug, and Isabella a slightly longer one.

"Joss, get some rest," Mara said, "but be ready. I'm coming by tomorrow. You need to talk to your parents. We need to figure out what to do."

I had no energy left to argue. I waved and headed around back through the side gate as they got back into the car and drove away. I dumped my bike in the side yard and went around to the back porch. It hit me. I couldn't ghost right now, and I didn't have a key. Keys didn't mean as much to me since I could walk through walls, but this was a real problem. If I knocked, I'd wake up my parents, and I had no interest in speeding up any awkward conversations.

I finally settled into one of our patio chairs and pulled out my phone. I flipped it out of airplane mode and set an alarm for 4:00 AM. I figured there was no way I'd fall asleep, but that maybe some rest would enable me to ghost again. I fell asleep in under ten seconds.

I woke to my alarm and immediately felt the burning itch of about seventy mosquito bites. I instinctively reggied and was back asleep before I'd even figured out if it had helped the bites.

Early dawn woke me the second time. I had a fresh collection of bites, but this time I felt human in spite of them. I reggied and the itchiness immediately disappeared. Maybe being a Seven was worth it after all. I got up and ghosted through the backdoor, unlocked it, and went back out to get my backpack. Back inside, I locked the door and crept across the family room to the stairs at the front of the house. I made it up to my room without seeing anyone and tossed my backpack in my closet to be dealt with later.

As I collapsed on my bed, I realized I was still in my work clothes. I struggled back up, stripped them off, and stuffed them under my mattress. I flopped back into bed wearing only my underwear and fell into a deep, normal sleep about a minute later.

The third time I woke up that morning, the sun was fully up and streaming into my room. That made no sense. My curtains had been closed. My eyes adjusted, and I saw that my mom was tying back the curtains.

"Hey, lazybones," Mom said. She gave me a big smile. "You feeling okay? Janey said you went to bed early. I wasn't expecting to wake you up at 10:00."

I sat up. "Oh, yeah, I feel great."

That was more or less true. My body felt great. It was my heart that felt sore.

"I've got some breakfast leftover if you want some," she said.

"Yeah, thanks," I said. "I'm gonna grab a shower first if that's okay."

Mom made a big deal out of sniffing the room and smiled. "I'm thinking a shower is a great idea. See you downstairs."

Once she'd left, I grabbed a change of clothes and headed across the hall to the bathroom. The shower seemed to wash away some of my worries along with the dirt and sweat. Once I was dressed, I checked my phone before heading downstairs. There was a text from Mara.

Called your dad. He's on the way home.
Coming over now.

Oh, no. I remembered Mara saying something about talking to my parents, but I hadn't realized she meant today. Now that I thought about it, she'd said she was going to come by the house today. How had that slipped my mind? I checked the text. It had been sent about fifteen minutes ago. Right on cue, I heard my dad's voice drift up from downstairs explaining to my mom why he was home. Maybe it was my imagination, but he didn't sound happy.

The doorbell rang, and my heart sank further. That

would be Mara. For a few seconds, I thought about blending and making a run for it. In some ways, talking to my parents seemed worse than facing Mr. Silver. I knew they loved me, but they were going to be so angry and disappointed. I'd managed to put my whole family in danger while supposedly trying to help someone. Again.

CHAPTER 13

CONFESSIONS

JANEY'S HEAD POPPED into my room. "Hey. I hear Dad downstairs. And someone's at the door. What's going on?"

"What's going on," I said, "is I'm so busted I don't even know if I can deal with it. "

"Cool," Janey said. "You coming down?"

"You know this means you're busted, too, right?"

She stepped into my room. "What are you talking about?"

"That's Mara at the door. It got really bad last night, and she saved me. But now she's gonna tell Mom and Dad everything."

She narrowed her eyes and tilted her head, like a little angry bird. "I'm sorry it 'got really bad' for you, but what does that have to do with me?"

"You were blackmailing me!" I said.

"Right. And?" She kept staring at me with her angry bird face.

"And, and, you're part of it."

"Joss, is that how it is? You get in trouble and you try to get me in trouble? Is that how we do things? I thought we looked out for each other."

That was insane. She'd looked out for me, sure, as long as I gave her what she wanted. But at another level, I knew she was right. I sort of hated the part of me that wanted her to be in trouble just because I was. I was better than that. I took a deep breath.

"No," I said. "Sorry."

She stepped over to me and looked up into my face. "I'm

121

sorry bad things happened. I guess I'll hear about it?"

"Yeah, probably so."

"Joss!" Dad yelled up the stairs. "Downstairs! Now!"

One last chance to run. I shoved down the thought. "Come on," I said to Janey, and headed out of my room.

Janey followed me down the stairs. My dad was waiting at the bottom, and waved me toward the family room. His face looked grim. For a second I thought he was going to stop Janey, but he seemed to change his mind and waved her after me.

Mara and Isabella were sitting on the couch when Janey and I walked into the family room with Dad right behind us. Mom was getting drinks or something in the kitchen. Isabella jumped up and ran over to Janey at the same time that Janey leapt toward her. They collided in this massive hug that almost looked painful. I nodded to Mara and she nodded back. She was wearing a t-shirt that had a picture of a steaming coffee mug on it and said CARPE CAFFEAM, whatever that meant. I wasn't happy to see her, but I owed her, and it was hard to feel angry at her.

About the time Isabella and Janey broke off their hug, Mom came in from the kitchen carrying a couple glasses of water.

"Hey, Mara," Janey said.

"Hi, Janey," Mara said, taking a glass from my Mom.

I glanced back at my dad. He still had the grim look on his face, and seemed about ten years older than usual. I looked away before he could make eye contact. I knew my dad was a lot older than me, but at that moment he looked like an old man, and it made me feel even worse. I'd done that to him. If he keeled over with a heart attack or something, it'd be my fault.

Mixed in with the guilt, however, I felt the pinprick heat on my neck of a rising anger. I'd been beaten on the head and shot the previous night, all because I'd tried to help someone. Bobby wasn't even a friend, but he had a terrible situation at home, so I'd tried to help. And now everyone was going to come down on me like I was a big problem.

Isabella sat back down on the couch and took a glass from Mom. Janey sat down between the Torres sisters, and Mom sat on her recliner. I wasn't quite sure what to do, so I stayed where I was. Dad walked around me and stood near his chair, but didn't sit.

"So," he said. "So. I got a call from Mara this morning, Joss, and I'm not going to lie, I'm about to lose my mind."

He was looking at his feet, not me, as he spoke. It almost made it worse. Until he looked up and held my eyes with his, and I realized that was far worse. There was a tightness around his eyes and a slackness in the rest of his face that said he was angry but also very sad.

"I need to know what's been going on, right now," he said. "From your mouth. All of it."

I had a moment where I stood on the brink. I hated to see him looking like that, all sad and hurt and angry, but I was getting angrier by the second. He didn't need to react that way. He could come alongside me and help, but I knew that wasn't going to happen. Instead, he'd blame me. All I had to do was blend and ghost, and I could go. None of them could stop me. I was the Seventy-Seven. I didn't have to spill my guts and confess everything going on. I could be gone in a moment. I didn't have to obey.

For some reason, my mind flashed back to when I was little, an early memory, when I'd fallen out of a tree. It hadn't been a trip to the hospital or anything, but it had hurt. Dad had been there, and after he'd hugged me tight and checked things out, he'd told me it would be okay. I'd believed him, and it had made it so much better. It'd still hurt, but I'd known it would work out.

I blinked, and my vision cleared up. Everyone was looking at me, like the whole world was holding its breath, waiting on my answer. So I told them everything, except the parts involving Janey. I could see her tense up and then relax as I skipped the part about her blackmailing me. I started at the beginning and worked forward to the Warrior and the chair and the escape. Being shot with a silver bullet that had shattered my lower leg. Mara rescuing me and bringing me home. I tried to tell them how scary Mr. Silver had been, but it was hard. I didn't really have words for his evil, hard eyes.

I looked at my feet as I spoke. When I got to the part about Mara having to pull the bullet out while pinning me to the ground, my stomach tightened up, and I heard Mom sob. Dad let out a slow hiss of air. I plowed through it, and when I finished I looked up just in time to brace myself for Mom as she swept me into a tight hug. She was still crying, which made it feel even worse. My dad wasn't crying. He looked like he wanted to hug me and then kill me. After a long minute, Mom let go of me and went back to her seat.

"Thank you for being honest," Dad said. "That, ah, description of events is so utterly outlandish I have no doubt you were telling the truth."

I opened my mouth to speak, but he held up a hand to stop me.

"That said," he said, "I am so disappointed in you. Which part of 'don't do anything without talking to us' did you not understand?"

His eyes betrayed how frustrated, hurt, and angry he was. Normally, Mom would step in if she thought Dad was showing too much anger, but not this time. She sat in her chair and quietly wept.

"I told you I'd let you know about anything new," I said. "The whole Bobby Ferris thing wasn't really new."

"That's your excuse?" Dad's voice could have chipped rocks.

"Well, it's true!" I said, but I wasn't sure I believed it.

"The truth goes deeper than your words, Joss." Dad turned toward the couch. "Mara, thank you for bringing all this to my attention, and thank you for saving Joss last night. Is there a reason you didn't call me yesterday?"

Dad kept his voice level, but he sounded intense. Mara leaned forward as he spoke and crossed her arms.

"Do I owe you a reason?" she said.

Dad took a deep breath. "No, not really. But I would have appreciated it."

She sagged back into the couch. "Fair enough. I acted on

what I knew to save him. It seemed like the right thing to do."

Dad took a moment to stretch his neck from side to side. "But you didn't tell me."

"True," Mara said. "But I'm not your child, he is. I did go hundreds of miles out of my way to save him. That needs to be enough for you."

Dad closed his eyes for a long moment and drew in a deep breath through his nose. When he opened his eyes he looked sad.

"You're right," Dad said. "Sorry. And thank you. From the bottom of my heart, thank you." He looked over at Isabella. "Thank you, Isabella."

Everyone else was sitting, so I dropped to the floor. While they'd spoken, the warmth in my neck had spread, and my chest felt tight. Sure, I hated to see my mom cry, and thankfully she seemed to have stopped, but there were limits. I wasn't some stupid little boy. I was Joss the Seven. Isabella had called me that back when we'd met, and I liked it. It was way better than Bullet Boy. I was going up against horrible, powerful men. It wasn't some kind of kid's game, like I'd messed up on a prank. These were evil criminals, and they needed to be stopped.

"Mara," Mom said, "we've heard from Joss. Is there any more you can tell us?"

"Not much," Mara said. "I managed to get a quick look in the main part of the warehouse where those trucks were. I saw Silver. Big guy like Joss said, with a green mask. There were other men around, a lot of them, but Silver was only talking to one guy. Medium height and build with dark hair cut short, and a short beard just starting to go white. His jeans and shirt were pretty tight, so we can't rule out him being a Seven."

My mouth dropped open. She'd just described Nick Stanton. I was shocked. He'd been the one who hit me in the head and given me to Mr. Silver? I'd read him when he'd ghosted through me a few weeks back and felt total honesty. I'd trusted him. How was that even possible if he was working for Mr. Silver? Had he gone bad in the past couple days? It made no sense.

"Let me untangle this." Dad's voice cut into my thoughts. "Joss decided he'd help his friend's dad, Eddie Ferris, but the first night he ended up almost getting some cops shot and not much else. Then he tried again the next night, got knocked out, presumably by a Seven who was blending, got roughed up by this Mr. Silver, threatened, and then rescued by you, Mara."

"You left out the parts where I saved Mara," I said. "Oh yeah, and the part where I got shot with a silver bullet. Being a Seven didn't stop the pain, okay? I felt everything."

"You suffered. Acknowledged. And somewhere along the way you and Thomas discovered you were being followed by officers Young and Malick, who aren't cops, but work for some task force on the, what was it?"

"DOSN," Mara said. "Department of Seven Normalization."

"Right. DOSN." Dad rolled his head from side to side again, like he was trying to loosen up a cramp. "Some governmental organization I've never heard of. And we kicked off the week with a meeting with the Guild, promising to meet weekly with them."

"The only thing that matters," Mom said, "is that Mr. Silver, this Mocker, has promised to turn Joss or kill all of us. And he's got a Seven Thief and a Seven Warrior, plus lots of other men. Men that were firing silver bullets. I've got to think that means they're trained to deal with Sevens. That's what matters. How do we stop him before he finds out who Joss is and where we live? Do we call the police? The Guild?"

"It might be too late for that," I said, and everyone's eyes pivoted to me. Part of me didn't want to say anything, but the stakes were too high. "Okay, do you remember that guy I told you about, that time I was breaking into the Guild offices but didn't know it? The Thief?"

Everyone looked at me blankly. Had it really only been two and a half weeks ago?

"When Janey got kidnapped," I said, "and I told you what all had happened, and told you how one of my missions ended up being to steal from the Guild for Jordan, but I didn't know it, and it was all a setup, and this Thief tried to stop me? That guy?"

One by one, they nodded. I guess I hadn't emphasized it much at the time.

"I remember," Isabella said, and she gave me a tight smile.

"Okay, when the Guild came by the house, what, two days ago?" I said. "He was here."

My dad's eyebrows pulled together, and a muscle started twitching in his jaw. "He was here. A Seven." He shook his head. "And we're just hearing about it."

I stood up. I'd just about had it with being blamed for stuff. "Yeah, you're just hearing about it."

"Joss," Mom said. "Watch your tone."

I ignored her and kept staring at my dad.

"Go on," Dad said. "There was a Seven Thief here. So I'm guessing he was invisible."

"Yeah, he was blending," I said. "He was supposed to be watching for me, in case I hid. We talked. He sort of warned me about jumping into the Guild."

"And you didn't tell us," Dad said, "because?"

"Because I don't know!" I said. "But that's not the point. He was here at the house. He knows me. And I trusted him, because when I was robbing that office a couple weeks ago, he ghosted through me. I sensed him. He was a good guy. I know he was."

My dad brought his fist down on the arm of his chair like a hammer and stood up. "You knew he was good. Dear Lord, Joss, you don't know how to tell the truth, but know how to feel when someone is good?"

"I know how to tell the truth!"

Mom stood up and took Dad's arm. He had this vein standing out in his neck. It didn't look healthy.

"It'd be nice if you tried to prove it," he said.

Mara stood, and Janey and Isabella stood with her.

"I need Joss to finish," Mara said. "You met this Seven here at the house. What was his name?"

"Nick Stanton," I said, "but he goes by Stanton."

"So I have a bad feeling I know what you're going to say," Mara said, "but go ahead and say it."

Everyone turned to me. Mom looked like she was going to be ill, but she still clung to Dad's arm, which was probably a good thing. He looked ready to tackle me. In the back of my mind a little voice thought it would be funny to see him try. Anger was throbbing in my blood. My chest felt as tight as a drumhead. I needed an outlet before I lost my mind.

"The person you described," I said, "the guy with Mr. Silver. It was Stanton. He must've been the one who knocked me out and gave me to Mr. Silver. And he already knows where we live."

Dad threw his hands in the air and walked in a quick circle around his chair. His face had turned red and splotchy. He stopped, stared at me for a moment, and took a step toward me. He'd lost his temper with me a few times and had to apologize for it, and I'd done the same a hundred times more. But this felt different. Not that I was scared. I was too angry to be scared. I'm not sure what I was planning to do, but it didn't include backing down.

Mara was between us in a moment. She didn't shift, but stood there with her arms outstretched. Dad glanced down at her.

"Deal with your son later," Mara said, "once we know everyone's going to still be alive, okay?"

Dad paused. "Fair point, Mara. We'll deal with the boy later."

Something snapped inside. I'd been shot and had my leg shattered less than twelve hours earlier. I'd paid the price for my decisions. I didn't need someone telling me how to be a superhero. I thought about going all Thief and just disappearing, but tossed the idea aside. I wanted to make a point. I needed the Warrior. I kinneyed and bruised. I really wasn't sure what I was doing, but I was going to make an impression.

The world shifted to extreme slow motion. I stepped around Mara. My dad's eyes tried to track with me, but they couldn't keep up. I was so angry. He was right there in front of me. Mom was off to the right, between their two chairs, her hand covering her mouth. I wanted to hurt something. To destroy. I glanced at my dad, but looked away. I couldn't go there. But I needed something.

I leapt forward and kicked his chair at full speed while bruising. The chair exploded outward as it flew backwards. I watched for a moment to make sure none of the fragments were heading for my mom and released the kinney.

It was violent chaos. The chair blew up as it flew back and slammed into the breakfast table, carrying it partly through the wall to the laundry room. Simultaneously, chunks of wood and leather flew up and out in all directions. Fragments stuck in the ceiling, broke a window in the breakfast area, and pretty much messed up that whole part of the house.

No one moved. No one seemed to breathe, except me. I was panting. I glanced at my dad. He didn't look angry anymore. More sad and scared. I turned to my mom and my heart clenched up. A line of blood cut across her cheek below her eye. I must have missed a fragment of wood.

I reached toward her and she flinched away from me. "I'm, I'm sorry, Mom."

She nodded at me, her mouth pulled in a tight line.

"Go to your room. Now."

Dad's voice was quiet. Cold. I turned, ignoring everyone, and headed for the stairs. I'd go to my room, but I wasn't planning to stay there.

CHAPTER 14

CALLING CARDS

HALFWAY UP THE stairs, the anger started to drain out of me. What had I done? What if I'd really hurt my mom? And how was I going to keep them safe if Mr. Silver came for them? I trudged upstairs, my burning anger rapidly replaced by a dead weight in my stomach.

I pulled my door closed behind me and paced my room. I'd have to trust that between Mara and my parents they could figure things out and stay safe. I needed to get to Stanton. But how? His face kept flashing behind my eyelids whenever I blinked. He'd seemed to truly care about me. Had it all been an act? He'd even said he would leave me a mobile number.

I stopped pacing and wracked my brains. Where had he said he'd put it? The pillowcase. I grabbed my pillow and yanked it out of the case. A small white card fell to the floor. I dumped my pillow on the bed and picked up the card. It was blank except for a phone number printed in small type on one side.

But what could I do with it? I needed help. I needed to talk to Thomas. I grabbed my work clothes from under my mattress and stuffed them into my backpack. Swinging my backpack on, I pulled open my window and climbed out on the roof. After closing the window, I crept along the roof to the part above the garage, and dropped down to the side yard. I didn't bother bruising or ghosting. Sure, Battlehoop had been a con Jordan used to manipulate me, but it had also taught me a lot of cool skills including the fine art of falling.

As I rode my bike across our yard and out the cul-de-sac, I half expected someone to run out of the house and try to stop me. No one did, and I was pretty disappointed. I hadn't planned to stop, but it would have been nice if someone had at least tried. The rest of the ride to Thomas's house was boring and hot. The only upside was that there were no cops tailing me that I could see.

When I arrived, I dropped my backpack by the front door and went full Thief, ghosting and blending. I walked through the front door and dropped the ghosting, but held the blend. I found Thomas in the family room, lying on the couch and reading a book. I didn't hear his mom—I hadn't expected to, given how much she worked—so I dropped the blending.

It had a nice effect, me popping into sight standing over him. Thomas shot up so fast he lost his hold on the book and launched it up and over me. I kinneyed, stepped backwards, and plucked it out of the air.

"What the heck, Joss?" Thomas said as I dropped the kinney.

"Here." I glanced at the cover as I handed the book to him. *The Worm Ouroboros.* I'd never heard of it.

He took it after a moment's hesitation. I headed back to the front door and grabbed my backpack. Hopefully no one would steal my bike.

"What's going on?" Thomas asked when I got back to the family room. "What happened last night?"

"Total disaster," I said. "Someone saw me when I was blending and hit me on the back of the head. Knocked me out."

"Another Seven?"

"Must have been, right? I woke up in this room, chained with silver. This guy, Mr. Silver, came in…" I stopped. Was his name on purpose? "Anyway, he pulls off his mask—"

"He was wearing a mask?" Thomas asked.

"Yeah, this green lucha libre mask," I said. "Crazy, right? He pulls off his mask and tells me how he never shows people his face except his inner circle or something.

A Thief, a Warrior, his daughter, and maybe someone else. And then he threatens to kill me and everyone who knows me if I don't join him."

Thomas sat down hard on the couch. "I know you."

"You and my parents and Janey," I said. "He left the room to let me think it over, and Mara suddenly busts through this window high up on the wall. She's a gorilla and takes out the two guards."

"Wait," Thomas said, "there were guards? How did Mara know you were there?"

"Yes, on the guards, and remember that app she had me install?"

Thomas snapped his fingers and pointed at me. "The app. Got it."

"Mara finds a key on a guard and unlocks me. She changes to a hawk or something and circles around to fly through the window, when the door just explodes in. I kinney, and I see this guy step in. He glances up, sees Mara, and launches himself at her. His leap was perfect, Thomas. He was, like, a master."

"He was kinneying?"

"Oh yeah, and bruising to come through the door like that," I said. "Mara had wedged a chair in to hold the door, so when I see him jump, the chair was flying by me, so I just"—I pantomimed grabbing the chair, whipping around, and throwing it—"threw it at him. Totally wiped him out. Mara got away, and I ran."

"Whoa," Thomas said, and held a fist out. I bumped it.

"I get out the other side of the building, and there are these other guys, and right when I'm about to escape, one of them gets lucky and shoots me in the leg. Just blew it up, right below the knee. It was a silver bullet, so I couldn't heal."

Thomas's eyes went huge and flickered down to my leg. "And?"

"Mara swoops in as a huge eagle and grabs me. She gets us out of there, takes me to her car, and does, like, surgery on my leg while I'm taking the pain. Gets the bullet out so I can reggie. It was rough."

"Joss," Thomas said, "not gonna lie, when you said it was a disaster, I wanted to say I told you so. But not after that. I'm, uh, really sorry. You okay now?"

"Yeah, it healed up when I reggied."

Thomas shook his head. "If Mara hadn't shown up..."

I nodded. "Would have been bad. But then Mara called my dad today and came over. We sort of had it out."

"What does that mean?"

I told him as I walked back and forth across the room. All of it, even the part of me losing control and destroying the chair and hurting my mom. All the leftover anger drained out of me as I told him about it. When I was done, I had this overwhelming need to tell my parents I was sorry. I should have never snuck off and tried to help Bobby's dad. What had I been thinking? I wasn't ready to go up against criminals or gangs or Mockers on my own.

"Man," Thomas said. "Just, wow. You gotta be careful. What if you'd really hurt your mom?"

"I know!" I said. "I know, and I'm sorry, but it's not enough. I've got to figure out how to make it right."

Thomas stood up and started pacing with me. I needed Thomas to come through for me. I was a good schemer. Gifted, really. But I was so wrung out from everything that had happened, I couldn't think straight.

Thomas stopped. "You've got a number for Stanton, right?"

"Yeah."

"And didn't DOSN duo give you their contact info? Do you have that?"

I frowned. Young and Malick? Oh! They had given me a card with a phone number, and I'd stuck it in my backpack. I dropped to the floor and pulled open my backpack, digging through it until I had both cards in hand. I held them up.

"Not sure how this helps," I said. "I like the whole 'DOSN duo' though."

"You need to get to Stanton, right?"

I nodded.

"And he's a Seven, who works for a Mocker," Thomas said.

I nodded again.

"And you happen to know two people who make a living hunting Sevens and Mockers, so…"

I jumped to my feet. The icy claw that had been holding my stomach loosened its grip a little bit. I was feeling something strange. Maybe hope.

"So we set up Stanton with Young and Malick," I said.

Thomas nodded. "Pretty much. It's really our only play that I can see. You've got to rope Stanton in. We set up a meet, and get them to grab him. They have to know how to do that, right, or how can they go up against Mockers? Anyway, doesn't matter. Maybe you grab him and hand him over. He doesn't know all your talents, does he?"

"I don't think so."

"You can go all Warrior on him and catch him yourself. It doesn't matter who catches him, as long as he's caught."

"I get it," I said. "I'll improvise. So we get him. Squeeze him for info, right? Figure out where Mr. Silver is. Take the fight to him."

"Pretty much," Thomas said. "I don't know what else you can do. And at least Stanton'll be out of it. We can get the DOSN guys to take him away. They'll do it, right? I mean he works for a Mocker."

"Might as well find out," I said.

"Right. And if Stanton's gone, that's got to simplify things, right?"

I nodded. "Grab Stanton. Find out about Mr. Silver. Take him down somehow. I mean, if we can pull that off, then we just need to figure out Mr. Ferris."

"That's got to be easier than all this other stuff," Thomas said. "Let's figure out what you're gonna say, then you've got a couple phone calls to make."

We talked through the phone calls, and what would come next. At some point we decided to have Thomas call the DOSN duo in case he picked up on something I'd miss, given how wired I was. Once we'd sorted it out, I held up their card so Thomas could dial the number.

He put his phone to his ear. "It's ringing."

There was a short pause, and he stiffened up a bit. "Uh, hello. Officer Young?" Pause. "Yes, this is Thomas. You know, one of the guys you've been following around?" Another pause. "Right. So, here's the deal. We've found a Seven, a Thief, who works for a Mocker named Mr. Silver. We think we can help you catch him, but it has to happen this afternoon. Can you help?"

He listened for a little, then gave me a thumbs up. "Great. But here's the deal. We need to talk to him after he's caught, okay? We need some info." Pause. "We're aiming to meet him in the mall parking lot, over on the south side away from the mall itself. We figure there'll be lots of cars to provide cover." He paused again. "Yeah, okay, and you know how to—" He stopped talking and listened. "Okay, we can do that. Can I text this number when we know we're on?" Pause. "Cool. I'll confirm the time as well. Okay, bye."

Thomas waited a moment, and hung up. "Good to go. Your turn."

"Hold up," I said. "What'd they ask about?"

"It was Young. They want us in with the cars and not all the way out in an empty parking lot," Thomas said. "And then something about knowing how to deal with Sevens."

"That doesn't sound good, but I guess it's what we need." I took a deep breath. "Okay, Stanton. Here goes."

I got my phone out and dialed Stanton's number. It rang, and rang some more. I hadn't even thought about what we'd do if Stanton didn't answer, but it made sense. The guy had knocked me out and given me up to Mr. Silver. He knew where I lived. Why would he bother talking to me on the phone.

For a split second, I thought the call had gone to voicemail. "Stanton here. This Joss?"

I had a moment of panic. That definitely wasn't voicemail. Why had I thought it was a good idea to talk to a guy who'd almost gotten me killed?

"Joss," Stanton said, "is that you? We need to talk."

I forced myself to speak. "Yeah, this is Joss. We do need to talk—"

"Look," Stanton said, cutting across what I was saying, "last night was out of control—"

"But," I said, trying to get back in control, "not on the phone. In person. Somewhere safe for both of us. How 'bout the mall near my house?"

Thomas leaned in toward me, his shoulders pulling up in anticipation as I waited for the answer.

"Yeah, okay," Stanton said, "I can meet you there. What part of the mall?"

"The parking lot on the south side, away from the mall itself," I said. "At 3:00 PM. Can you do that? I'll be there. Look for me."

"Yeah," Stanton said, "I'll be there. But Joss, you need to know that—"

I hung up on him. It's one thing to talk to someone who tried to get you killed. It's another thing to listen to everything he has to say.

"We good?" Thomas said.

I nodded and held out my fist. Thomas bumped it.

"Let the DOSN duo know we're on for 3:00 PM," I said.

Thomas texted for a moment, waited, and then texted again. He looked up after staring at his phone for another minute.

"We're locked and loaded," he said.

"Speaking of which," I said. A memory of our conversation with Young and Malick the day before had come to mind. "What's that about you being a natural born shooter?"

Thomas shrugged. "Dad and I go to this one shooting range the weekends I'm with him, and I didn't think I was anything special, but the owners and regulars say I've got something. The whole breathing thing we did with our Battlehoop training actually helped. Breathing right steadies your heartbeat, which steadies your hand, which makes you a more accurate shot. But I guess I was pretty accurate to begin with."

I nodded and smiled. "That's pretty cool. Sure came in handy when it all went down with Jordan."

"Yeah, I guess it did," Thomas said. "Listen, you want to call your parents or anything before we do this?"

"What's the point?" I said. The ice in my stomach had gotten much worse the moment he'd mentioned my parents.

"Um, like earning back their trust?"

I kept seeing the chair explode and go flying. What had I done? I'd let my anger own me, was what. "I don't think a phone call's gonna do it. Let's just get over there."

Thomas grabbed my shoulder to stop me as I headed for the front door. "Get your backpack. I don't want to have to explain it to Mom."

"Sure," I said. I picked it up and slung it over my shoulder.

He grabbed my shoulder again. "You sure about this?"

"What're my options?" I said. "I've got to get out in front of this before Mr. Silver shows up at my house."

Thomas nodded. "Six months ago, if you'd told me you were a superhero, or even a sort of decent hero, this isn't what I would have pictured. It's so complex, you know?"

"Yeah," I said, "I'm with you." I shrugged. "It is what it is. Let's do this, okay?"

Thomas nodded, and we headed out. He met me around front with his bike, and we rode toward the mall in silence. Once we crossed the large street and got to the mall parking lot, Thomas pulled up next to me.

"How's this going down?" Thomas said. "You gonna do the Warrior thing?"

"Probably," I said, "but I've been thinking about it. Stanton knows I'm a Thief, and I think he knows I can bruise. So the thing is, as long as he ghosts, he probably figures I can't touch him with the bruising, right? So I'm betting he's gonna ghost the whole time."

"Oh," Thomas said. "I hadn't thought of that. If you're both ghosting, you'll be like two normal guys fighting, right? That's not good. I mean, I know you can hold your own, but still."

"It's not gonna be a fair fight," I said. "I'll kinney just enough to beat him. I kinda think it'd be better if he didn't know about the whole Seventy-Seven thing. So I kinney just enough to beat him down. Maybe he thinks I'm really fast."

"Like Janey."

"Like Janey," I said. My heart hurt saying her name. What had I done? What would Isabella think? And why was I worried about Isabella when I'd messed things up so badly with my family?

We pulled up in the shade of a small tree on a tiny oasis of green surrounded by parking lot. Beyond the tree, the cars thinned out, but we had lots of them parked nearby. I leaned my bike against the tree and dropped my backpack on the ground. I didn't see anyone in sight, so I blended and ghosted. The blending was to keep an eye out for Stanton if he was blending. The ghosting was to get me out of the heat.

"You still here?" Thomas said.

"Yeah. Keeping an eye out for him in case he comes in blending."

Thomas nodded and pulled his phone out of his pocket. "Text from DOSN guys. They've got eyes on us and are ready to move." He looked up at me, except he was probably looking about a foot to one side. "Joss, they probably just saw you blend."

I looked around and saw nothing. Apparently, they knew what they were doing. "Oh well. What's the time?"

"Five 'til."

I nodded and looked around again. A man was getting out of a car on the edge of the parking lot. It was hard to see him in the glare of the sun off the asphalt, but it looked like it might be Stanton.

"Can you see him?" I said.

"Yep," Thomas said. "He's not blending."

"You ready?"

"Sure," Thomas said. "I mean, not really. I don't have anything to do."

"Just be ready," I said.

Stanton walked toward us at an angle so that he ended up a row over. About ten cars away, he cut between two minivans to come over to our row. When he stepped out into our row, Thomas coughed. He coughed again. I realized he was speaking as he coughed.

"Blending."

At least that's what I thought Thomas was saying, and it made sense. It's why Stanton had cut between the minivans, so he'd be out of sight when he made the transition. I'd seen him the whole time because I was already blending. Stanton zeroed in on me and walked over, stopping on the other side of the tree. He squinted at me.

"Why are you ghosting?" he said.

Then, as my dad would say, all heck broke loose.

CHAPTER 15

A DEAL WITH DOSN

I DIDN'T KNOW where they'd been hiding, but Young and Malick rushed out from behind cars on either side of us. They were both wearing black goggles that stuck way out on their faces, and both held what looked like massive, fat guns. The barrels were big enough to hold my fist, and I decided I didn't want to find out what they shot. I simultaneously dropped the ghosting and blending while kinneying and bruising in their place. It was probably the fanciest work I'd done as a Seven.

In the slowed down world I entered as I kinneyed, the guns made a loud woomph sound, and what looked like large, silvery bean bags shot out of them. As they rocketed toward Stanton and me, they opened up. Stanton immediately disappeared from sight. I pushed off the tree and shot backwards. I dropped the kinney but held the bruising as I landed on my back and skidded along the pavement. I came to a stop just past Thomas.

The silvery bean bags turned out to be silver nets that opened up to probably ten feet across and enveloped Stanton and the tree trunk. The moment the silvery material touched him, he popped back into sight. That meant it was real silver. His talents had been cancelled. I scrambled to my feet and ran past the stunned-looking Thomas back to the tree. I got there just as Young and Malick came in from each side,. The goggles and net-guns had been discarded, and I guessed the little black devices they each held were tasers.

"Wait," I said. "I've got to talk to him."

Young looked around, and gave Malick a quick nod.

"Twenty seconds," Malick said. Both agents put their tasers up to Stanton's neck.

"This is a mistake, Joss," Stanton said to me. "I'm not who you think."

"Oh, I figured that out after you knocked me out," I said. "Where's Mr. Silver?"

"It wasn't supposed to happen like that," he said. "I was going to free you later, but you were gone."

"You were going to free me?" I said. "After capturing me?"

"We don't have much time," Stanton said. "Here's what you need to know. I've been deep undercover for the Guild for months. Silver wasn't supposed to be there last night. I had to maintain my cover. I was going to catch you, then make sure you got loose. No harm, no foul. But Silver showed up."

"No harm?" I said. "I got shot with a silver bullet!"

"Time's up," Young said.

"Wait!" I said. "I need answers!"

With calm efficiency, they tased Stanton as I spoke, and he collapsed, still wrapped up in the silver nets.

Young tossed him over a shoulder and carried him to a nearby minivan while Malick picked up their abandoned gear from the parking lot. I followed Young to the minivan.

"Officer Young," I said, "You said I could talk to him."

"You did." Young opened the side door and dumped Stanton into a seat. It was rigged with silver restraints. Young started locking him in place.

"I needed more time. I need to know where Mr. Silver is!"

Young glanced at me, and then resumed restraining Stanton, who had started moving around. "We'll take care of it, Joss. Appreciate your help though. I think you've earned it. We'll strike you from our report."

Malick patted me on the shoulder and I jumped. I hadn't seen her coming over to the minivan.

"Good work," she said. "It was the right call to involve us."

"But I've got to get to Mr. Silver." I was starting to feel desperate. "He's going to come after my family!"

Young finished with Stanton and slammed the door shut. He turned to me.

"You want to fill us in?" he said. "Tell us what happened with Jordan? Tell us how you know Silver?"

I looked from Young to Malick and back. It felt like I was looking at two predators. Tigers, maybe.

"Some pretty fancy moves back there," Malick said. "I'd pegged you as one of those ghosters, along with the blender thing. But you moved awful fast when we came in."

"No raspberries, either," Young said. He shrugged. "A guy slides twenty feet across pavement, you sort of expect some torn clothes and road rash."

My breathing was speeding up. Definitely tigers. I needed their help, but I couldn't bring myself to talk to them about my talents. My mind felt foggy and slow. I was pretty sure I was starting to panic. If they took Stanton away, I was hosed, with no way to get at Mr. Silver, or Silver as everyone else seemed to call him.

Thomas stepped up next to me. Our shoulders bumped as he came to a stop. Well, my shoulder bumped his upper arm. The guy had several inches on me in height. Anyway, I was pretty sure he'd done it on purpose, because it snapped me back to reality. I glanced at him and gave a quick nod. I'd suddenly realized I had something they'd want.

"Do you know what he looks like?" I said. I could still feel Silver's heavy stare when he'd taken off his mask. A mask he'd claimed he always wore.

Young's eyes narrowed. "Do I know what who looks like?"

"I'm betting," I said, "you've only seen Silver with the mask on, right?"

Malick tilted her head and pulled her mouth to one side, staring at me. She shook her head. "There's no way you've seen him. Not his face. He's too careful."

I shook my head. "Not when he's threatening to kill you.

When the mask comes off, he either trusts you or kills you."

Young and Malick looked at each other for a moment, and Young finally shrugged. They turned back to me.

"You can identify him?" Malick said.

"Easily," I said. "Just show me a picture or something."

"It's not that simple," Malick said. "But we'll get to that. What do you want?"

"I need to talk to him." I nodded toward the window of the minivan. The tint on it was so dark I couldn't see Stanton. "I give you Silver, and if I ask, you let him go."

Even Thomas looked shocked at this, but I'd been chewing on it ever since they'd nabbed him. I was sure Stanton had been honest a few weeks ago. I needed to see if he'd changed. If it was still true, if he was still true, this was all a big mistake. Sure, he'd gotten me caught and given me a nasty bump on the head, but that was worth it, even to me, if it took down a Mocker. And that's what Stanton had said he was doing.

"We'll need more," Young said.

"What do you mean?" I said. "I don't have more."

"I think you do," he said, "or you will. We need something to pin on him. Evidence. If we can figure out who he is, we need his books."

Thomas and I looked at each other.

"His books?" Thomas said. "Like, all of them? What if he reads a lot?"

Young pulled his mouth in a line and shook his head.

"His accounting books," Malick said. "His records."

"Oh," I said. I looked at Thomas. "Everybody wants me to steal stuff for them." I looked back at Malick. "How will I find them?"

"Let's see if you can identify him first," she said. She pulled out her phone, picked an app, and handed it to me. "Draw him."

I looked down at her phone. A blank oval sat on the top half of the screen, and lots of options on the bottom half. Hair, ears, eyes, and every other facial feature. I started tapping around and picking options. Each selection made a change to the oval at the top, and it gradually took shape. There seemed to be nearly infinite choices, but it was easy once I got the hang of it.

There were options within the options. Once I'd found the right set of eyes, I was able to make them slightly smaller to match what I remembered of Silver's face. I flipped back and forth between the features, and his face gradually appeared in the top half of the screen. After about ten minutes, I held it up to Malick. Young leaned over and looked with her at the screen.

"That's him," I said.

Malick took the phone from me and tapped the screen a few times. "It will take a few minutes," she said. "Give it a moment."

Thomas looked like he was going to say something, but snapped his mouth shut. We stood around for a couple minutes that felt longer than my eighth grade year of school.

"Swipe to the side," Malick said, and handed me the phone again. "Tell us if you see him."

I took the phone and looked at the picture. The guy in the photo could have been Silver's cousin, but it wasn't him. I swiped, and another guy who sort of looked like him appeared. I swiped, and swiped, and swiped. Apparently, the DOSN had lots of pictures of guys who looked a lot like him. The pictures were all different types. Some looked like those mug shots you see online. Others looked more like my dad's driver's license photo. And they kept going.

Suddenly, I was looking into the hard, dark eyes of Silver. I swiped past him before I could stop my thumb and realize what I'd seen. I glanced up at Young and Malick. They were watching me intently. On an instinct, I looked back down at the phone and kept swiping. After about thirty more photos had gone by on the screen, I looked up.

"I've got him."

Malick leaned forward to look at the phone. "Him?"

"Nope," I said. "You give me a moment with Stanton and I'll show you who it is."

"I told you," Young said, "we need more."

"I know," I said, "but you get nothing if I don't talk to him."

Young and Malick gave me hard looks.

"So we do it in two phases," Malick said. "You identify Silver for us, and we let you talk to Stanton. Then you get us evidence, and we'll let him go."

"Sure," I said. I figured that I may not even want Stanton to get free after talking to him.

"Deal," said Malick.

I flipped back to the picture of Silver and held the phone out to Malick.

"That's him," I said.

She glanced at the phone. "You sure?"

"Positive. It's him. Now let me talk to Stanton."

Young glanced around, then pulled the minivan door open. Stanton was draped in silver netting and held in place by silver cuffs. His eyes through the mesh looked wild.

"I need one of his hands free," I said. Young and Malick both looked at me, but neither of them moved. "Guys, I'm not trying to rescue him, okay? I called you, didn't I?" I gestured toward Malick's phone. "I told you who Silver was. I need one of his hands free of the silver."

Stanton had zeroed in on me while I spoke and looked a little less crazy. He'd probably figured out what I wanted to do, and he didn't seem worried about it. That was probably a good sign. Young went to work pulling back the netting from Stanton's hand.

"Joss, I had to make a tough call." Stanton watched Young working on the net as he spoke. "Maybe I did the wrong thing. I'm sure I did, given what happened. But at the time, I didn't know Silver was going to be there."

Young got the net free of Stanton's arm and unbuckled the silver strap. Stanton reached toward me. I clasped his hand in mine, and concentrated on ghosting just my hand. I hadn't tried to ghost a part of me in weeks. It hadn't gotten any easier, but I did it.

Stanton played it perfectly. He held his hand rigid, as though our hands were still clasped, but now my hand overlapped parts of his and I got hit with that full sense of him. It was a complex mess, but underlying all of it was a strong sense of honesty. I pulled my hand away and released the ghosting. He was telling the truth, and I'd gotten him captured by DOSN.

"Joss," Stanton said, "I'm not sure what's going on, but you need to straighten things out. I'm not talking about me, okay? I'd guess it's your family or something deeply personal."

Oh, crud. I'd forgotten he'd sense me at the same time. He must have felt the lump of guilt and anger burning in my chest. For a moment, the anger flared up. I was trying to help him in spite of what he'd done, and he was going to give me advice? The moment passed, though, and I realized he was simply living up to the honesty I'd felt in him. I gave him a quick nod.

"He doesn't know that I know you," Stanton said, "but he's clever. He'll figure out who you are, and then he's coming for you. I would have helped, but"—he shrugged and glanced down at the silver netting—"I don't think I'm much use to you."

Young stepped between us, pushing me away from Stanton.

"Hey!" I said. "I still need to find out where Silver lives."

Young didn't turn around, and I guessed he was locking Stanton's arm back in place. Malick answered for him.

"We can give you his home address. Office, too, but we're guessing his home will have what we need."

I turned to her. "You can?"

She held her phone up. "All the info right here."

Young stood up straight and slammed the minivan door shut. He turned to me, Malick right beside him. Thomas stepped forward so that the two of us stood together facing them. It felt good to have a friend by my side because I had no idea what to do.

"Are you going to give it to us?" Thomas said.

"Of course," Malick said. "When you called earlier, was that your mobile?"

Thomas nodded, and Malick messed around on her phone for a second.

"Sent," she said.

Thomas pulled out his phone and angled it so I could see the screen. A second later, a text came in from Malick. Thomas opened it, and we saw an address and a name. Gregory Goram.

"Got it," Thomas said. "Are we done here?"

"Get us evidence," Malick said, and nodded toward the minivan, "and he goes free. No questions asked."

"What if we need help?" I asked. I had no idea how I was going to turn an address into evidence.

"Call if you need something," Young said.

"Okay, but—"

"Let's go, Joss," Thomas said. He turned back toward the tree where our bikes were.

I followed him, but glanced back at the minivan. They were already getting in the front seats. By the time I'd picked up my backpack and gotten on my bike, they were driving away.

"I didn't see why we should drag that out," Thomas said as we rode home. "They've got Stanton thanks to us. And you ghosted when you took his hand, right? Is he telling the truth?"

"I ghosted," I said. "He's telling the truth. I'm not saying he should have hit me in the head and gotten me caught. He doesn't even know I can reggie. It could've messed me up. But I believe him when he says he's trying to take down Silver, or Gregory Goram, or whatever his name is."

"So what do we do? It didn't happen like we wanted, but we've got the info, right?"

"Well," I said, "either I get over to his house somehow and find his books for the DOSN duo, or I do something more drastic."

Thomas glanced over toward me as we rode. "What does that mean?"

"I have to stop him, right? What if we can't find any evidence? Do I just wait for him to come for my family, or do I take the fight to him?"

"So, what? You go in and kill him? Like, an assassination?"

"Well, what would you do?" I said.

"Not that," Thomas said. "Listen, the only person who's actually harmed you was Stanton. You can't decide to kill people based on what you think they might do. That's way beyond wrong. It's evil."

I took a deep breath and thought about it. Thomas was right. I'd had these thoughts running through my head about stopping Silver, and I'd felt trapped, like I had to do anything it took. Thinking about it made me feel sick in my stomach. But my parents had hammered into me over and over growing up that you don't try to use evil to do good. Hearing Thomas call it evil made me realize I didn't have to go that far, and I was relieved. Maybe things would turn out horribly and I'd have to live with that, but I wasn't going to become some psychopath.

"Thanks," I said. "That helps."

We turned onto Thomas's street, and a large bird swooped down ahead of us in front of his house. There was a twist and Mara was standing where the bird had been. We pulled up next to her.

"Cool entrance," I said.

Thomas looked around. "Hope the neighbors didn't notice."

"Boys," she said, nodding to each of us. "We need to talk."

CHAPTER 16

WE

"Maybe inside?" Thomas said. "Mom shouldn't be home for a while."

Mara waved an arm toward the house. "Lead on."

Thomas took us around through the side gate to the backyard. I left my bike against the side of the house out of sight from the deck. Mara followed the two of us around and into the house through the backdoor.

"So, Joss," she said once we were standing around the kitchen island, "that was—"

"I know," I said, butting in.

"Uh-uh," she said, and took the glass of water Thomas had poured for her. "You don't get to shut me up, not after the show you put on."

"Water?" Thomas said to me, and I nodded.

"Your parents are worried sick," she said. "Let me ask you something. Are you parents your parents only as long as they're stronger than you?"

"Of course not," I said, and avoided her eyes.

"So if you keep growing, like normal boys do, and one day you're stronger than your mom... heck, you may already be there. But whenever it happens, is she still your mom?"

"Yeah," I said, taking the glass of water from Thomas.

"And do you need to be her kid still?" Mara said. "You know, honor and obey and all that?"

I gulped down my water to buy time. I didn't like this conversation one bit.

"Yeah, all of that," I said when the water was gone.

"I see," Mara said. "And if your dad got hurt, and was in a wheelchair or something, would he still be your dad?"

I looked up at her. Her eyes were narrowed in anger. "Yeah, Mara, he'd still be my dad."

"So being stronger than you isn't really what makes them your parents, is it?" she said. "But you get a few talents, some extraordinary abilities, and you think you can pop off at them? Just do your own thing?"

I looked away and didn't say anything. Thomas was sipping his glass of water and staring at the countertop. Mara slammed her fist down.

"Do you know what it makes you?" Mara said. "What you did? Scaring them? Even hurting your mom?"

I looked her in the eyes. "Yeah, I'm pretty sure I do."

"And what's that?"

"A lousy son," I said.

Mara glared at me, and I held her eyes. Finally, her face softened a bit. "Yeah, Joss, a pretty lousy son. And lousy sons grow up to be lousy people. And that's not you, is it? So get this through your head. They're still your parents, even if they don't know how to parent a Seven. And you don't get off the hook for being their son just because you're the Seventy-Seven."

"I get it," I said. "Okay?"

Thomas stood up straight and looked from me to Mara. "This has been great, Mara, really helpful"—his voice got louder as he spoke—"but I feel like we need to turn our attention to keeping everyone alive!"

Mara gave Thomas a hard look. "Don't push, Thomas."

"Push? I find out this morning my life's in danger, and I want to do something about that, and I'm 'pushing' too much?"

"It's a fair point," I said, and Thomas gave me a quick nod.

Mara took a deep breath. "Okay, so, after the whole thing this morning at the Morgan house, it looks like you two have been busy. What just went down at that parking lot? I saw a Seven get caught by someone."

I felt shocked. "You were watching the whole time?"

"Of course," Mara said. "Did you really think your parents would let you run off like that? I convinced them to let me tail you more discretely."

"You were, like"—I pointed up—"flapping around?"

"Mostly," she said.

"Mostly?" Thomas said. "Wait, were you in my house? Like, as a mouse or something?"

Mara shrugged. "Far as you know. Now, tell me what all went down. Assume I don't know any of it."

I looked at Thomas and he shrugged. We filled her in on what we'd known about Stanton, and how we'd called the DOSN duo, and the rest. Mara started slowly shaking her head partway in and never stopped.

"So you just eliminated the one person who could probably really help you?" she said when we were done.

I shrugged. "Pretty much, but we know where Silver, uh, Mr. Goram lives, and we know what we have to do next."

"So you're going to stroll into his house and have a look around?" Mara looked over at Thomas. "You going with him? Just take a cab or something?"

"Well," said Thomas, "we were planning to ask you for a ride. And I wasn't going in. We're not crazy. I was going to be a lookout."

"You really think I'll have a hard time going in there?" I said. "Me? The Thief?"

"Joss, take a deep breath and think." Mara grabbed my shoulder and squeezed. "He goes by Silver. He locked you in silver chains, remember? He deals with Sevens. Do you really expect his home to be unguarded? Just an open door for a Thief?"

I was stunned. I hadn't even considered any of that. I'd figured I'd go in blending and ghosting, find his stash of accounting books, grab them, and get out. Mara must have seen it on my face, because she gave my shoulder another quick squeeze and dropped her hand.

"We're going to assume that ghosting is out as far as

getting in," she said. "Remember how Jordan was building out that warehouse with wire mesh? I bet you he learned that from Silver. I'm betting it's in the walls, doors, whatever."

My heart leapt at her words. Sure, she was demolishing all my plans, but her first words had mattered most.

"We?" I said. "Not me?"

"Yeah, Joss, we." Mara sat down on one of the stools next to the kitchen island and took a drink of water. "Look, I'm not going to get all emotional here, but you, you helped me get Isabella out. You helped us get free of Jordan. We lost two years of our lives to that animal, and you put it all on the line to help us. I'll never forget that, okay? Never. Just because I think you've got straw for brains doesn't mean I won't do everything possible to help you. Why do you think I showed up last night?"

Maybe she'd said she didn't want to get emotional, but her eyes sure looked sparkly when she was done talking. I gave her a grin and held my fist out toward her. She hesitated, then bumped it. I felt a rush of hope that almost choked me up. It was probably insane, but I felt like Mara and I could take on the world. Silver and his goons were going down.

"Let me add that this could be crazy dangerous," Mara said. "I just don't see an alternative. Your family's lives could be at stake if we don't move fast."

"So what do you think?" I said. "I'm not sure how we really make a plan when we don't have anything to work with but an address."

"We've got more than that," she said.

"Which means…" I raised my eyebrows in question.

"The DOSN duo," Thomas said. "They said to call if we needed help."

"There you go," Mara said. "So what might help?"

I snapped my fingers. "We need Silver out of there. I'm guessing his Sevens hang with him pretty close. If he had to go into a risky situation, I bet he'd take his Warrior with him."

154

"Right," Mara said. "So we need them to somehow bring down the Feds on him, like, right now. Get him away from his house."

I turned to Thomas. "What do you think?"

He shrugged. "Worth a try, right? I'll call them."

Thomas pulled out his phone and hit the redial on Young's number. "Officer Young?" Pause. "Yeah, hey, we need your help. Can you guys do something to force Silver out of his house, like, today? And make him nervous?" Another long pause. "Cool. So, when would that happen?" Pause. "Okay, thanks!"

Thomas hung up. "They're going to send cops to bring him in. Young said he'll lawyer up and they'll have to let him go, but he'll be gone for at least a couple hours."

"When?" Mara said.

"They'll aim for 5:00 PM. So we've got a couple hours to kill."

"Maybe," Mara said. "Depends on the address. Let me see it."

Thomas held out his phone to her with the info on Gregory Goram. Mara mapped the address.

"Thirty-minute drive with traffic," she said, "so we leave at 4:40 sharp."

"Cool," Thomas said.

Mara shook her head. "Not you. I'm not bringing you, Isabella, Janey, or anyone. Just Joss and I."

"What're you talking about?" Thomas crossed his arms. "I'm not getting sidelined again."

"Yeah," Mara said, "yeah you are. Take a look at this."

She held out her phone with the map on satellite view. It showed a huge property with a large house in the middle surrounded by what looked like a large wall of some kind. From the size of the shadows, the wall had to be pretty tall.

"It's a fortress," Mara said. "Joss and I need to search it top to bottom, but I'm betting it will be crawling with Silver's men. We're not going to have the luxury of looking around unless we neutralize everyone first."

"Look," Thomas said, "I'm not claiming I'm going to

'neutralize' anyone, but I can keep a lookout and let you know when we're out of time."

"And what happens when we're out of time," Mara said, "and we have to run? Just flat out flee for our lives? You think it's going to help us to have you along then?"

I could see the muscles in Thomas's jaw working. He slapped the counter. "What the heck? I hate this! I hate being the normal guy who has to be protected."

He turned away from us. I reached out and grabbed his arm, but he jerked it free and walked out of the kitchen. I looked to Mara and shrugged.

"Give him a sec," she said. "It's tough."

"What's tough?" I said, keeping my voice low.

"Being your friend."

I frowned. "What does that mean?"

"It means being around you makes Thomas feel worthless because he can't do the stuff you do."

"What?" I had not expected that. Thomas and I had been friends forever. "He's cool with it. Really."

Mara shook her head. "He's acting cool with it, and he wants to be cool with it, but I promise you it gnaws at him. Leaving him behind pretty much throws it in his face."

"So let's not leave him."

"Joss, he's got a mom who expects him home today. Not to mention she probably expects him to be alive tomorrow. We can't take him. It's too risky."

I grimaced. "But you just said that throws the whole 'doing special stuff' in his face."

"Yep," Mara said, "but I didn't say there was anything we can do about it. You're going to have to be a good friend to him, even if he's not very happy with how some of this goes."

I slumped onto a bar stool. None of the comic books I'd read had prepared me for the stupid stuff superheroes really had to deal with. Parents. Friends. I shook my head. I just wanted to get myself out of this whole mess and have things go back to normal. But not really. I liked being a Seven, and I didn't want to give it up. But what if it cost me my friends?

There had to be something I could do about it.

"Thomas is a good friend," Mara said. "He'll rise to the occasion. But keep in mind that just being your friend asks a lot of him, okay?"

"That's really not fair," I said.

Mara shrugged. "Is it fair that you're the Seventy-Seven? What's fair really got to do with it? Just be his friend, okay? And part of being his friend is being aware of what he's going through."

So lame. How were my powers something that Thomas had to deal with? And what was Mara expecting of me with this whole 'being aware' thing? Didn't she know I was a teenage boy? We hung out. We had fun. We didn't think about each other's feelings. The whole thing was ridiculous.

"I can see it written on your face," Mara said. "I know, teen boys aren't exactly the most sensitive people. But you know what? Tough. You're going to have to rise above that, or you're going to lose friends. Understood?"

"I guess," I said, but I didn't understand, and I wasn't totally sure I wanted to.

"Just think about it, okay?"

I nodded. "But not right now. I think I'm gonna grab some rest before we go."

"Sure," Mara said. "Crash on the couch. I'll hang with Thomas."

A thought hit me. "Hey, where's Isabella?"

"Hanging with Janey," Mara said. "After your little tantrum at your house, I'm sure they're telling stories about you and giggling."

I shook my head. I didn't need one more thing to worry about, but I couldn't help wonder what Isabella thought of me now. Again, Mara seemed to read my thoughts.

"Just move forward with a healthy perspective," she said. "Ask for forgiveness. No one's going to hold a grudge."

I nodded, and headed to the couch in the family room. Thomas was nowhere to be seen. I figured he was upstairs in the game room, which would be directly above me. A funny thought hit me, and I stopped just before laying down. Mara was leaning on the door to the kitchen, watching me. I held my hand up to ask her to wait, then blended, and kinneyed.

The world around me slowed down. Mara's eyes slowly flared open as I disappeared. I crouched down and leapt. As I floated up toward the ceiling, I ghosted. Just as I'd thought would happen, I ghosted up through the ceiling, but slowed down rapidly, so that I stopped going up with about half my body sticking through the floor of the game room.

Thomas was sitting on his couch, playing XBOX. He sort of looked angry and sad all at once. I had a sense of seeing something private, like I was spying on him. It didn't feel right. I ghosted back down through the floor as fast as possible and dropped to the floor of the family room, where I released all the talents. Mara had her head quirked to the side when I popped back into sight.

"Checking on Thomas," I said. "He's playing XBOX." I pointed up. "Didn't look super happy. Maybe you're right."

"Wait," Mara said. "How'd you check on him?"

I walked her through how I'd used kinneying, blending, and ghosting. Her eyebrows got higher and higher as I spoke.

"You can do all that?" she asked when I was done.

I shrugged. "I guess."

"But you couldn't have done that a couple weeks ago when I left, right?"

"Nope. Not a chance," I said. "I've been practicing a ton."

"Sure," she said, "but there aren't enough hours in the day to get in that much practice."

"There are when you only sleep a couple hours a night. You're the one who taught me the trick."

Mara stepped into the room and put her hands on her hips. "What trick?"

"You know," I said, "the whole reggie when going to sleep to refresh yourself super-fast."

Mara's mouth dropped open. I didn't know what the big

deal was. She was the one who'd told me to do it in the first place.

"I, I've never done that," Mara said. "Not for normal sleep. I sort of reggie automatically, but only when injured. Sometimes, if the injury's bad, it helps to sleep. But I'd never thought to force the reggie when I wasn't injured."

"Huh," I said. "Well, it works like a charm. It's what I'm about to do when I lie down."

"This is huge," Mara said. "I'm stunned. I can't believe I never thought of that."

I shrugged. "Glad I can help. But I'm grabbing some sleep, okay? Go check on Thomas if you want."

Mara nodded, but it looked like she was in a trance. Her eyes were too wide, and she wasn't focused on anything. She turned and drifted toward the entry with the stairs. I smiled and shook my head. I hadn't expected to teach Mara any new tricks. With that thought, I reggied and fell asleep.

Mara woke me about an hour later. I felt great, and hopped up to do some stretches. Thomas came in from the kitchen and brought me a cup of coffee.

"Thanks, man," I said, and he cracked a grin.

"My contribution for the evening," he said, and gave a sweeping bow.

I took a sip. He'd put in just the right amount of sugar, maybe four spoonfuls, along with a bunch of half and half. And it wasn't too hot. I didn't have time to sip hot coffee. I gulped it down instead.

"It is a most favorable contribution," I said. "My thanks for the service."

Mara watched us and shook her head. "Okay, Joss, get your work clothes on. We need to roll."

I retrieved my backpack and blended while I changed clothes. Sure, the clothes would pop in and out of view, but I was completely invisible. It still felt a little weird to be in the middle of Thomas's house, standing in front of Mara and changing, but I rolled with it.

"We got a plan yet?" I asked when I was done.

"About 200 feet of it," Mara said. "Thomas dug up some

really solid rope from the garage. It's in my car already. I'm seriously good at knots, so we keep the plan simple. Go in strong. Hope your DOSN buddies actually got Silver and his Warrior out of there. Incapacitate everyone, and search the place."

"Hey," I said, "that's way more detailed than 'rob a bank,' right? Let's do this."

"Good luck," Thomas said.

He held out his fist, and I bumped it.

"I'll get your stuff out of sight," Thomas said, waving toward my clothes and backpack.

"Cool," I said. "Thanks. For everything, Thomas, okay?"

He grinned and smiled. Mara waved me toward the front door, and we headed out. Her car was parked out front now.

"You were busy while I slept," I said. "I take it you talked to Thomas?"

"Yeah, and he's a really good friend to you," Mara said. "I also ran by your house and got my car. Hop in."

I settled into the passenger seat while she cranked the car and got underway. "Did you, ah, see my folks?"

"Briefly," she said. "We can talk about it later. We need to focus. I need an update on what you can do."

I gave her a quick rundown on how I was coming on the various talents while she drove.

"I'm still a little surprised you can't shift," she said. "When this is all over, I want you to try shifting with me again. Maybe that will get you past the block."

"I hope so," I said.

"Okay, let's talk approach," Mara said. "I'm going to park a few blocks away and fly in so I can drop the rope where we can get to it. I want you to go straight in. Try to ghost through the gate to see if I was right about the silver. Otherwise, do that kinney jump thing you've worked up, and I'll meet you in the courtyard."

I nodded, and sat back, trying to calm myself. My stomach had tightened up into a knot. What if there was a Warrior there? What if Silver hadn't left? What if he had, but we couldn't find his stuff?

I clamped down on my thoughts, and pulled my mask on. I'd felt so much confusion today about who I was and what I was supposed to be as the Seventy-Seven. As a son. As a friend. But not tonight. Tonight was about kicking some butt. For my parents. For Janey. For Thomas.

Mara pulled over a while later by a park in a super wealthy-looking part of town. The park was surrounded by homes that looked closer to castles than the houses in my neighborhood.

Mara pointed. "One street over. Take a right. Fourth house, or estate, or whatever these things are on the left. Get in there and blend and ghost until I show up. Got it?"

"What about you?"

"I'm going to take the rope and find a private place to shift and get airborne."

I nodded, and blended. While Mara got out on her side, I ghosted through the door and held the ghost to fend off the heat as I headed toward Silver's house. A street over and four houses down, I found it. I could see the top story of what must have been a three-story mansion. A huge white wall ran in front of the property, with wrought iron spikes sticking out the top of it.

I headed down the wall to a driveway off the street that ended in a huge, wooden gate set into the wall. I was still ghosting, so I tried to step through the gate. It was like I was trying to walk through an actual wall even though I was ghosting. I hit something solid about an inch into the wood and came to a stop. Mara had told me to expect this, but it was still a little shocking. I was glad, though, that the silver worked that way with ghosting and hadn't actually made me stop ghosting while partly in the wood.

I stepped back toward the street and looked up at the top of the gate. It had the iron spikes mounted like the rest of the wall. I took a deep, calming breath, and kinneyed.

"Yolo!" I said, and jumped.

I sailed over the wall and dropped my kinney as I cleared it. I fell to the ground, switching from ghosting to bruising, and landed with a loud thud in the middle of absolute chaos.

CHAPTER 17

JOSS THE WARRIOR

DETAILS FLICKERED INTO view as I glanced around. Seven or eight men burst out of all sorts of doors in a huge, white home that stood about fifty feet away across a stone-paved courtyard. A large roll of rope bounced as it hit the ground about ten feet in front of me. A man with a large, black telescope thing on his face pointed directly at me and yelled. The other men raised all sorts of weapons and pointed them at me, including a couple of those huge-barreled things that the DOSN duo had used to fire silver nets at Stanton.

I pondered my situation for about a tenth of a second and decided it was time to panic. I knew I couldn't kinney for long, but if I didn't use what I had right now, I was finished before I started. For that matter, was blending going to do much more than tire me out if I was moving full speed? I was already bruising, so I dropped the blending and kinneyed. Time to see what Joss the Warrior could do.

I leapt toward the man pointing at me, angling up at about a forty-five degree angle. The men all reacted to my sudden appearance and movement, eyes flaring open, heads moving too slowly to keep up with me. As I slowly sailed up and toward the house, one of the men with the big net guns fired it, and a silver bundle shot out and expanded. I twisted in the air as the net opened and avoided it.

I glanced up and saw a huge eagle plummeting in slow motion toward the men on my right side. Good. I'd take the guys on the left and leave the others to Mara. I looked back to the man with the telescope goggles and realized I'd aimed too high and was going to go over him into the wall of the

163

house. I'd never jumped this far, but the adrenaline must have kicked in. There was nothing to do with it but try to conserve energy.

I tucked into a ball and released the kinney. Time snapped back to normal and I was shocked how fast I was moving. Definitely a lot of adrenaline. I hit the house about five feet above the main doorway goggle-man was standing in. There was a large window above the door that I glimpsed as I rocketed forward. I hit the edge of the window and brick wall, blowing out glass and brick as I ricocheted into the house.

I screamed as pain ripped through my back, and to my horror I realized I was no longer bruising. Silver. There had been silver in the wall. I'd lost a lot of speed hitting the brick, but not enough. Everything was a blur as I shot across some sort of room, arcing down toward the floor.

I bruised again just as I slammed into a staircase. Mercifully, though the wood crumpled under me as I came to a stop, I didn't come into contact with any silver. The pain was overwhelming, and for a moment I couldn't do anything but breathe. My senses were hollowed out by the pain. My vision was only a pinprick of light, my hearing a confusion of loud noises.

I reggied, and relief flooded my body along with an intense weariness. I sat up and looked around. I sat in a small crater about four steps up a winding staircase that led from an entry hall to a balcony overlooking the front doors. The noise came into focus. It sounded like a war was happening just outside the open front doors.

My mind lurched back into action. Mara! I kinneyed and surged forward, just as three men came through the front doors. I had no idea which three they were, but it didn't matter. The man in the front, dressed in a dark suit with no tie, held one of the net-guns. He was swinging it up toward me as he came into the house. Behind him, the man to the left held a handgun with a silencer. The man to the right was holding a silvery-looking sword.

What. The. Heck. It was like a bad joke my dad might

tell. Three men entered a bar. One had a net, another a gun, and the third a sword. Or something like that. Whatever. The joke was going to be on them. I leapt, aiming for the ceiling almost directly above them, and trying to make sure I didn't jump too hard. As I flew upward, I bruised again.

I twisted in the air and hit the ceiling on my hands and feet. Thankfully, I'd jumped with the right amount of force and didn't bust through to find the silver hiding within the ceiling. Instead I pushed off, angling toward the wall directly above the door and below the window I'd destroyed. I managed to twist around again and hit the wall feet first. I pushed off and flew toward the back of the three men, who'd come to a stop but hadn't had time to turn toward me.

Bowling with bad guys. It was a new game I'd just invented. I spread out like a spider monkey to try to maximize the impact as I slammed into them and released my kinney. I don't really know what happened next, except that I came to a stop near the stairs again after bouncing a couple times. The three guys were scattered around the room, crumpled in heaps, unmoving. I was pretty sure I'd heard some bones breaking as I'd flown through them.

I looked down at my arm and was shocked to see a deep gash through my shirt sleeve and across my forearm. The moment I saw it the pain hit, like the wound had been waiting to get my attention before crying out. I must have hit the sword on the way down. I dropped the bruising and reggied. The wound closed up like a zipper, but the sleeve hung open.

I was utterly exhausted. I wasn't much of a Warrior if I could only handle three men. That meant four more were out there with Mara. I looked around the room, and glanced up toward the balcony. A drop-dead beautiful girl, or teenager, stood leaning over the railing, watching me. I blinked to check if I was seeing things, but she stayed put.

Her hair fell in dark curls past her shoulders, surrounding a face that made it hard to breathe. I couldn't see much more than that looking up at her, but it was enough. My teenage boy mind sort of locked up and started stumbling around, wondering what to do next.

"You might want to get moving," she said in a musical voice. "I think your friend needs some help out there. And between you and me, I'm pretty sure Greg's got a few more men lurking around somewhere."

Her eyes flickered toward a door on one side of the entry hall. I followed her gaze and saw two men burst through the doorway, guns drawn.

"Good luck," I heard that magical voice say as I blended and rolled to the side.

The men fired at the spot where I'd been lying, missing me by inches. On instinct, I immediately rolled back toward that same spot, just as both men stepped to the side and peppered the areas on either side of me with gunfire.

I thought about ghosting, but with my luck they were using silver bullets, and I was spent. I wasn't sure how long I'd be able to use two talents simultaneously. Instead I got up and ran as silently as I could toward them. They'd stopped shooting and stood about four feet apart, scanning the room. I really hated dealing with nameless bad guys. I decided to call the one on the left Dumb and the guy on the right Dumber. I kicked Dumb with everything I had right in the crotch. It was a cheap shot given I was blending, which was exactly what I wanted.

He crumpled to the floor, but I wasn't watching. I immediately leapt to the floor, aiming toward Dumber. The moment I'd kicked Dumb, Dumber had swung around toward him. I slid under where he was pointing his gun and did a sweep kick. My foot took Dumber's ankles from the side, and he actually got fully airborne for a second as he crashed to the floor.

I was already up and leaping out of the way by the time he landed, which was a good thing, since both men fired simultaneously toward where I'd been. Too bad for them I was gone because they hit each other. For a moment, I thought I was witnessing the death of two men, and the horror of what I'd done was overwhelming.

Thankfully the men swore and looked hurt, but neither seemed inclined to die. I figured they were wearing bulletproof vests under their suits. That would explain why they looked so thick. I'd thought they were a bit overweight when I'd first seen them. I stepped forward and kicked Dumber in the side of the head. It felt like I'd broken a toe, but it looked a lot worse for Dumber. He collapsed to the floor and stopped moving.

Once again, I didn't wait around to see what would happen. As Dumber's head rebounded from my foot, I leapt as best I could off my other foot, directly toward Dumb. I barely cleared the line of fire as he squeezed off a couple shots in rapid succession just over Dumber. I let go of my blending and bruised as I came down on top of Dumb and punched him in the side of the head with a hardened fist. His head bounced off the floor and I felt his body go limp.

I released my bruising and rolled over onto my back, panting, still on top of Dumb. I stared up at the high ceiling and noticed it was painted to look like a cloudy sky. That was interesting. From there, my gaze drifted up, which carried it over to the balcony, where that girl was watching me. She was still beautiful, even when viewed upside down.

"Nicely done," she said. "If your friend survived out there, I'm thinking there's only one more to deal with."

I nodded, like this was a totally normal conversation. Just two people chatting, one of them casually watching a small battle play out, the other sprawled exhausted across an unconscious man. I slowly lifted my hand and gave a thumbs up.

"So I'm thinking you have more talents than normal."

She said the word "talents" like it was special. Like she knew about Sevens and our talents. That was way more interesting than the ceiling.

"By my count," she said, "you've used four so far. I'd say you've kinneyed, bruised, reggied, and blended."

I forced myself to get moving and stood up. I was so tired, and I wobbled a bit before I could catch my balance. Who was this girl that she knew so much about Sevens? I'd sort of figured she was Silver's daughter, but who used their dad's first name?

I heard several shots fired just outside the door and remembered Mara. I blended once more and ran toward the courtyard. I almost hit the doorframe as I struggled to stay upright. Just outside the door, a man in a dark suit stood over Mara, holding a gun pointed down at her. She was laying on the ground, crawling on her elbows away from him, leaving a trail of blood. I didn't hesitate, or count the cost, or think about my actions ahead of time, or any of those other things that my parents are always telling me to do. I dropped my blending and used everything I had to kinney.

I doubt I got going more than four times my normal speed, but I used all of it to throw myself at the guy's shoulders and head. The moment I launched, I dropped the kinneying. I had nothing left to bruise, and the impact was incredible. My shoulder met his head as our bodies slammed together. There was a wrenching tear, and for a moment I thought I'd torn my arm off. The pain burned brighter than the sun for a split second, and then cut off. Gone. It was like I was floating in warm water. I careened off of him and hit the paving stones hard, bouncing my head on the ground and knocking the breath out of me.

I lay there frozen, unable to breathe and feeling nothing but a searing pain in my head for what felt like eternity. I wanted to scream, but that took air, and I didn't have any. I wondered if I'd knocked out the guy who'd shot Mara, or if he was about to shoot me. If he did, at least the burning need to breathe would go away.

I heard someone speaking, but it didn't sound like a man. Then it was quiet. My vision was getting dark around the edges when my lungs finally started working again and I sucked in a quick gasp of air, followed by another. I breathed, and breathed some more. I tried to sit up, but I couldn't seem to move. Nothing. I reggied, but again, nothing.

I lived that way for what felt like hours, lying with hot stones against my cheek under a bright sun. My head was looking off to the side toward the large, white wall. I heard some sounds toward the house, where Mara had been. Then the voice was back, and I recognized it. The girl on the balcony. I tried to picture her face, but it wouldn't come to mind.

Tears leaked out of my eyes, dripping into my mask, a few escaping to the paving stones through the eyeholes. Why couldn't I move? What had happened? Was Mara still alive? Would I still be lying here, crying, when Silver came back?

I closed my eyes, breathed, and waited. The pain was horrible in my head, but I couldn't feel anything else. I knew my shoulder must have been terribly injured, but there was no pain, no feeling at all, from it or any other part of my body.

Gentle hands lifted my head and a hand shaded my eyes as I cracked them open. I was looking up at balcony girl. From the view, I guessed that my head was now lying on her lap. That seemed awkward, but since I couldn't move, I decided to roll with it.

"Hey, Joss," Mara said, from just out of sight.

The girl shifted the position of my head, and Mara came into sight. She was kneeling by my waist. I wouldn't have known where my waist was if I hadn't seen it, which was terrifying. Mara reached out and pulled my mask off, tucking it into my chest pocket with my phone. She put a hand on my injured shoulder, but I didn't feel anything.

"Listen, you need to reggie," Mara said, "but I'm guessing you've got nothing left or you would have already done it."

I tried to reply, but couldn't seem to reply. Nodding my head didn't work either. Tears started leaking out of my eyes again instead.

"Just relax," Mara said. She glanced over her shoulder for a moment, but I couldn't see what she was looking at. "You really came through, Joss. Pretty sure you saved my life with that last move. He was firing silver bullets. But I think you may have broken your neck."

CHAPTER 18

JASMINE

I FOUGHT TO move anything. My feet. My hands. My head. I could only blink and raise my eyebrows a little. After silently fighting a little bit longer, I discovered I could flare my nostrils. So there was that.

"Joss!" Mara said. "Look at me!"

I shifted my eyes to her, but it was hard to see anything through the tears. Balcony girl stroked my hair, which felt pretty good, except for when she touched the huge lump on the side of my head where I'd hit the ground. I decided it was worth it, not that I could do anything about it.

"Don't panic, okay?" Mara said. "You're going to reggie. I just need a few minutes to tie these guys up and get something from my car. Jasmine and I are going to carry you inside, and she'll stay with you while I'm gone."

"I don't think you're supposed to move people with spinal injuries," Jasmine said.

"You're not," Mara said, "but he's going to heal himself. Let's get him in there."

I didn't have much to say about the plan since I couldn't speak. Mara and Jasmine cradled me between them and carried me back into the entry hall of the house. It felt better to be out of the summer sun, even if I hadn't been able to feel it on anything but my face. They lay me on the floor near the stairs, my head once again lying on Jasmine's lap.

"Be back soon," Mara said. "No more than fifteen minutes. Jasmine, can you tell him what you told me?"

With that, Mara was gone. Jasmine looked down on me with her lovely face and made me feel awkward. She stroked my hair and carefully wiped my eyes when a tear leaked out.

"I'm not really Greg's daughter." She was looking off into space now. "I was his step-daughter. My mom married him when I was eight. I think they were happy for a while, but she didn't know who he really was." She looked down at me again. "When she figured out what was really going on, she tried to leave him. When I was twelve, she finally divorced him. But Greg did something. Threatened people, or maybe paid them off, to gain full custody of me."

She stopped speaking for a little and looked off into the distance again. "I didn't understand what was going on at first, but now I know. I'm pretty much a hostage to ensure Mom keeps her mouth shut. For four years I've lived with this psychopath. He's remarried, and I've played along to survive."

My mind drifted back to my meeting with Silver. He'd said there were five people he trusted. His wife and daughter had been two of them. I guess Jasmine had pretty much pulled off pretending to be loyal. That couldn't be an easy way to live. Her hand brushed my hair, and my eyes snapped back to hers. She was looking at me. I tried to say something, and my jaw moved a little bit. Progress, but still no words.

"You were impressive," she said. "Not like Vance. He's, he's a monster. Don't ever try to fight him, okay? But you did good. And you're young. What are you, thirteen?"

I couldn't move much, but she must have seen me trying to frown.

"Fourteen?"

I relaxed my face.

"Fourteen, then," she said. "Anyway, I'll show Mara where Greg keeps his books. That's what Mara said you needed."

Jasmine leaned over closer to me, her dark eyes capturing mine, her dark hair almost touching my face.

"Destroy him, Joss. He's a monster."

I wanted to say something, to say I would take him

down, but I still couldn't speak. My jaw was moving more and more, but my voice wasn't back yet. She held my eyes for a minute, and nodded.

"Good," she said, and leaned back against the stairs.

We stayed like that until Mara came back into view. I wasn't really sure how long it had been. I was having trouble judging time. She knelt beside me.

"This really isn't a healthy thing to do," Mara said, "but you took to it pretty well last time." She held up a small can of 300MINUTE ENERGY DRINK. "Blink twice if you think you can swallow it."

Last time I'd drank two of the 300MINUTEs, and it had felt like my body was built out of different pieces that were falling apart, with my head floating around on its own. It'd been a terrible feeling, but had helped me push through when I was worn out.

I focused on Mara's question, and realized that I hadn't been choking on my own saliva, so that meant I could swallow. I blinked twice and cracked open my mouth. Mara popped the lid off and gently held my head while pouring the nasty fluid into my mouth. The taste was worse than I'd remembered.

I managed to swallow most of it down, and Mara wiped off my face when I was done. She reached out of sight, and held up her hand with a second bottle of the stuff. I tried to give her a look that said, "Are you crazy?" She shrugged, popped the lid off, and poured that one down me, too.

"Sit tight, Joss," Mara said, and stood up. "If it hits you like it did a couple weeks back, you'll hopefully be able to reggie in ten or fifteen minutes. I need Jasmine to work with me for a couple minutes so I can get started on the safe, okay?"

That was not okay. I did not want to be left on the floor of some psychopath's house with a bunch of unconscious guys all around. Since I couldn't shake my head, and my voice wasn't working yet, I moved my eyes from side to side. Mara must have gotten the message, because she knelt back down.

"The men are secured, Joss," she said. "You're safe here. Jasmine will be right back."

"Okay," I said. I didn't think Mara heard me, but I was positive I said the word.

With Mara's help, Jasmine lifted my head a bit and got out from under me. Mara laid my head on the floor, and they both headed up the stairs that I'd partially wrecked. I lay there staring at the cloudy sky on the ceiling and waited for a burst of energy. I never felt one, but after a few minutes I started to feel shaky, like my eyes wanted to roll around independently. That had to be the 300MINUTE drinks.

It was time to reggie, but I was terrified. What if it didn't work? What if I'd burned out or something? Mara had told me weeks ago that it wasn't possible to burn out as a Seven, but how could she really know? I worked my jaw, flared my nostrils, and wiggled my eyebrows. I could do this. I closed my eyes, took a deep breath, and reggied.

Mara shook me awake, and I jerked up off the floor. My head felt like it was floating a few inches above my body, which had to be the 300MINUTE drinks. A burning pain was centered on my shoulder, and I shuddered with relief. I was moving. I could feel pain again. My spine must have healed when I reggied, even if the rest of me was still doing badly. I turned toward Mara, and realized Jasmine was sitting on the bottom stair right next to me. She must have been watching over me.

"He's back!" Mara held out her fist, and I bumped it. "You still hurting?"

"Everywhere," I said. "Especially my shoulder."

Jasmine stood up next to Mara. She was taller than I'd expected. Not as tall as Mara, but she had at least an inch on me. I glanced around the room. Brick and glass were scattered around from my entrance through the window earlier, but the men were all gone.

Mara pointed toward the side door two of the men had entered. "Tied up. We need to grab the safe and get out of here."

"And tie me up," Jasmine said.

"Agreed," Mara said.

"Agreed?" I said. "Why do we agree? She's helped us!"

"Which is why," Mara said, "we need to make sure that Silver thinks she was captured by us like the rest of his men."

"I asked if she'd do it," Jasmine said.

"Oh," I said. "I get it. Sorry."

"We need to move, though," Mara said. "We've been here too long. Joss, you able to help?"

I did some quick stretches and discovered I was definitely not good to go. My shoulder seemed to move pretty well, but burned deep in the joint, and motion made it worse. A lump still adorned my head. I was pretty much one big bruise. On top of all that, the 300MINUTE ENERGY was making each part of my body feel like it wanted to do its own thing.

"I'll get by," I said. A thought hit me. "How'd you reggie if the bullets were silver?"

Mara nodded toward Jasmine. "She did some minor surgery on me with some tweezers and salad tongs."

"I'll go throw up now," I said.

Mara shrugged. "It wasn't any fun for either of us, but you'll learn. You can tolerate a lot more pain than you'd expect if you know it'll be over soon. She dug the bullets out, I reggied, all good."

I frowned. "I don't feel all good."

"You were pretty busted up, but you'll get there. We need to get to work." Mara headed toward some large double doors underneath the balcony and across the room from the front door. "Follow me."

"Good luck," Jasmine said. She smiled and I tried to return it, but I think it may have looked more like a grimace. I was really hurting.

I followed Mara through the doors into a huge hallway. The place looked expensive. Lots of wood paneling that looked hand-carved with vines and stuff.

"How do we know where we're going?" I asked.

"Jasmine showed me," Mara said, and pointed at a large door at the end of the hall. There'd been some other doors along the way, but she'd ignored them. "Master suite. I've already knocked out as much of the wall as I could, but there's a lot of silver."

"How'd you knock out any of it if there's…" I stepped into the bedroom behind Mara and my voice trailed off. It was pretty obvious how she'd busted up the wall. Every heavy piece of furniture in the room, including the bed frame, was smashed to bits and scattered around the room. A huge chunk of wall to the right side was destroyed, a safe standing out in the midst of the devastation. Silver mesh was poking out here and there among the ruined wall.

"So," I said, "Mara the gorilla had some fun while I was sleeping, huh?"

"Pretty much." She grabbed a large coil of rope just to the side of the door and held it up for me to see. "Leftovers after I took care of the men." She stepped to the safe and peered at it. "It's attached to the structure of the house. I'm thinking we yank the whole thing out and take it with us."

I stepped up next to her. The safe was maybe a foot square on the front and extended back into the rubble of the wall. I frowned. That was no normal wall. It was way too thick.

"So what do we do?" I said.

Mara held one end of the rope and dropped the remaining coils on the floor. "Dig your hand into the wall on your side. I'll try to hand the rope through."

"But the silver," I said.

"Yep," Mara said. "No talents, just your normal arm and hand."

I shrugged and started worming my hand back along the safe, reaching further and further into the wall. Mara did the same on the other side, holding the rope. I had to pull a bunch of broken bits of wood and wall plaster out, but eventually I felt the back corner. Mara was up to her shoulder in the wall, so she must have gotten further than me.

"I think there's a cavity behind it," Mara said. "Try to catch the end of the rope when I swing it."

"Got it," I said, and Mara raised an eyebrow. "Well, I don't have it yet, but I'm ready."

I held my hand open, and Mara managed to flip the end of the rope over so it smacked my palm. I grabbed for it, but missed.

"Sorry," I said, and shrugged. "One more time."

Apparently, she was really good at flipping rope, because a second later the rope hit my palm again. I grabbed it and quickly pulled it out of the wall as Mara fed more rope through on her side. Mara took the end of the rope and tied it off to itself, so the rope was in a loose loop around the safe. Then she tugged the loop so the knotted end rotated back behind the safe and out again on my side. She untied the knot and pulled more rope through until there were a few feet of rope free of the wall, with two loops around the safe, and another twenty feet or so of rope still coiled on the floor.

"Cool," I said. "What now?"

"I'm going to shift to something big and strong." As Mara spoke, she knotted the two free ends of the rope together. "We have this loop of rope here in the room"—she held up the completed knot—"with two loops of rope around the safe. You're going to secure this big loop around me, and I'm going to haul the whole thing out."

"You talking, what?" I said. "An elephant?"

"Even I can't shift to something that big," Mara said. "I'm going for an ox. Just make sure the rope is secure on me, okay?"

I took a big step away from her. "So what's the difference between an ox and a cow?"

"Oxen work," Mara said. "Cows are for dairy and meat. But it doesn't really matter."

"So they're the same kind of animal?" I said, but Mara had already shifted.

Ox Mara sure looked a lot like a big, ugly cow. She was a dingy brown with darker blotches on her backside. I grabbed the rope and slung it over her shoulders, looping it around her huge neck so it wouldn't slip off. It was weird looking into those giant bovine eyes and knowing it was Mara.

She turned away from me and lurched forward. The rope snapped tight and there was a horrific screeching sound. The safe didn't come out, but I'd have sworn it shifted a bit. Mara relaxed for a moment, and surged forward again. The whole wall seemed to tremble, and the noise was almost painful. For a moment, everything seemed frozen in time. Mara straining forward, the rope thrumming with tension, the safe hanging on by its fingernails. Then something gave, and the safe pretty much leapt out of the wall.

It crashed to the floor and landed facedown, tilted to the side because of the knobs on the front. It was deeper than I'd expected, and stood about two feet tall. My peripheral vision caught a movement, and I looked back at Mara. She'd shifted back to normal and was getting untangled from the rope. I stepped over to it and tried to lift it. It was heavy, but not as heavy as I'd expected, and I got it an inch or so off the floor before my shoulder felt like it had burst into flames.

"I'm going to tie Jasmine up," Mara said. "Then we get out of here."

Mara headed out of the room, and I sat down on the floor and massaged my shoulder. How was it that as a superhero I was getting all these horrific injuries? Between bruising and ghosting, it should have been impossible to hurt me, but instead I'd barely survived. Maybe it was that I'd started fighting well-armed grown men since I'd become a Seven instead of pulling pranks on kids. That had to be it.

It definitely gave me a different angle on having my talents. I couldn't just go flying into every situation assuming I'd come out okay. I had to learn to think it through. To plan better. To count the cost, as my dad would have said. But I'd purposely not counted the cost when I'd thrown myself at that guy to save Mara, and I was pretty sure I'd done the right thing, even if I'd gotten horribly injured. There had to be a balance, but I didn't seem to be very good at finding it. Maybe that was what I needed to sort out with my parents. Maybe I needed their help, even with the superhero stuff.

While I was sitting there thinking about stuff, I put my mask back on. It felt better to be anonymous while robbing some powerful crime lord's house in broad daylight. My sleeve was pretty much ruined by the sword cut, and was flapping around. I figured the first time I ghosted through a wall I'd leave a big chunk of it behind.

Mara burst into the room, interrupting my thoughts. Her eyes were wide and looked intense. Not good.

"Up! We need to be gone! Silver's pulling in."

CHAPTER 19

IN THE GUTTER

I JUMPED TO my feet, wrenching my shoulder again and gasping in pain. Mara was already busy with the safe, tying more loops of rope around it on all sides.

"Garage is detached." Mara said. "Driveway runs around the side of the house at the other end. We have a tiny bit of time."

"How do you know all this?" I asked. I stepped over to her to help with the knots, but there wasn't anything for me to do.

"I flew in, remember?" She pulled a last knot tight. She'd left a long loop of rope hanging off a bundle of knots. "Listen, we need to go. I'm going to fly this thing out of here and get back to the car."

"You can carry that?" I said.

Mara gave me a flat look. "Joss, I carried you last night. Do you really think this weighs more?"

"Oh, yeah," I said. "That makes sense. What do I do?"

"You help me dump this through that window"—she nodded toward a large window on the wall behind the remains of the bed—"and then flee. Can you kinney enough to jump the wall?"

I took a moment to calm myself and tried to kinney. I was pretty sure I wouldn't be going anywhere near my top speed, but I could do it.

"Yeah, I'll jump the wall," I said. "Meet you back at the car?"

Mara nodded and stood. She grabbed the loose loop of rope and started pulling the safe toward the window. I got behind it and pushed with my good arm. Once we got it next to the window, we lifted from either side and tossed it through the glass. Mara shifted into a small bird of some sort and flew through the broken glass after it.

"So why didn't you do all this as a gorilla?" I asked.

"You're not the only one running low on energy," she said from outside. "Now bruise and get out of here."

I tried to bruise and discovered I could pull it off. I scrambled over the broken shards of glass through the window and landed in a private garden area. Leafy, flowering plants surrounded the grassy area where we stood, with a path leading toward what I guessed was the back of the house. Mara was already an enormous eagle, and she hopped onto the loop of rope, grasped it in her talons, and leapt into the air.

The safe tore up the grass as it slid along the ground for a few feet before lifting into the air. A moment later, Mara got it high enough to clear all the plants and it disappeared from sight. Right then, I heard the bedroom door bang open back in the room. That was a problem. I immediately dropped my bruising and blended.

"Vance!" a voice roared. That was Silver calling for his Warrior. I took off running, heading down the path, looking for a way to the wall. I figured I might only have one good jump before I was wiped out again and couldn't kinney. I broke free of all the plants into a huge yard along the back of the house. Across the yard, I spotted the garage. A pool and cabana sprawled across the back of the yard. And behind the cabana, the white fence.

On an instinct, I cut off the path the moment I cleared the plants and headed directly back toward the wall. I saw a blur of motion in my peripheral vision back on the path. It took me a moment to realize I was seeing someone kinney and race along the path. It had to be Vance, and he was moving with blinding speed. It didn't look like a person so much as a blur. In a few seconds he'd zoomed through the whole backyard and disappeared around front. I didn't even want to know what would have happened to me if I'd stayed on the path and he'd run into me.

I jogged toward the wall. I was still feeling weird from the energy drink, but reggying seemed to have tamed the worst of it. With Vance running around, I desperately wanted to keep blending while I kinneyed, but I had that horrible wide-awake-exhausted feeling and wasn't sure I could pull it off. If I failed, it would be disastrous. I decided not to risk it and dropped the blending as I got near the wall.

Digging deep, I kinneyed. As the world slowed, I leapt, and the moment my feet cleared the ground, I let go of the kinneying and hoped for the best. I also blended again in case I'd been spotted. Blending took nothing compared to kinneying.

I shot in a high arc over the wall and hung for a moment at the peak. I flicked my eyes to each side as I started to drop. A large truck was coming down the street from the right with its diesel engine revving loudly. It wouldn't be a problem. I'd have plenty of time to land and get across the street before it ran over me. I was about to drop the blend and bruise when a blur of motion caught my eye. I flicked my eyes back to the left along the wall, and the blur came to a sudden stop, resolving into a huge man, his hands on his hips, standing still and scanning the street right where I was about to land. Vance.

No time to think. Instead of bruising, I held the blend and reached with my toes toward the ground like they'd taught us at Battlehoop. Only we hadn't actually fallen fifteen or twenty feet onto pavement for practice. But one more gruesome injury sounded better than being dead at the hands of some psychopath Warrior, so I figured I'd roll with it. Literally.

I tried to redirect my momentum forward into a shoulder roll as I hit the ground, but the road was not kind to me. Something in my left ankle made a loud cracking noise, and pain swallowed me whole. My shoulder roll turned into more of a flop, and I skidded to a stop after a few feet of sliding feet first on my back. My work clothes held up pretty well, so I didn't lose much skin.

I probably screamed the whole time, but it was hard to tell. There was too much noise coming from the giant truck that was about to run over me. I glanced toward Vance. He was walking back the way he'd come, facing away from me. I'd have to risk it. I released the blend and bruised like my life depended on it just as the huge front wheel of the truck ran over me.

I'm not sure what the truck was carrying, but it turns out most of the weight was in the rear. The front wheel bounced over me, and I wondered if I'd ever breathe normally again. My ribs felt like I'd been hit with a baseball bat. Then the two pairs of rear wheels redefined for me just how badly ribs could hurt. I must not have been bruising very well, because I was pretty sure I had at least a couple broken ribs by the time the truck was done with me. In spite of the blinding pain, I had the good sense to immediately blend again after releasing my bruising.

It was really too much. I rolled over and over until I hit the curb, and that was it. I was done. My ankle was on fire and there was no way I could walk on it. Each breath was agony as my ribs creaked. I needed to reggie, but I was pretty sure I'd pass out if I did, which would leave me helpless, lying in the gutter by Silver's compound. I decided to keep blending, which still left me helpless in the gutter, but at least no one could see me.

I'm not sure how long I lay there. Time got weird for me as I struggled with each breath. I think I heard the dog before I saw it. Sort of a snuffing sound that got louder and then quieter, and then louder again. I let my head flop over to the side, and it took me a moment to figure out what I was seeing. The whole world was sideways, but I eventually realized it was one of those long-eared, short dogs that are good at tracking things.

It wandered around until it got right up to my face, still sniffing. It paused by me for a minute, wagging its tail. Then it turned and ran off the way it had come. It wasn't sniffing around anymore, but running flat out, ears flying this way and that. So that was weird.

A mom and her kid came walking toward me on the sidewalk next to the gutter. I tried to stop whimpering while they were near me, and I guess I succeeded, because they walked right on by. Then it was back to whimpering and waiting. I wasn't sure what exactly I was waiting for. Maybe nighttime so I could let go of the blend and Mara could find me. She'd probably fly around as an owl looking for me. It wouldn't take her long. I'd be okay. I just had to keep breathing through the pain.

Cars drove by me now and then, but no more giant trucks. I took my mask off and stuffed it in my pocket at some point to get a little relief from the heat. I heard another car drive by, but something sounded off. Like, the sound didn't taper off. I rolled my head away from the sidewalk to check the street. There was a car stopped beside me, its engine idling. Mara's car.

The passenger door pushed open a couple feet. Mara was leaning across to the passenger seat. "Joss, can you get it?"

"Yeah," I said. "I'm moving."

I couldn't get up. I couldn't even crawl without messing with my bad ankle, so I edged along on my butt until I could pull myself up into the passenger seat. Mara got ahold of my arm and helped me. I pulled the door shut and sagged back into the seat. The cold AC, the soft seat, the shade, it all felt wonderful.

Mara dropped the car into gear and started driving. "What happened?"

I dropped my blend and leaned forward to check my ankle. Unfortunately, I couldn't reach my ankle without my ribs catching fire. I sagged back into the seat.

"Your back's a mess," Mara said. "Give me an update."

It was hard to speak. "Jumped the wall, but Vance was there, so I had to blend and couldn't bruise. Landed hard and may have broken my ankle. Then a huge truck ran over me. Managed to bruise in time, but I'm pretty sure I broke some ribs."

"And you couldn't reggie," she said, "because you were

worried you'd pass out."

I nodded.

"Rough day, Joss," Mara said. "I'm sorry. I'd really expected to get through this better, but Silver was prepared. Hit the reggie, okay?"

I didn't need to be told twice. I reggied, and the world went black.

I woke up in my bed, still wearing my torn up work clothes, my desk lamp spilling a little light into the room. It was dark outside. I must have slept for hours. I sat up and felt surprisingly good. My ankle, shoulder, and ribs were still sore, so I reggied again. Healing swept through my body. It was an amazing feeling. I hopped out of bed and cut across the hall to the bathroom. I wasn't going to talk to anyone until I'd had a hot shower.

My work clothes were a complete mess. Between the sword cut, sliding on the street, and being run over, they'd pretty much been destroyed. The cool ninja shoes were in good shape though, so there was that. Twenty minutes later I was cleaned up and dressed in some normal clothes. The shower had worked its own magic, and I was feeling good as long as I didn't think about talking to my parents. For a second, I thought about leaving the house. A quick blend and ghost, and I'd be gone. But that wasn't the right answer.

Instead, I headed downstairs to see who was home. I got to the family room, and stopped in shock. Somehow I hadn't realized how much damage I'd done. Dad's chair was gone, but the kitchen table was still embedded in the wall, the window beside it boarded up. The ceiling and surrounding walls were beat up and had fragments of wood sticking out. All in all, it was horrible.

My parents were on the couch facing toward me. Janey and Isabella sat opposite them on the floor, and all four were playing a card game on the coffee table. Or they had been. At that moment, all four were staring at me. My mom got up and stepped around the table toward me.

"Honey, would you like some hot tea?"

My dad stood up and waved me toward him. "Come here, son."

I took a step, and another. He met me halfway and pulled me into a huge hug.

"I'm sorry, Dad."

I was fighting back tears and winning. No way I was going to cry in front of Isabella. He held me for a minute, then ruffled my hair.

"We'll figure it out," he said as we stepped apart. "Your mother and I had a chance to talk this afternoon. Hopefully the three of us can talk soon." He glanced around the room at the others. "But not right now."

We stood there, side by side, surveying the room until Mom came back with my tea. She handed it to Dad and pulled me into a big hug. I apologized to her, too. It felt like a huge weight had lifted off my chest.

"Sorry about the room," I said, taking my tea from Dad.

"Yeah, I think we're going to have to partner on getting it repaired," Dad said. "It's not going to be cheap."

I took a small sip of tea. "I don't have that much money, but I'll give you what I have."

"We'll figure it out, honey," Mom said. "Let's not focus on that right now."

I set my tea cup down on the coffee table, where Isabella and Janey were still sitting. I gave them each a nod in greeting, and Isabella's face lit up with her awesome smile in return. I was pretty sure I'd come out ahead on that one.

"I can give a little bit of help right now," I said, and walked over to the breakfast area.

The ceiling between our family room and breakfast area was lofted and sort of sloped down toward the kitchen. The largest piece of wood in sight was stuck in the ceiling about fifteen feet up and dangling down like it wanted to fall. I glanced back and saw all four of them watching me as I centered myself under it.

I kinneyed and jumped. I was getting much better at judging how hard to jump, which was a good thing since I didn't want to throw myself through the ceiling. I floated up and grabbed the wood at the top of my jump. It pulled right out and I came back down. I held the kinney the whole way to make sure I landed as softly as possible.

When I dropped the kinney and glanced at my family, they were all staring at me with their mouths hanging open. Isabella was still smiling. I held up the piece of wood and glanced around the ceiling. All the other wood fragments looked like they weren't at risk of falling.

"How'd you do that?" my dad asked. "I thought I knew all your powers."

I set the piece of wood down on the remains of the breakfast table. "I kinneyed. I've figured out how to use it to jump and stuff."

"That. Was. Awesome!" Janey said. She was on her feet now, and Isabella got up to stand beside her.

It suddenly hit me that Mara wasn't around. How had I missed that?

"Where's Mara?" I said.

Mom and Dad glanced at each other before turning back to me.

"She headed over to see Thomas," Dad said. "She said he'd be able to help contact the right people to deliver a safe."

What was wrong with my brain? I hadn't noticed Mara was missing, and now I realized I didn't know what time it was. I pulled my phone out and checked. 8:15 PM.

"How long ago did she leave?" I said.

Dad glanced at his watch. "Mara left, what, two hours ago?"

Mom nodded. "That sounds right."

"Should I try to help her?" I said. "Hate to make her do stuff without me."

"You should finish your tea and maybe eat some food," Mom said. "Come take a seat." She gestured toward the couch.

"Your mom's right," Dad said before I could argue. "Mara's got it under control. I bet she'll be back soon." His phone chimed, and Dad pulled it out and glanced at it.

"Speak of the devil. She just texted. On her way back now."

Isabella scooted over toward Janey so I could sit by her. Dad went to the dining room and brought back a chair, which he set where his recliner had been. Mom headed to the kitchen and I heard the microwave run for a minute or so. She came back in with a glass of water and a big plate of spaghetti.

"Leftovers from dinner," she said, and set the plate and glass in front of me on the coffee table. "Should be pretty good."

Mom and Dad sat down in their chairs, and everyone watched me take a few sips of tea.

"So?" Janey said. "What happened? Mara said it was rough, but you got what you needed."

"Joss," Mom said, holding up a hand to stop me from talking. "You don't have to relive every detail, but I'd prefer to hear about any traumatic injuries now instead of finding out bits and pieces for the next several weeks." She took a ragged breath. "Let's just get it over with."

"Okay," I said, "but, uh, you sure? 'Cause… it's bad."

Mom closed her eyes for a long moment. She opened her eyes, pursed her lips, and gave me a firm nod.

I drank my tea, ate my spaghetti, and told them about our assault on Silver's house. I didn't drag out the tough parts, but I didn't leave them out either. Isabella gasped when I got to the part about Mara being shot with silver bullets, but my parents never made a noise. I noticed a muscle twitching in my dad's jaw, but that was it. I finished my story and the spaghetti at about the same time.

"You know," I said at the end. "I never asked her, but the dog must have been Mara looking for me, right? I bet she'd guessed I was blending."

"Joss," Dad said in a voice that sounded like broken glass, "have you noticed that you tend to underestimate the men you're going up against?"

"I don't mean to be disrespectful, but I don't think I estimated them at all," I said. "I mean, I doubt Mara underestimated them. We just didn't have much choice, so we did it." Dad's left eyebrow raised as I spoke, so I added, "But I get your point."

"Enough," my mom said. "Joss, into the kitchen. I want to look you over."

Mom was a physician's assistant, so I didn't argue. She didn't want to hear me say I was okay. She wanted to see for herself. As I stood, Isabella reached out and squeezed my arm.

"Thank you, Joss," Isabella said. "You were *mi hermana's* guardian angel today."

I patted her hand. "More like she was mine."

"Okay," Dad said. "Joss, get into that kitchen and let your mom convince herself you're okay."

Mom checked me out top to bottom. She put me through this thing called a concussion quick check, tested my range of motion, poked and prodded me almost everywhere, and finally decided I was okay.

"I just can't believe…" She drifted off and frowned at me. "Are you sure you were paralyzed?"

I shrugged. "Far as I know. I reggied, now I'm better."

"I'm still getting used to this," Mom said, shaking her head. "It's, it's amazing."

"Yeah, the getting better part is. The getting hurt part pretty much sucks."

She gave me a big hug. "Alright, let's head back out."

We went to the family room together and I was startled to see Mara standing with the others, Isabella's arm wrapped around her waist. "Mara? Didn't hear you come in."

She gave me a smile. "Good to see you up. Your parents gave me a key, so I let myself in."

The doorbell rang, and rang again. Mara glanced around at everyone.

"I'll get it," she said. "Just in case."

We all crowded into the wide doorway between the family room and entryway while Mara unlocked the door and swung it open. Thomas burst into the room, followed by Bobby Ferris. Mara took a quick step back to avoid being shoved. My stomach tightened up in fear. Nothing good could cause Thomas to push his way into our house at night.

"Thomas—"

That's as far as Dad got before Thomas spoke over him.

"Silver knows! He'll probably be here any minute!"

CHAPTER 20

MANO A MANO

"THOMAS," MOM SAID, "who's this with you?"

Thomas looked at her, his mouth hanging open. "Didn't you hear me?"

"I did," Mom said.

Thomas looked from Mom to Bobby and back. "It's Bobby." He turned to me. "Silver knows. He knows who you are."

"Ma'am," Bobby said, nodding to my Mom.

"Take a breath, Thomas, and give us the short version," Dad said.

"Shouldn't we be running or something?" Janey asked.

"Hold on, Janey," Mom said to her.

"Bobby?" Thomas said.

Bobby stepped close to Thomas and leaned in toward him, but I could still hear him. "Do they know? About Joss?"

"They all know about me, but I appreciate you checking," I said. Ice had filled my stomach. I nodded at each person as I introduced them to Bobby. "My parents, Mr. and Mrs. Morgan. My sister Janey. Our friends, Mara and Isabella. So, what's going on?"

"Right," Bobby said. "So, I'm Bobby Ferris. I was in eighth grade when Joss got to the Beedle as a seventh grader. Joss has been trying to help my dad. He's gotten mixed up with some really bad people. Uh, my dad has, not Joss. Anyway, last night, Dad got home earlier than normal, and he was, like, in this rage. Said the whole thing had gone to, uh, heck, and that the boss guy had shut the whole thing down. Something about huge losses, and no more work.

Dad was freaking out. I was trying to calm him down, let him know people were looking out for him, so, I told him. About Joss."

"Oh," I said, and I'm pretty sure several other people said it at the same time.

"Yeah," Bobby said, staring at his feet. "Sorry."

"I'm realizing I don't really know how things got started between the two of you," Dad said. "Bobby, may I ask how you knew about Joss?"

Bobby looked from my dad to me. I gave him a shrug, and he turned back to my dad.

"Well, I didn't know any of this at the time, but Joss decided to try to help my dad a few weeks ago," Bobby said. "So he pretended to be a guardian angel. And I think it worked. Dad was getting things sorted out, but then things got weird."

"I see." Dad said. He was looking at me, not Bobby.

"Yeah, but I'm really glad Joss tried," Bobby said, staring at his feet. "It might've worked out if this freaky guy, Mr. Silver, hadn't showed up at our house tonight. He was wearing this crazy green mask, and he had this big guy with him who, like, did impossible stuff. He moved so fast. Too fast. It completely freaked out Dad, and he just started talking. Told them you did it all. Told them about your powers, you know, being invisible. All the stuff he'd heard from me. And they totally believed Dad, which didn't make any sense."

"And then?" Mara said.

"Well, I was listening in from the hall," Bobby said, "so when I figured out what was going on, I bailed through my bedroom window and ran to Thomas's house. I didn't know where you guys lived, but Thomas's mom and my neighbors go way back, so I'd met him and, I don't know, I must have heard where he lived and I remembered. He brought me here."

"Loaned him my mom's bike so we could make good time," Thomas said. "Speaking of making good time, can we go now?"

"Mara, Joss," Dad said. "This Silver. He's the guy whose house you just raided, right?"

"Yeah, and the Seven's got to be Vance, that Warrior I saw at Silver's," I said.

By this time, Thomas was sort of bouncing on the balls of his feet like he had to take a leak. Mom and Dad ignored him.

"What are we saying?" Mom said. "Warrior? What's that again?"

"Warriors can usually kinney and bruise," Mara said. "Joss has seen him kinney. Pretty sure he can bruise. So, he's deadly."

"I thought you guys had taken down Silver," Janey said.

Mara shrugged. "We did, but it'll take some time to play out. I talked to the DOSN guys when I dropped off the safe. They think they'll have the evidence they need by tomorrow to build a case and take him down."

Dad held his arms up to quiet everyone down. "Do we think he'll find our house?"

"Yes!" Thomas said.

Mara shrugged. "I think we need to assume he will."

Dad nodded, and looked toward Mom. They did that weird thing where they acted like they could talk to each other with their eyes. They stared at each other for a moment, and Mom nodded.

"Okay," Dad said. "Let's go. Everyone to the garage. You too, Thomas, Bobby. We'll take both cars."

Dad waved Bobby and Thomas ahead of him and locked the front door. I stepped to the side of everyone as they shuffled into the family room and waited for him. Dad stepped in beside me and herded everyone forward toward the kitchen to go to the garage. I felt it just before it happened, though I didn't really know what it was. A tug, maybe, down in my gut. A sense of something slightly out of phase with reality. I kinneyed, not truly knowing why. Everything slowed to a stop. We were all cutting across the family room. My mom was stepping forward, her foot two inches off the ground, then an inch, then—

Before her foot reached the ground, the front door to the house blew up. I whipped around to look as Vance came through it, wood exploding outward into the house. He'd probably hit it on the run, kinneying and bruising. I leapt forward to block my dad from flying bits of wood and bruised. I tried to impersonate a spider monkey, spreading my arms and legs out to block the biggest chunks of wood flying toward my dad while tumbling through the air.

A small piece caught Dad in the shoulder and tore through him, blood spraying out of the wound. Another small, blocky piece clipped him in the head, and his eyes rolled shut as he started the long, slow fall to the ground. Most of the rest of the wood hit the walls above and around the doorway to the family room.

I tumbled through the air, hit the ground, and rolled to a stop about five feet in front of Vance. Up close, he wasn't any less scary than he'd seemed at Silver's house. He was a big guy with straight, brown hair cut short in front, but hanging down to his shoulders in back. He wore a pair of jeans, boots, and a black t-shirt. One hand was on a hip, the other hidden behind his back.

I jumped to my feet, breathing in short gasps. The cold pit in my stomach had become an iceberg. I'd seen Silver's face, I'd busted up his home, and now he'd sent Vance to finish me. And not just me, but everyone with me. But I wasn't just a Warrior. I was the Ultimate Warrior, the Seventy-Seven. I blended, because the Ultimate Warrior was terrified and thought it was a good idea to be invisible.

Vance whipped a pair of night vision goggles like the guy had had at Silver's house from behind his back and held them to his face with one hand. They looked like big, black goggles with a mini-telescope sticking out right in the middle. I'd learned a few weeks ago that infrared could see Sevens when they were blending, so I figured the goggles had IR. For a second, I thought he was going to strap them on, which would have been stupid. They were too big to be pulled in with his kinneying like his clothes, and they'd whip off his face the moment he moved fast.

Vance didn't strap them on. Instead, he held them firmly in one hand to his face and looked right at me. He was big and scary, but I had a faint glimmer of hope. If we were both bruising and he could only use one hand, I had a chance. I'd practiced fighting with Jordan a ton at Battlehoop, so I had a sense of how to fight defensively with someone much bigger than me. I could do this.

I really wasn't sure how fighting while kinneying would work. Maybe it'd be like fighting on the moon. I needed to make sure I stayed on the ground, because once I was airborne it would take a while to fall back down. That didn't really matter normally, but I had a feeling it would be critical when fighting another Warrior. I took a defensive stance, arms up, feet spread shoulder width apart.

Vance laughed. It was weird to hear normal sounds while kinneying, and see normal movements. All the other sounds people made were super-low pitched, like the sound waves were spread way out and slowed down. Not Vance's laugh. Which made me realize that I must sound like a bee or something to everyone else when I was kinneying. Maybe just a high-pitched buzzing. Which also made me realize I was terrified, and my mind was looking for distractions.

Vance stopped laughing and threw a punch at me. I dodged to the side, but his foot came out of nowhere, a high kick that clipped me on the ribs. I immediately learned three things. First, I'd been right about fighting while kinneying. It was ridiculous. When I jerked away from him, I accidentally launched myself, and once I was off the ground, I was totally out of control. Second, bruising worked like ghosting and blending, so that when two Sevens did them, they sort of cancelled out. It felt like he'd really kicked me, as though I hadn't been bruising. Third, Vance's boots had steel toes or something built into them. They felt like a hammer. A couple of my ribs shattered.

I screamed as I spun through the air, but the sound cut off in a strangled, choking sound. It hurt too much to scream. I couldn't remember reading about any superheroes that spent half their time screaming and getting injured. I figured I was special. The pain was horrific, and it was all I could do not to pass out. I hit the floor curled up in a ball, sliding through the opening from our entryway to the dining room, trying to protect my ribs. I slammed through the chairs and table legs. Wood snapped and splintered as I slid under the table and hit the far wall.

Vance walked toward me as the table collapsed in slow motion, the goggles still held to his face. I dropped the blending and bruising for a moment and reggied. The ribs healed and the pain was instantly quenched. Relief flooded through me. Vance stopped and and stared, then pulled the goggles off his face.

"Did you just—"

He cut off as I blended. I leapt to my feet and charged him. I had to catch him off guard or I was doomed. I couldn't kinney for long, so avoiding the fight wouldn't do any good. Vance didn't bother putting the goggles to his face. He leapt straight up, and I stumbled past underneath him. By the time I came to a stop, I was back in the entryway. My dad was finally finishing his fall to the floor, Mara had turned and was leaping toward him, and everyone else was staring in my general direction looking shocked.

I turned back toward Vance in time to see him land hard on the floor. He must have pushed off the ceiling to have that kind of speed. He had the goggles on again, held in place with one hand, and marched toward me. We truly fought then, though I'm not sure Vance would have agreed. Even with one hand holding the goggles, and his limited view of me, he overwhelmed me.

Kicks and punches came at me, and it was all I could do to dodge and deflect them. Even with one arm, he would have destroyed me if he could have seen me well. Thankfully, the IR goggles slowed him down and made him less accurate. We fought, but the ending was pretty much inevitable. I was going to lose. It would only take one good blow to my head, and it would be lights out.

What else could I do? I struggled to stay clear of his blows and desperately tried to think of something that would change the dynamic. If I could break the goggles, or injure one of his arms, I was pretty sure I could take him. But how was I supposed to do that? I was barely surviving as it was, jumping around, throwing weak kicks and punches back at him when I could.

I was also running out of time. I could feel the fatigue setting in. If I dropped any one of the kinneying, bruising, or blending, I was doomed. I was doomed anyways, but I'd be doomed instantly if I dropped any one of the three talents I was using.

Then I noticed it. Vance seemed to be slowing down slightly, moving a little less confidently. We were still going at it like crazy, but he took his first step backward, further into the dining room. And then another step. And it hit me. Maybe he was wearing out just like I was. Mara had said Seventy-Sevens were unusually strong with the Talents. I'd just been assuming Vance could Kinney all day. Maybe I stood a chance if I could outlast him.

I redoubled my efforts, dodging, parrying, punching, kicking, and Vance retreated another step. He looked shaky. Was I really going to do it? To be a Warrior, mano a mano? It seemed crazy, but it was happening.

Vance suddenly leapt backward, his free hand pointing directly at me, and laughed. It was a horrible sound. The sound of confidence, like he knew something I didn't. Something that mattered. I whipped around to steal a glance behind me.

Three of Silver's men were just inside the broken front door, each with one of those big net guns pointed directly at me. Silver stood behind them, still partly outside, his green lucha libre mask covering his face. Reality smacked me upside the head, as my dad would have said. Vance hadn't been losing. He'd been drawing me away from the door, delaying me, so these guys could get in position.

I leapt straight up in a desperate gamble just as all three fired their guns. The silver nets exploded out of the barrels and opened way too fast. They'd aimed them so they overlapped and filled the space. I shot up toward the ceiling and was enveloped in one of the nets.

Instantly, all my talents switched off. Time snapped back to normal as I slammed into the ceiling and fell back to the floor. Someone was screaming. It made sense. I'd been hearing this low rumble for most of the time I'd been fighting Vance. Probably my mom trying to warn me about Silver's men.

I hit the floor, tangled up in the net, unable to land properly. Pain exploded in my hip and shoulder, and the air was driven out of my lungs. I thrashed around on the ground, trying to breathe. Footsteps approached, and Silver came into view, his mask looking down at me from high up. Then Vance was standing beside him, and he gave me a gentle kick to the head.

CHAPTER 21

THE PRICE OF FREEDOM

"COME ON, JOSS. You're gonna be okay. Please wake up."

The voice was a low hiss, intruding on the beautiful quiet of my dream. It sounded familiar. I struggled to place it.

"Please, Joss. We need you."

Another voice. A girl. A lovely girl with an accent. Isabella. I cracked my eyes open, and it felt like the light was going to split my head open. Pain lanced from a point behind my left ear to my forehead. The room spun.

"His eyes are open," Janey said.

I glanced to my right. Janey was sitting on the floor, her hands bound with silver manacles attached to a chain. A chain that ended in a silvery spike that had been driven deeply into the floor. I remembered the setup at the warehouse. The spike probably went down into the concrete foundation.

I looked around as my head stabilized. The pain settled down to a quiet roar, and the room stopped spinning. We were all in a broad circle on the family room floor, bound with silver manacles attached to spikes driven into the floor, well off to the side of the doorway to the front of the house. Janey, my parents, Bobby, Thomas, around to Isabella just to my left. Something was off. I looked around the circle again. Mara was gone.

"They didn't know who was a Seven," I said. My throat was dry, my voice raspy.

"Joss, sit quietly," Dad said. He scooted around his spike so he could lean toward me. "Come closer."

I followed his example and scooted toward him, leaning in close. We got within a couple feet, and dad spoke under his breath so I could barely hear him.

"You've been out for a little while. Lots happened. Mara disappeared when everything went down, but she's made sure we've seen her. She's still here. Keep it quiet, okay?"

"Yeah, okay," I said in my quiet, raspy voice.

I looked around, but Dad made a low hissing sound to get my attention again.

"Thomas did an amazing thing. He texted the DOSN guys when he was coming over here. Gave them a heads up about Silver. They showed up in force just after we were all chained like this. I think Silver's figured out that you're something beyond a normal Seven. He wants you, Joss. He wants you bad. Probably why we're all still alive. Anyway, there's going to be war out front of our house any minute. Silver's got his men out there. I think the DOSN people, or cops, or whoever are bottling up the cul-de-sac. Not sure what's happening."

I saw a flash of motion near me—something small and furry—and Mara was crouched next to me. She held her finger to her lips and looked around the circle at everyone, making sure they stayed quiet.

"Need to get you out of these," she said, glancing down at the manacles.

"You have the key?" I asked.

"Not this time, no," Mara said. "But we need you. I can't take on Vance."

"But if you don't have a key, I'm stuck, right?"

Mara gave me a long look, her mouth pulled in a line. She put her hand on the side of my face, like my mom would do. "There's another way."

"There is?" I said. "Cool. Good. Let's do this."

Mara turned toward my dad. "I need your belt."

"What are you doing?" Mom said. Her voice was low and urgent.

"If Joss isn't free, right now, some of us—maybe all of us—will die," Mara said. She was looking at the floor, avoiding my mom's eyes. "I'm doing what has to be done. The belt."

My dad fumbled his belt off with his chained hands and gave it to Mara. She wound the belt in a loop and then pushed it flat so it was several layers thick.

"Open wide and bite down on this, okay?" Mara held the wad of leather out toward me.

I panicked. People bit down on things in movies when the pain was out of control, like having surgery a couple hundred years ago with no pain killers. I yanked at the manacles, trying to free my hands, but the silver loops were too tight. Mara put a hand on my shoulder, and I looked up at her.

"We're going to be okay. You can do this, Joss."

"Mara," Dad said.

She glanced at him. "Please. It will be okay. Trust me."

I was terrified, but I did trust Mara. With my life if it came to that. And I needed to escape. No delays. I looked at my mom and dad, and tried to smile.

"It's cool," I said. "I'm the Seventy-Seven."

What a load of bunk. I was utterly terrified, and I didn't even know what was about to happen. I took a deep breath and opened my mouth wide. Mara jammed the folded up belt into my mouth. It tasted really bad. I hadn't eaten much leather in my life, so I wasn't totally sure what it normally tasted like, but the belt tasted horrible. While I sat there thinking about my tasting notes for the belt, Mara gently took my shackled hands in hers.

My heart raced. I was pretty sure I was going to vomit, and started worrying about how it would get out my mouth with the belt blocking the way. Fear seemed to pull my stomach up into my chest.

My voice finally came back. "What are you doing?" Except that's not what it sounded like, since I had a mouth full of belt. It came out as more of a long, sad grunt.

"Joss, listen. There's only one way to do this. I've got to change to a gorilla, okay?"

I grunted in response. My throat was closing up again.

"I'm sorry. But we're out of time."

I panicked and tried to yank my hands free of her, but she'd changed into a gorilla as she finished speaking, and her massive hands held mine in a vice-like grip. Somewhere in the distance, as though at the far end of a tunnel, I heard my parents freaking out. Mara the gorilla looked into my eyes for a moment, nodded, and flexed. In a single, swift motion she crushed both of my hands. Bones snapped. A lot of them. Maybe all of them. I didn't really count. I was too busy trying to scream around the belt in my mouth.

The pain. Unreal. Unimaginable. There were no words to describe it. Mara was no longer the gorilla. She tugged at my right arm, and my hand popped free of the manacle in a starburst of white hot pain. I stopped screaming because I could no longer breathe.

In that silence, I heard someone nearby getting sick. Mara took my other hand and pulled it free. My entire existence narrowed down to my two hands. It was like twin suns, burning brightly on each hand, fiery pain lashing through my body. Then, lurking among that living, breathing pain, I sensed something. My talents were back. I reggied. Full-blown, deep healing.

Bones knit together in a sickening rush. I gagged and collapsed to my knees, my hands cradled to my chest. I sat there, hunched over, and sobbed. The belt fell from my mouth. Pain echoed in my head, so loud that I almost didn't notice the source of pain was gone. I struggled for control, and finally stopped crying. I looked up.

Mara stood beside me, her hand on my shoulder. My dad's face was contorted, as though he was the one in pain. Mom was looking directly at me, tears leaking out of her eyes. Bobby was wiping his mouth, and the floor near him was a mess. Thomas looked almost sickly he was so pale, but he held my gaze and nodded. I sucked in a ragged breath.

"Well done, son," Dad said, and held up his hands, one of them in a fist.

I made a fist, but couldn't bring myself to bump his. The

memory of that pain had attached itself to me.

"Oh. Right." His hands dropped to his lap. "Sorry. Don't know what I was thinking. Way too soon. Listen, both of you." He looked from me to Mara and back and held up his shackled hands. "I, I hate this. I can't do anything. But I trust you two, okay? Put an end to this. You understand? Joss, you are deputized to misbehave."

I nodded and stood. Intense weariness washed over me. I rocked on my feet, and Mara grabbed my upper arm to steady me.

"Tired?" she said.

"Yeah." I stretched my neck. "That took a lot. I'll be fine."

I wasn't sure that was true. I felt beat, but the fiery heat, the living pain that had moments ago engulfed me, was slowly being replaced by a burning anger. It energized me. They'd attacked us in our home. They'd threatened my family. I'd had enough. The only problem was I didn't know what to do about it.

"Can we talk?" I nodded toward the fireplace, well out of sight of the entryway.

Mara nodded, and we moved off to the side.

"Listen," I said, "I have no clue how to take down Vance. Any ideas? I'm running on empty. We've probably got one good shot at this."

"Okay, so I've been thinking about it," Mara said, "and, yeah, I've got an idea."

"Good to hear," I said. "What is it?"

"You kinney and blend, then shift into a gorilla. You'll be way undersized, maybe a third the size of a full-grown male. But pound for pound, they're way stronger than a man. Sucker-punch him as a gorilla, he'll drop."

My stomach almost hit the floor. "Mara, so, that's a problem. I can't shift. I was hoping for something, you know, I could actually do."

She put a hand on my shoulder and looked me straight in the eyes. "I'll make the shift so you can see it. You just follow my lead."

I shook my head. I felt desperate. How could our plan come down to me doing the one talent that was impossible for me? I'd worked hard at it. I simply could not shift. It was out of reach.

Mara's hand tightened on my shoulder. "You can do this."

I sought another angle, another way to take Vance, but there was nothing. I had no energy left, and even at full strength, he'd man-handled me. My head sagged.

"I can't. I've tried."

"Look at me, Joss," Mara said. "Look at me. Don't think about whether you can do it. Just think about what's needed. What you have to do."

"How's that going to help me?"

"Just do it. And look around. This is it. Go time. What's needed?"

For the first time since I'd gotten free, I really looked around the room. Janey looked terrified, but tried to smile at me. Her manacles were too tight, and she kept shifting her arms around, trying to find a position that didn't hurt. Bobby was utterly miserable. His wrists were scraped up and bleeding. He'd probably tried to pull free and failed. I had an intuition that he blamed himself for the whole mess.

"Not your fault, Bobby," I said on an impulse.

He looked at me, his eyes wet, and nodded. Thomas leaned over and bumped his shoulder to Bobby's. I couldn't believe Thomas had thought to contact the DOSN duo. It was the one reason we even had a chance to fight back. Actually, I could believe he'd thought of it. In some ways, Thomas was more of a superhero than I was, he just lacked the talents.

Mom and Dad had both recovered from the whole gorilla crushing their son's hands right in front of them experience, and were nodding encouragement to me. Mom still had a narrow scab across her cheek that I'd given her. Yet they'd forgiven me. My heart felt full.

"*Ve con Dios*," Isabella said, whatever that meant, and she somehow mustered a smile.

I smiled back at her. It wasn't about what I thought I could or couldn't do, but what I had to do.

"I'm ready," I said to Mara.

"Good," Mara said. "I checked things out while you were out. "They're set up in the cul-de-sac. The DOSN crew have it blocked off with cars, but Silver's got his men behind a perimeter of four vehicles out in front of your house. I don't think Silver wants an all-out war or he'd have already sent in Vance. It's almost like he's buying time."

"Got it," I said. "I'll blend, get out there and find Vance, then you shift where I can see it, and, you know, I shift. Rest'll be easy, right?"

Mara reached up on the mantle and pulled a fake flower out of an arrangement in a vase. She handed it to me. "Put it under your shirt. When you're ready for me to shift. Toss it in the air. Be looking toward your house. When it hits the ground, kinney. Got it?"

"Yeah, I got it." I tucked the flower under my shirt and tucked in the front of my shirt so it would stay put.

"I'm heading out through the back," Mara said. "I'll be ready for your signal."

I nodded, and stretched my neck.

"Joss?" Mara said.

"Yeah?"

"Wouldn't want to do this with anyone else. They won't even know what hit them."

"They'll know," I said. "Once I rip that ridiculous mask off Silver and look him in the eyes, they'll know."

I strode through the room as Mara headed for the back door. I fist bumped Dad as I went past him. I was Joss the Seven. Guardian Angel. Maybe even Bullet Boy. Time to earn those names. Time to finish Silver and his ridiculously scary sidekick Vance.

And what was up with that name? It was even worse than Gary, and I'd thought that was the absolute low point for gangster names. Didn't matter.

I blended, took a couple quick breaths, walked into the entryway, through the ruined front door and into a small battlefield.

CHAPTER 22

LAST STAND

I TOOK IT all in with a glance by the greenish-yellow light of the cul-de-sac's one streetlamp. Four SUVs were parked in a line across the cul-de-sac out in front of our house. A bunch of men crouched behind them. It was hard to say for certain, but I was pretty sure they were armed. Further out at the entrance to the cul-de-sac, cop cars sealed off the road, red and blue lights flashing brightly.

Two men stood in the middle of our yard facing away from me. A big man wearing a dark mask, and a man in dark clothes and boots. I didn't need better light to know the mask was green. Silver and Vance. Their heads were close together, and Vance was nodding. Probably scheming.

I thought about kinneying and bruising. If I could launch a surprise attack against Vance, it could be over in a heartbeat. But I remembered that feeling I'd had right before Vance had come through the front door. I'd known. I'd sensed that he was kinneying. I had no idea how it really worked, and I'd never sensed another talent, but I'd felt him kinney. I had to assume he'd know if I kinneyed.

I looked back at the other men huddled behind the SUVs. If I got over to the side and attacked at just the right angle, I thought I could knock them all senseless before they knew what was happening. Except for the part where Vance would know the moment I kinneyed, and would come over and kick me around. No, I had to deal with Vance first.

I was stuck with Mara's plan, which involved the minor twist that I had to do the impossible. I had to shift. It was so unfair. I was already bone weary. Even if everything went perfectly and I dropped Vance, I'd have nothing left. I'd pretty much be at the mercy of Silver and his other men. His well-armed men. There was no point thinking about it, since I had no idea what I was going to do. First, Vance.

I edged closer to Vance and Silver, pulled out the flower from under my shirt, and tossed it toward the house. It hung for a moment, and dropped toward the grass. A shape swooped down from the roof of my house, and I realized how exposed she was. She was going to shift right there in the middle of the yard where everyone could see her. It was madness.

At the exact moment the flower bounced lightly on the grass, Mara shifted back to herself. She did it flawlessly, so that she was standing on the grass after the twist and blur of the shift. I kinneyed and bruised, time slowed, and a moment later I felt a gentle tug behind me. Vance had just kinneyed. I was about to be destroyed. Sure, I was invisible, but he had those IR goggles. I stared forward, my eyes locked on Mara, hoping she shifted before I was taken out from behind.

Mara shifted, and I saw it all. The shift took almost a full second to my speeded up senses. I saw Mara morph into a gorilla. Saw the hair explode out of her skin. Saw her arms lengthen and thicken, her legs shrink. It was fast, but nothing like the normal blur when she shifted. Watching it happen in slow motion made all the difference. Something clicked in my mind, and I knew I could do it.

Vance's foot took me between the shoulder blades. My head snapped back, pain searing down my spine, and I was thrown forward. In the weird physics of kinneying, I wasn't knocked down, but went tumbling end over end through the air.

The pain in my shoulders was severe, and I was tired down in my bones. On top of that, I was terrified my family would be harmed. But a new emotion welled up as Vance's foot launched me. I was fed up. I was so sick of being literally kicked around.

I dropped my blending. Given how tired I was, I needed

everything I had to shift while kinneying and bruising. I painted the mental image of a gorilla. Focused on it. Poured all of me into it. Tried to ignore my slow rotations as I soared across our yard. Energized by pain and anger, I willed myself to shift. I fought through the pain, the fear, the exhaustion. I was going to be a gorilla. No, not any gorilla. Donkey Kong. Or maybe Donkey Kong, Jr.

I shifted.

"Yes!" I said, but it came out as an inarticulate roar.

I was still spinning through the air, a few feet from the bushes out in front of the house. I lashed out a long arm and jammed my fingers into the lawn, yanking myself to a stop and slamming into the ground. I stood, leaning forward on the knuckles of my two massive hands, and faced Vance. He skidded to a halt a few feet away from me, his mouth hanging open, his eyes wide.

I leapt with all the primal strength and violence contained in my ridiculously strong gorilla-self right at his face. His eyes flared even wider, and he dove to the side. It was too late. I snaked out an impossibly long arm and grabbed his shoulder in a bone-crushing grip as I flew by.

There was probably some complex physics to explain what happened when I latched on to him, but we basically went whipping through the air, spinning around each other. I flexed, and was shocked how effortlessly I yanked us together. Mara had been right. Gorillas were crazy strong. I was crazy strong.

Vance's free hand whipped around toward my face, a short, fixed-blade knife clutched in his hand. Where had that come from? He held it mostly in his hand, with the blade only extending a fraction of an inch beyond his fingertips. Of course. If he kept it next to his body, my bruising couldn't stop the blade from piercing me. I grabbed his wrist with my free hand, stopping the knife a couple inches from my eye. Right then we hit the ground, bounced, and slid across the pavement. I caught a glimpse of a couple men go flying just before we slammed into one of Silver's SUVs. We must have been moving insanely fast, because the side of the SUV crumpled on impact.

I had his knife hand still gripped in mine. Vance strained against me, and I knew I was on the edge. I couldn't keep the kinneying, bruising, and shifting going much longer. There was also the minor problem that we had come to a stop in the middle of Silver's men.

I was out of time. Time to roll the dice. Clinging to Vance's knife hand, I let go of his other arm and raised my hand high. He immediately jammed his freed hand into the back of the knife, driving it toward my face. I yanked my head back and pushed desperately on his arm to deflect the path of the knife. Simultaneously, I brought my other hand down like a hammer, long fingers curled in a fist.

The knife missed my face by an inch and plunged into my shoulder, just as my fist connected with his forehead. His head bounced off the pavement, and his hands went slack and slid to the ground, leaving the knife sticking out of me. My gorilla throat made an inhuman cry, and I reached up and yanked the knife free.

The pain was shocking, and all my talents snuffed out. My senses weren't prepared for the double-whammy of simultaneously having time snap back to normal and no longer being a gorilla. I drifted for a time in a foggy place as blood pooled around my shoulder.

I struggled back toward reality, focusing on the pain in my shoulder like an anchor in a storm. A massive roar filled my ears, and the wind whipped against me like I'd landed in a tornado. I opened my eyes and tried to figure out what was going on.

I was still partially under an SUV out in the cul-de-sac, wedged in between it and Vance, who was out cold beside me. In fact, Vance's big body was mostly blocking my view of what was going on, but that hopefully meant no one could see me. I gritted my teeth against the pain and lifted my head to take a quick look around.

Two men lay nearby, unmoving. Bright lights swept over me, the noise reached a crescendo, and the wind raged all around. I squinted, and my eyes and brain finally got on the same page. I realized I was seeing a helicopter land on our front lawn. Silver was crouched with two men off to the side, waiting for it. That's what he'd been waiting for. Once he'd realized we had reinforcements with the DOSN duo, he'd been buying time so he could escape.

It also meant I'd been zoning for a while. I took a deep breath and prepared to reggie, but stopped and thought. What if I passed out when I reggied? I was tapped out, and had a major injury. I couldn't risk being sidelined. It felt like the right time to do some math. There'd been ten men, plus Vance and Silver. Two men were lying near me, and two were with Silver. Vance was down, so that left six men. And Mara.

Gunshots rang out. Every instinct I had screamed that I should curl up under that SUV, reggie, and hope for the best. I was so tired, my shoulder was in agony, and Silver's men were probably firing silver bullets. What could I do? But Mara was out there with up to six men, and Silver was about to get away. No way. Not on my watch. Not at my house.

I squeezed out over Vance and jumped to my feet, or tried to. My legs felt like jelly. I lost my balance, caught my heel on Vance, and fell back against the SUV. It probably saved my life. Some maniac was charging me from off to my left, firing a gun at the spot where I'd been standing. I snarled and kinneyed. There was a moment's hesitation, the man's gun drifted toward me as he took aim, and finally the world slowed.

I ducked low, stepped in, and slapped the gun away. I was moving fast, so it was a supersonic slap, and his hand bent in a weird shape as I hit it. I really didn't want to think about hands being broken at that moment—broken hands were still too fresh for me—so I stepped around him and gently nudged him at the base of his skull. His eyes slowly rolled up into his head and his knees went soft.

Just past him, crouched behind another SUV, a shadowy man was firing his gun out toward the cops at the entrance to the cul-de-sac. Flashes of light from the muzzle of his gun accompanied the whip-crack sound of the shot. I stumbled forward and gave him a tap at the base of the neck.

Four more. I looked back the other way, past Vance's motionless body, and saw Mara fall in slow motion from the night sky onto a group of men. At least, I assumed the blurring shape that was suddenly a gorilla was her. Hopefully that group was the other four men. Hopefully she'd neutralize them and live to tell the tale. Hopefully we'd sit around eating pancakes tomorrow morning. With bacon.

I blinked and tried to focus. My eyes had somehow gotten crossed. I was drifting again. I had to drop the kinney. I was bleeding, in agony, and had nothing left to give. I had to stop. My eyes uncrossed, and the helicopter came into view. Silver and his men were scrambling into it, moving in slow motion.

I snarled and stumbled forward. I had a hand clamped on the stab wound, blood leaking out between my fingers. The pain had faded into the background. It was like a buzzing insect, irritating but not the focus. Silver. Silver was the focus. That man was not going to simply fly away and haunt my fears.

Five steps, and I launched myself. Once my feet left the ground, I was done. There was nothing left to do, except muster enough strength to bruise as I tumbled through the air. I closed my eyes, let go of my wound and stuck my arms and legs out in every direction, dropped the kinney, and reached down deep for that diamond steel.

I bruised, and the world went black.

CHAPTER 23

A FULL DAY

I WOKE TO the smell of bacon. Dream-like memories floated just out of reach behind my eyelids. Someone shaking me awake and making me reggie. Had that happened twice? I opened my eyes to late morning sunlight flooding my room. Someone had definitely been in to see me. Probably my mom. She was all about opening curtains.

Instead of rushing downstairs, I went across the hall and grabbed a shower first. I had this vague worry, like I was forgetting something, but the shower felt great, and I couldn't quite figure out what was wrong.

After getting dressed, I headed downstairs. The entryway came into view as I neared the bottom of the stairs. Plywood and boards were nailed over the gaping hole that had been our front door. Memories rushed in at the sight of the repairs. I sat down hard on the bottom stair.

Silver and Vance. My shattered hands. The helicopter. The last thing I remembered was hurling myself at the tail of the helicopter and trying to bruise. I hopped up and pulled back the curtain of the narrow window by what had been the door. A helicopter sat on our front lawn, it's tail bent almost ninety degrees to the side.

"Whoa," I said under my breath, and headed for the kitchen.

"Joss!" Mom said from the entrance to the dining room.

She rushed over and pulled me into a tight hug. Behind her, I heard other voices. Mara, Janey, and Isabella.

"It wasn't a nightmare, was it?" I said.

"No, dear." She stroked my hair. "But it's over now."

She took a step back and held me at arm's length. I knew what was coming. A full-blown medical inspection. I reggied, and felt a warm glow, but no major healing taking place.

"I'm fine, Mom. Just reggied. Nothing really happened."

"Still not used to that." She tousled my hair. "We're all in the dining room about to have a brunch. We were going to let you sleep, but your timing's perfect. Dad's just bringing in the food." She gave the destroyed front door a look. "We both decided to take the day off."

I stepped into the dining room and got mobbed by three more ladies. Hugs from Mara and Isabella, and a high five from Janey. Mara was wearing a t-shirt that said DESK JOCKEY, PLAY THROUGH THE PAIN and had a line drawing of a hand holding a computer mouse with one of the fingers bandaged. The remains of the dining room table were gone along with the broken chairs. In their place was our big folding table placed end-to-end with the card table. Four folding chairs had been substituted in for the broken chairs.

Dad stepped into the room carrying a big plate of scrambled eggs in one hand and pancakes in the other. He saw me, and a grin split his face.

"Alright! Places, everyone." He set the food down and stepped over to me. "Come here, bud."

He grabbed me in a hug so strong I thought about bruising to protect my ribs. Instead, I hugged him back.

"You were a hero last night, Joss," he said. His voice was low, for my ears only, but intense. "The real thing. The absolute, honest-to-God real deal."

He gave me a final squeeze that made my ribs creak and released me. Mom, Dad, Janey, Mara, Isabella, and I sat down together at the tables, and Dad said grace. I tucked into the bacon right off, because bacon, but it all looked great. Everyone was in a good mood, the food was delicious, and nothing horrible was looming over me.

"So what happened last night?" I said. "When I threw myself at that helicopter, I sort of blacked out."

Dad opened his mouth to answer, but Janey jumped in. "We saw it, Joss! It was insane."

"What?" I said. "I don't understand. You were chained in there." I hooked a thumb toward the family room.

Janey started shaking her head before I finished. "Nope. Just after you went out there, one of the DOSN agents came in through the window. He was incredibly fast at picking locks. Freed us all."

"And when she says 'came in through the window'," Mom said, "she means in the literal sense. It's boarded up for now. All part of the mess we've got to deal with."

"Yeah," Janey said, "but he freed us, so Dad had us all run through the entryway and get upstairs. We watched from an angle through a window, so, you know, we couldn't be hit by any gunshots."

I looked around the table for confirmation. Dad shrugged and nodded.

"So what did you see?" I asked.

"We thought you were dead," Isabella said.

"Yeah, we couldn't find you," Janey said in between mouthfuls of pancake. "Mara filled us in. You'd just taken out Vance and were stuck under the car."

"We saw you climb out just as that man started shooting at you." Mom looked like the words hurt her. "You were looking away from him, but dodged backwards just in time. It was… stunning."

I stopped mid-bite in my next piece of bacon. "Oh, well, that wasn't really me dodging anything. I was, you know, dizzy and weak. I'd had to reggie so I didn't bleed out from being stabbed. Lost my balance and tripped over Vance."

"Wow," Janey said as Isabella let out a low whistle.

"Stabbed?" Mara said. "But you were bruising, right?"

"Yeah," I said. "When I was a gorilla—and bruising—Vance tried to stab me in the face. He was holding the knife so the blade was along his hand and bruising with him, I guess. I managed to, like"—I pantomimed pushing the knife away from my face and into my shoulder—"redirect it."

Mom's fork clattered to the table.

Dad reached over and put his hand on her shoulder. "It all worked out."

Mom looked up at the ceiling for a moment. "Let's just gloss over some of the details for now and hit the high points." She gave my dad a look and raised her eyebrows.

"Right," he said, "well, there's not much more to tell. You, ah, dodged backwards, then did your thing where you move too fast to really see. A couple guys near you collapsed. Next thing we know you're slamming into the back of the helicopter. You flopped off of it and just lay there on the grass. By that time Mara had taken care of several of Silver's men, and the DOSN guys came flooding in. They secured everyone, including Vance. They had silver for him."

"So, I was just out?" I said.

"Joss, we didn't know if you were alive," Mom said. She'd picked her fork back up, but hadn't used it.

"But you were," Dad said, "and we managed to rouse you enough to get you to reggie. You've been sleeping since."

"What about Silver?" I said.

"DOSN took them all away and left a couple guys behind to help me board up everything. They'll be back to take our statements later today. Oh, and they said they'll release that Stanton guy."

"But Joss," Mom said. "You need to know. Mr. Ferris, well, he made his choices, and he was arrested last night."

My heart sank. After everything, it hadn't been enough. I said as much, and my dad shook his head.

"Joss, we do what we can. You can help, but you can't fix what others want broken."

"And Bobby?"

"He stayed at Thomas's house last night," Mom said. "I'm sure CPS will be involved. It'll get sorted out."

"And Joss," Mara said, "there's one less Mocker out there. Mockers create sad stories, one after another. I think we can celebrate that much."

After that, we all ate in silence for a while, but eventually

I started feeling better. It was hard not to with bacon, eggs, pancakes, and no immediate threats on our lives. Soon enough we were all chatting as we ate, and there was even some laughter to go with the food.

"I have some news," Mara said, and waited for all of us to quiet down. "So, when Jordan first brought us to the U.S., he pulled strings and got me a green card through some super-expedited and probably very illegal and even unethical process. And then he fast-tracked me toward citizenship. I think he believed it would make life easier for himself in the long run. All that to say, I found out two things these past two weeks. First, I have the opportunity to naturalize as a U.S. citizen this coming month."

Mara paused while we all cheered and congratulated her, but soon held up a hand to quiet us. "There's a reason I'd like to become a citizen, and that's tied to the second thing I learned this past week. When Jordan opened Battlehoop, he set it up as a full-blown business. Financial accounts backing it and everything. And, for some reason—maybe to keep things looking legit—he put me as a second owner on the business. He never even bothered to tell me. It was all a front for him, but the actual paperwork was real. All that to say, when he died, I ended up as the sole owner of a well-funded business to train kids in the martial arts. Uh, right here in town. I have, like, a twenty-year lease on that building Battlehoop's in and cash in the bank."

She looked around at us, and gave a crooked smile. "Hopefully you won't mind seeing more of me because I think I'm going to give it a shot."

"That's incredible!" Mom said, and got up to give Mara a big hug. "Do you need him"—she nodded toward Dad—"to look over the books or anything."

"I was hoping you'd be willing," Mara said. "I don't know the first thing about business finances."

"Absolutely," Dad said. "But Mara, may I ask about, uh, Isabella?"

Isabella smiled radiantly as we all turned toward her. "It is all okay. We have a plan. And it is a real plan, not a 'rob a bank' or 'drop Joss out of the sky' plan."

"Phew!" I made a big show of wiping my forehead. "What is it?"

"Well," Mara said, "I'm hoping to adopt her so she can gain citizenship herself and stay with me."

"Wow," Janey said. "Just, wow."

Isabella shrugged. "It won't be perfect, but we have talked and agree it is best."

Not perfect? It sounded perfect to me. My mind was spinning. Isabella was going to live in my town. She wasn't going back to Mexico forever. And it'd be nice to have Mara around, too. Maybe she could get me through my shifting block. And Isabella.

"This is incredible!" I stood up and raised my glass of milk. "A toast. May Mara be a fantastic business owner and a, uh, wonderful mother."

Isabella giggled, but everyone lifted their glasses and gave a cheer. After that, breakfast turned into a real celebration. I ate way too much, and discovered that reggying couldn't make me feel less full. Silver was gone. DOSN had him along with Vance, and I had to believe that was enough. Sure, I'd set out to help Mr. Ferris, but I'd known from the start he didn't want help.

Maybe my work wasn't done. Bobby and I would be in high school together in a few days. He'd need a friend. Maybe there'd be a way to help him without using any of my talents. I nodded to myself. Sometimes, superpowers weren't really what was needed.

"Joss?" Isabella said. "What are your thoughts?"

I looked up and smiled. "Normal thoughts. I start high school next week. Was thinking about maybe checking in on Bobby."

"And by 'checking in' you mean?" Dad said.

"Saying hi to him. Trying to be a friend."

Dad smiled and nodded. "Your normal thoughts are good ones."

"Alright, everyone." Mom pushed back from the table. "Today's going to be full. We better get this mess cleaned up."

The day was full, but in the best sense of the word. The DOSN duo came by in their role as local police investigators and got everything moving, including the helicopter in our front yard, which was loaded onto a giant trailer and towed off. Agents Young and Malick talked to my parents for a long time and reached an agreement to be there the next time the Guild showed up. I wasn't positive, but I was pretty sure my parents were angling to play them against each other, to keep both the DOSN and the Guild honest.

While DOSN was dealing with the helicopter, a contractor came by with a crew of men, who did a first pass cleanup of our house. They removed the horrible silver stakes from our family room and installed a temporary front door. Dad also had a real heart-to-heart with our insurance agent, and got things sorted out to his satisfaction. We'd be able to get everything repaired, including the damage I'd done when I'd destroyed his chair.

After DOSN and the contractors left, Stanton came by. He wasn't ghosting this time, and introduced himself to my parents. They had some words to say about his decision to beat me over the head and get me caught by Silver, and he seemed truly sorry. He also promised to show up at the next meeting with the Guild.

Late in the afternoon, Thomas came by with Bobby. It started awkwardly, but pretty soon I realized Bobby was still feeling horrible about what his dad had done and wasn't mad at me.

"Dad, well, maybe this will work out for him," Bobby said as we sat in my room talking.

"Mom put him in touch with a great lawyer she knows," Thomas said. "She thinks he'll get off with minimum time served."

"He kicked the drinking," Bobby said. "At least, he seems to have. Maybe, I don't know, this'll push him to kick the crime."

I nodded. "I bet it does. I'm sorry I wasn't able to get it done."

Bobby shrugged. "Don't know many people who can be bothered to care about what happens to him. Least you tried."

"Thanks, Bobby," I said. "Seriously."

There was a loud knock on the door, and we all headed downstairs to see who else had come by. My dad was already at the door, talking to someone just out of sight. He saw me on the stairs, stepped back, and waved whoever it was into the house.

Jasmine stepped in, as beautiful as I remembered her. She was wearing a dress, and she wore it well. Mom, Mara, and Isabella came into the entryway from the family room.

"Joss, Mara," Dad said, "this young lady says she knows you."

There was a hint of a question in his voice.

"Jasmine." Mara stepped forward and gave her a hug.

I stepped off the bottom stair. "Mom, Dad, this is Jasmine. She's Silver's, uh, Mr. Goram's step-daughter."

"Ah," Dad said.

"Are things going to be okay for you?" Mara asked.

"Better than anything I'd hoped for," Jasmine said. "My mom's on the way to town. It'll take some time, but her lawyer is sure she'll be able to finally get custody of me."

Mom raised an eyebrow at me in question.

"Jasmine wasn't living with Silver willingly," I said.

"I was leverage," Jasmine said. "To keep my mom in line. Look, I'm not staying. Mara and I had exchanged phone numbers, and she texted me your address. I wanted to say thank you."

She looked me in the eyes, and my face suddenly felt hot. "Seriously. Thank you. What you went through, well, I know it was horrible, and I wanted to tell you, face to face, that it meant everything to me."

Dad looked from Jasmine to me, his brow pulled together slightly like it always did when he was thinking. "That's so good to hear, Jasmine. Thank you for taking the time to tell us."

Mom stepped over to Jasmine and gave her a quick hug.

"Do you have a place to stay?"

Jasmine smiled. "Oh, yeah. A house. A chef. A driver. I'm sure it will all go away, but Mom arrives tomorrow, and I'm set until then."

She took a small step toward me, hesitated, and gave me a hug. "Thank you."

She pulled away and stepped back to the door. "I need to go. Thank you for letting me talk to you all for a little. Goodbye."

With that, she was gone. Bobby and Thomas headed out next, and pretty soon I was winding down and heading to bed. The prior three days had been the longest, craziest three days of my life, and today hadn't been exactly normal. I was exhausted, and wanted to sleep the whole night.

I lay down, but I couldn't quite get to sleep. Maybe it was excitement over Mara and Isabella moving to town. Maybe it was gratitude that Bobby didn't blame me for his dad's situation. Maybe it was pride that I'd actually helped Jasmine.

Or maybe it was stark terror that in four days I started high school.

ABOUT THE AUTHOR

J. Philip Horne probably shouldn't be alive. Born in Florida, he grew up overseas for the most part, spending much of his childhood in Liberia and Micronesia. During those years, he experienced numerous attempts on his life. The wannabe killers included malaria, spinal meningitis, blood poisoning, a staph infection in his heel bone, a close encounter with a green mamba, and other cold-hearted foes.

From his earliest years, his parents read to him fantastical stories from wonderful worlds. Narnia and Middle Earth featured prominently, and had his youth been a generation later, he would have certainly encountered Hogwarts at a young age. Through his teen years he read stories by many other authors and experienced a host of new worlds.

After dabbling in writing for many years, he finally got serious and wrote his first novel in 2011. He has continued to write ever since. He currently lives in Dallas, Texas with his wife, four children, two dogs, two rabbits, and several literary aspirations. For news of upcoming works, please join Mr. Horne's email list at jphiliphorne.com or visit him at facebook.com/jphiliphorne.

63599025R00131

Made in the USA
San Bernardino, CA
21 December 2017